Praise for *Tempting*

"At turns witty and poignant, this hard-to-put-down book will appeal to a broad spectrum of readers."
—*Booklist*, starred review

Praise for *Sizzling*

"[A] tasty dish...Mallery's prose is luscious and provocative, and her characters worth following from book to book."
—*Publishers Weekly*

"*Sizzling* is simply dazzling! You'll laugh, you'll hoot, you'll raise your eyebrows, and yes, you'll cry buckets, so have those tissues handy.... Highly Recommended!"
—*The Romance Readers Connection*

SUSAN MALLERY
LIP SERVICE

HQN™

Recycling programs
for this product may
not exist in your area.

ISBN-13: 978-0-373-77372-5

LIP SERVICE

www.HQNBooks.com

Printed in U.S.A.

**Also available from
Susan Mallery and HQN Books**

**And don't miss the rest of the
Lone Star Sisters' adventures**

LIP SERVICE

CHAPTER ONE

"I'D LIKE YOU to marry my daughter."

Skye Titan was having enough trouble balancing a small tray with two drinks and a plate of appetizers in one hand while reaching for the study door with the other. A sudden inability to breathe only complicated the stability problem.

Thirty seconds ago she would have thought that nothing her father said could surprise her anymore. She would have been wrong.

Talk about humiliating, she thought, wondering if Jed Titan's statement was meant to buy a son-in-law or sell a daughter. With him, she couldn't be sure.

"Izzy?" the other man asked, his voice clearly audible, despite the thick door between them.

"No. Skye."

"Oh."

Skye waited impatiently.

"Oh?" Was that the best he could do? Annoyance grew as time ticked on.

"I guess that would work, too," the other voice said at last.

Skye practically growled in irritation. Words to make her heart beat faster for sure. So charming. How was she going to keep from *throwing herself at T. J.* Boone when she walked into the study?

If she had been any less the well-trained hostess, not to mention a dutiful daughter, she would have pushed open the door, tossed the drinks in both their faces and left the house, never to be heard from again.

"Egotistical jackass bastard," she muttered, not sure if she meant the insult for T.J. or her father. They both deserved it.

She forced herself to breathe slowly, then imagined herself sinking into the big tub in the bathroom off her bedroom. Bubbles up to her chin, a glass of white wine to take off the edge. She was calm and in control. She was going to do the right thing, because that's who she was. The good girl, dammit. The one who served drinks to men like T.J. and her father.

Skye opened the door to the study and stepped inside the room. The two men stood next to the pool table. Jed didn't bother acknowledging her while T.J. looked momentarily uncomfortable. As if he wondered whether she'd heard him condemn her with faint praise.

She smiled as she offered the successful businessman his drink, wishing she'd thought to spit in it first.

"T.J.," she said.

"Skye."

He was good-looking, in a blond, blue-eyed sort of way. Tall and well dressed. He was a Texas boy and was probably charming, but it was hard to notice when the unenthusiastic "I guess that would work, too" was bouncing around in her brain.

She set the appetizers on the table in the corner. "Is there anything else, Daddy?" she asked.

"That's all, Skye."

"Then I'll say good-night."

Her hostess duties completed, her temper still firing, albeit silently, she left the room and walked to the stairs. Once on the third floor, she made her way to the last room on the left. During the day, it was a bright open space done in primary colors. A big bed sat by the window overlooking the main pasture. At night, shadows closed in, but seven-year-old Erin was never afraid of the dark. She wasn't afraid of anything. A quality she must have inherited from her father, Skye thought enviously.

Now Erin lay sleeping, a tiny curled-up bump under the covers. Skye sat on the edge of the bed and stared down at her child.

"I love you, Bunny Face," she whispered.

Erin didn't stir.

Skye rose and walked the few feet to her own bedroom. Her younger-by-a-year sister, Izzy, sprawled on the big bed, watching television. She muted the sound when Skye entered.

"Don't you have a TV in your own room?" Skye asked.

"Sure, but using yours is more fun. Who's the guy?"

"T. J. Boone. You're the one he wants."

Izzy sat up, her dark curly hair a halo around her head. "What are you talking about?"

Skye walked to the bathroom and turned on the tub. While water thundered out, she poured in jasmine-scented bath oil that foamed and made bubbles.

"Jed told T.J. that he'd like him to marry his daughter. T.J. asked about you but Jed informed him that I was the daughter being auctioned off. T.J. paused for a *very* long time before agreeing that I would do." Skye returned to the bedroom, then swore softly. "Did I remember to bring up a big bottle of wine? Of course not."

Izzy bounced to her feet. "What are you talking about? Of course he wants you. You're gorgeous."

That was stretching it, but Skye wasn't going to refuse the compliment.

"It doesn't matter," she said with a sigh. "I'm not letting Jed pick a husband for me. Been there, done that."

"Bought the T-shirt," Izzy added helpfully.

She'd done more than that. She'd married the man in question because it was what her father wanted. Because it was the right thing to do, or so it had seemed at the time.

"I have a backbone," Skye said, feeling dissatisfied with her life and not clear on why. "I'm sure of it. If I didn't have a backbone, I couldn't walk upright. I'm twenty-six years old, a widow and single mother. Shouldn't I be the one running my life?"

"You are," Izzy said, then shrugged. "Sort of."

"How wonderful. I'm a role model for doormats everywhere."

"You're not a doormat."

Skye shook her head. "Sorry. This should be a pity party for one. I didn't mean to include you. Why don't you go downstairs and flaunt yourself in front of T.J.? Show him what he'll never have."

Izzy frowned. "Are you okay? I can stay and keep you company."

"No, thanks. I'm going to take a bath where I'll be floating in a sea of denial." Because her bad mood wasn't just because of T.J.'s obvious rejection. She wasn't interested in him or any man. It was her father assuming once again he could control her life. Because she'd let him…more than once.

"Sk-ye." Izzy drew the word out into two syllables. "Don't make me sing 'The Sun Will Come Out Tomorrow' until you beg for mercy, because I will."

Skye laughed. "Okay. I'll be good. Now run along and make trouble. We'll both feel better for it. I'll be fine. I just need to get some sleep. Everything will look better in the morning."

"Promise?"

"I swear."

Izzy hesitated, then left. Skye returned to the bathroom and turned off the water. She pinned up her hair, then undressed and climbed into the tub. But no matter that she closed her eyes and slowed her breathing, she kept hearing the conversation between T.J. and Jed. And kept getting mad. Mostly at herself. For being the kind of person who did what she was told.

Because she was the good sister. The one who followed the rules. Who did the expected.

"I hate people like that," she said aloud into the empty room. So why had she become one of them?

IZZY WAITED until T.J. stepped out onto the front porch of the house. She'd grown up lurking in shadows, spying on her older sisters, who seemed to have all the fun. She was used to being stealthy.

When she was sure he hadn't noticed her, she crept up behind him and said, "Hi," in a loud voice. It was hard not to laugh when he jumped.

"Jesus," he yelled as he turned. "You scared me."

"Good. I understand we're soon to be brother and sister. That's very cool. I've always wanted an older brother. You can teach me all kinds of things."

T.J. stood a good ten inches taller than her, but Izzy wasn't the least bit intimidated. She wasn't there to fight fair and would use every advantage to bring the jerk to his knees. Scaring him had just been a happy bonus.

"Brother and sister?"

"You're marrying Skye, aren't you? At least, that's what she said."

T.J. swore, this time more aggressively. "She heard. I didn't mean for her to."

He was standing at the top of the stairs. Izzy thought about giving him a big push, just for the thrill of watching him tumble. "You hesitated when Jed offered you Skye. I can't believe you had the nerve to think about it. She's worth ten of you."

"Wait a minute. My hesitation wasn't about Skye. She's a beautiful woman."

"So were you concerned about the size of your equipment?" Izzy interrupted with a smirk.

"I was making a point with your father." He leaned against the post by the stairs. "And for future reference, I've never had complaints about the size of my equipment."

"Most women are too polite to complain in person. We only tell each other when we're disappointed."

He raised a blond eyebrow. "You have sass."

"I have a lot of things you'll never see."

"Want to bet?"

Izzy liked that he gave as good as he got, but not that he was consorting with Jed, talking about marrying Skye and flirting with her.

"Jed won't take kindly to you playing his daughters against each other. Trust me, he's not a man you want to piss off."

"Maybe he doesn't care which of his daughters I marry."

"You couldn't catch me and even if you could, you couldn't handle me."

"That sounds like a challenge."

She ignored the statement. "Let me be clear. Hurt my sister again, T.J., and looking eye to eye with a snake will seem like a step up for you."

He stared at her feet, then worked his way up. "You think you could take me?"

"Even on a bad day. I fight dirty."

"So do I, little girl."

She filed that piece of information away for future reference. "I'll be reporting our little conversation to my sister. The Titan girls are very loyal to each other. Keep that in mind."

"You're full of advice. What makes you think I need it?"

"You have amateur written all over you."

MITCH CASSIDY PULLED to a stop at the entrance to the ranch. Although he'd grown up here, he hadn't been back in nearly nine years. He'd expected a few changes—life had a way of moving forward whether he wanted it to or not—but not this.

He stared at the words over the open metal gates. The gates, connected to nothing, were just there for show. "Cassidy Ranch. Home of certified organic beef and free-range poultry."

"What the hell?"

He wasn't sure what offended him the most. The phrase "certified organic" or the word *poultry*.

"Chickens? We have goddamn chickens?"

He hated chickens. They were loud and messy. And this was Texas. His family ran beef. They had for nearly a hundred years. It was the source of the Cassidy fortune. If some ranch wife wanted to raise a few chickens for eggs or deep frying, the stupid birds were kept out of sight and never talked about. They weren't bragged about in a sign.

His left foot ached. He reached down to rub it only to remember a half second later that he didn't have a left foot anymore. The below-the-knee amputation was the reason he wasn't a SEAL these days. It was the reason he'd finally come home.

He swore again, put the truck in Drive and headed for the main house. In a perfect world, he would quietly reappear at the ranch, easing into a normal life, without anyone noticing. However, though life was a lot of things, it wasn't perfect.

He drove down the nearly mile long private road. White fences lined both sides. There were horses on the right and prize bulls on the left. Prosperity on the hoof.

He rounded a curve, past a grove of trees and saw the house where he'd grown up. It was a sprawling two-story structure with a wraparound porch. Flowers grew waist high, swaying gently in the breeze. It could have been a picture from a postcard. Mitch almost wished it was.

Fidela stood on the porch, straining forward, as if wanting to know the second he arrived. She took off at a run toward the truck, forcing him to stop short of the house.

She might be pushing fifty, but she had the speed of a six-year-old and got to him before he'd awkwardly clambered out of the truck. He landed on gravel and nearly lost his balance as his leg muscles struggled to keep him upright on his new and painful prosthesis.

"You're back!" she said, tears filling her brown eyes. "Finally. I've been praying and praying since you left. God is tired of me asking for your safety. You could have helped, you know. Not done such dangerous work. But no. You like to test my faith."

She cupped his face, then ran her hands across his shoulders and down his arms, as if wanting to make sure he was real.

"You're taller since you left, but so thin. Mitch, such sadness in your eyes. But you're home now, yes? Home with me and Arturo. The ranch will heal you and I will cook all your favorites until you are too fat to ride a horse."

She smiled through her tears, then hugged him with a fierce strength that squeezed the air out of him.

She'd been a part of his life since before he was born. Arturo had brought her to the ranch as his young bride. She'd helped his mother and Arturo had managed the ranch. His parents had never enjoyed staying in one place for very long, and when they'd left on their many trips, Arturo and Fidela had been the ones to take care of him.

He hugged her back, slowly, tentatively, remembering and wanting to forget at the same time. He was careful to focus on staying balanced, with his center of gravity where it was supposed to be. All the easy things he'd once taken for granted.

"I made enchiladas and beans the way you like. There's pie and flan and all your favorite foods. Your room is ready, on the main floor. Just for now, though. That is what the doctor said when he called. Just for now."

Mitch wondered what else the doctor had said. Mitch knew he'd been a difficult patient. He wasn't interested in all the bullshit about how things happened for a reason and even when God closed a door, He opened a window. Mitch wasn't interested in a window. He wanted his life back the way it had been before the explosion that had taken off the bottom half of his left leg.

"I gotta go," he said, pushing away from Fidela and returning to the truck. "I'll be back."

She stared at him, her mouth trembling with an emotion he didn't want to identify. Pity, most likely. And why not?

He slammed the driver's door and started the

engine. He didn't know where he was going—as long as it was away from here.

He circled the barn and followed the dirt road toward the pastures. The fencing was new and in good repair. To his right he saw something that looked suspiciously like a whole lot of chickens, so he stared straight ahead until he'd crested a rise. From there he could see Cassidy land and the dark shadows that were the cattle. At this distance, the changes wouldn't be so noticeable.

He got out of the truck, then winced when he took a step. His stump ached. He'd done too much, too fast, ignoring the advice from his doctor and therapists. He was supposed to get used to the prosthesis over time, to use crutches or a walker. Not that he would.

He limped over to a big rock and sat down, then pulled up his jeans and unhooked the plastic and metal replacing what had once been flesh and bone.

His knee was all banged up, scarred and still red in places. The field surgeon in Afghanistan had done his best to save Mitch's leg, or at least what had been left of it. For that Mitch would always be grateful. Not happy, exactly, but grateful.

He hurt everywhere and on the days when he didn't want to bother getting out of bed he reminded himself that, compared to a lot of soldiers, all he had was a scratch and he needed to get over it. His buddy, Pete, had risked his life to drag Mitch to safety and had gotten shot for his efforts. So Mitch owed him, too. There were...

The sound of steady hooves caught his attention. He started to stand, remembered too late he was missing a foot and nearly fell over. He grabbed for the rock and managed to stay upright. But before he could strap his prosthesis back in place, a horse and rider joined him on the rocky ledge.

Mitch stared at the one person in all the world he never wanted to see again. Did it have to be now? With him holding his fake leg in one hand? Did he have to look like the cripple he was?

Anger welled up inside of him. Living, hot anger that wanted to explode and burn and destroy.

"Get the hell off my land," he growled. "You're not welcome here."

"Hello, Mitch," she said, not acknowledging his order. "I just heard that you were back."

Skye Titan drew her horse to a halt, slid from the saddle and onto the ground. She pulled off her cowboy hat.

Despite the years that had passed, she looked exactly as he remembered. Her dark red hair contrasted with her pale skin. Eyes the color of spring grass stared into his. She looked good. Too good, all curves and temptation.

"How are you?" she asked.

He motioned to the prosthesis. "How do you think I am? Go away. You're not anyone I want to talk to."

She wore jeans and a long-sleeved T-shirt, one that hugged her breasts in a way that irritated him even more.

"I don't think I'm leaving just yet," she said.

His gaze dropped to her left hand. He didn't see a ring. "What happened to husband number one? Daddy tell you to dump him?"

"Ray died," she said, her gaze never leaving his.

"Living life as the rich widow or has Jed married you off again? Who is it this time, Skye? An old tycoon or some international banker?"

THE MITCH CASSIDY Skye remembered had been a funny, easygoing guy who rode like the wind and could kiss her senseless in a matter of seconds. He laughed as hard as he played and Mitch had loved to play. She knew war changed a man, but she hadn't expected him to be a cold, mean stranger. His crack about a second arranged marriage hit close and hard. She took a step back.

"I'm sorry about your injury," she said.

"I'll sleep better knowing that."

"Is the sarcastic bastard act specifically for me, or are you sharing it with everyone?"

He turned his back on her.

She supposed that was an answer of sorts, even if she wasn't sure of the specifics.

She'd missed him, she thought sadly, staring at the familiar broad shoulders. His dark hair was military short, which suited him. The scar on the side of his jaw wasn't one she remembered and she remembered everything about Mitch's body.

He'd been her first love, her first lover and there had been a time when she would have walked through fire to be with him. But she hadn't been willing to defy her father. Had that been a mistake?

"I wish things had been different," she said, before she could stop herself. She meant the past, but then he spun toward her, his eyes narrowed, his mouth a thin line, she realized he thought she was talking about his leg.

"I don't need your pity," he growled. "I don't need sh—"

He lost his balance and started to go down. Skye reacted instinctively, springing toward him. She grabbed him around the waist as he reached for the rocks. The prosthesis dropped to the ground.

He was heavier than she'd anticipated and the weight of him knocked her sideways. Her foot slipped. She scrambled to stay upright, then they were both falling.

The ground was hard. She landed on her back, him on top of her. Rocks jabbed her but that didn't matter. She couldn't draw in air.

Mitch was off her in a second. "Breathe," he said, propped up next to her. "You're fine. Just breathe."

She sucked in a breath, then another.

"What's wrong with you?" he demanded. "You're

too small to hold me up. What did you think you were doing?"

He looked furious, which was oddly better than cold and sarcastic.

"I'm not weak," she told him. "I could so kick your ass."

"On what planet?"

"Zorgon."

One corner of his mouth twitched. "Don't, Skye. Don't try to make this okay."

Because it wasn't or he didn't want it to be? "I missed you, Mitch."

The humor faded and the coldness returned. "You should have thought about that before you dumped me."

"I didn't have a choice."

"Sure you did. Daddy asked you to jump and you got out the ruler to make sure it was high enough."

She sat up. "You don't know what you're talking about."

"How much did I get wrong?"

Nothing and that's what annoyed her most. "Mitch, please."

"Please what?"

They were both sitting, facing each other. She could see all the colors that made up his irises, the individual hairs of his lashes. The scent of him was familiar, as was the heat rising inside of her.

He was so different, yet she recognized every part

of him. It was as if the nearly nine years between them vanished and there was only this moment and the man she had once loved with a desperation that had left her weak.

"Mitch," she said, then grabbed him by the front of his shirt, closed the space between them and kissed him.

For a moment, there was nothing. Just the feel of his lips against hers, but no reaction. She pressed harder, wanting him to want her, wanting him to respond. When he didn't, she knew she'd made a mistake. That whatever she'd been longing for, it had been on her side alone. He hadn't missed her at all.

She drew back.

Heat climbed her cheeks. She released him and started to get to her feet.

He grabbed her around the waist and pulled her down next to him. He leaned over her until she was forced to sink onto the ground.

"There is no way this is going to happen," he told her.

Then he kissed her. His mouth moved on hers, all desperation, taking and claiming.

He kissed with a need that stole her breath far more effectively than her recent fall. His arms wrapped around her, she clung to him and everything was exactly as she remembered. It was hot and hungry and perfect.

He thrust his tongue inside of her mouth. She welcomed him with darting strokes. They teased and danced, relearning, discovering.

She ran her hands up and down his back. He was stronger than she remembered, the muscles thicker. He'd filled out even as he remained lean. He shifted closer, his body bumping hers. She turned toward him and felt the thick ridge of his erection.

The proof of his desire thrilled her. She hadn't been with a man since Ray. For a while, she'd thought that part of her was dead. Recently it had tried to surface, but she was a single mother with a lot of responsibility. Sex wasn't possible in her world.

But now, with Mitch, desire flared to life. Liquid ache poured into her belly, moving lower as she recalled the feel of him filling her, taking her beyond this reality to a place that was pure pleasure.

He continued to kiss her, circling her tongue with his. Then he pulled back enough to move his mouth along her jaw. He pushed up her T-shirt and jerked down the cup of her bra, exposing her left breast. He bent over her and sucked on her nipple, drawing it in deeply, flicking the tight tip with his tongue.

She gasped and strained to get closer. Her skin burned for more and her body throbbed with pent-up need. She dug her fingers into his back, then moved lower so she could cup his rear. His arousal surged against her.

He shifted her onto her back, unfastened the front of her jeans and shoved his hand under her panties.

They were outside in the middle of the day, with her horse standing close by and the sky above them.

She should have been shocked or embarrassed, but she could only hold her breath until his skilled fingers slipped between her legs, into her wet, waiting heat.

He didn't disappoint. Even as his thumb settled on that one, sensitive spot, he pushed two fingers inside of her. She was already swollen and desperate. The second he began to rub, she felt herself losing control.

It was too fast, she thought as he stroked her, at the same time moving his fingers in and out of her. Too fast and too much and so incredibly perfect she didn't want him to stop. She arched her hips to get closer, to take more. She moaned and writhed. Wanting filled her.

He abandoned her breast, then shifted so that he could kiss her again. She welcomed him in her mouth, then closed her lips around his tongue and sucked until it was his turn to groan.

He moved his hand more quickly—rubbing and pushing, taking her closer and closer. When she was within sight of her release, he drew back.

"You're going to have to get on top," he told her.

What?

He rolled onto his back and undid his jeans. Rational thinking returned just enough for her to realize he probably didn't know how to be on top. Not yet, anyway. And who on earth cared?

She jerked off one boot, pushed down her jeans and panties, pulled one foot free, moved the clothing out of the way and settled herself on his erection.

He filled her completely, perfectly, and her body responded with a sigh. She rode him a couple of times, letting herself stretch around him, taking in the sense of being with a man again. This man who had taught her the pleasures possible.

"Lean forward," he said.

She did as he suggested. He reached under her shirt and unfastened her bra, then cupped her breasts in his hands.

Rocks cut into her knees and her palms, but she didn't care. Even as he teased her nipples, she moved up and down, filling herself with him, letting the heat rise between them. The wanting. Everything faded except the feeling between them.

She felt him getting closer, felt herself responding to each deep thrust. The sun was hot on her back. Muscles tensed, she strained forward. Then he dropped one hand, slid it between them and rubbed her with his fingers.

She came with a sharp cry that silenced the birds. Her orgasm crashed over her, making her ride him faster and faster as she drew out the experience as long as possible. Her thighs clenched, her hips moved up and down. There was nothing but the perfection of being with him again.

Beneath her, Mitch met each of her movements with a hard thrust that satisfied every part of her. He grabbed her and steadied her rhythm, then tensed and lost himself in her. When she was sure he was done, she slowed, then stopped. And then it was just their breath in the air, both of them recovering.

Reality returned in the form of an ant climbing up her arm. Skye brushed it away, then stood, feeling exposed and awkward. She had one boot on, one off. Her pants and panties hung on one leg. Her bra was loose under her shirt. Mitch zipped up and was dressed in about five seconds. She was left with her ass hanging out for all the world to see.

While she struggled to dress, he stood and leaned against the rock, watching her.

His jeans hung empty on the left side, but she was the one who stumbled and couldn't get herself together. Finally she was dressed and pulled on her boot. She straightened, not sure what to say.

There were a thousand things she almost blurted out. Like, "that wasn't supposed to happen." Or, "I don't have sex with strangers." Except Mitch wasn't a stranger. Not exactly.

His dark eyes gave nothing away. She couldn't read him at all. Finally, one corner of his mouth lifted.

"Thanks, babe. I needed that. Next time you're feeling like you want to get laid, give me a call and I'll see if I can fit you in."

The verbal slap landed with perfect precision. She flushed, as shame filled her. She walked toward her horse, grabbed her hat, shoved it on her head, then swung up into the saddle and rode away.

It was only when she was a mile or so from the

rock outcropping that she allowed herself to give in to the tears burning in her eyes. She cried all the way to the barn—some for herself, some for Mitch, but mostly for how young and in love they'd once been and how much had been lost.

CHAPTER TWO

AFTER GETTING his prosthesis reattached, Mitch got into the truck and drove back toward the house. He stopped a half mile or so from the buildings that made up the heart of the ranch. He wasn't ready to face Fidela again. Or anyone.

When he'd awakened on the naval hospital ship and realized what had happened, all he could think was that it was time to go home. That after nearly nine years, he was ready to go back where he belonged. But now that he was here he realized it wasn't home anymore. Everything had changed...including him.

He turned off the engine and leaned back in the seat. He hurt all over, but the worst throbbing came from the part of his leg that didn't exist anymore. He'd been told that would happen and given pages of instructions on how to deal with the pain. Everything from massaging his stump to some stupid-assed hand-rubbing energy woo-woo crap he hadn't bothered reading. He was strong—he would will the pain away. Eventually. Until then he would deal.

The sun had moved in the sky and long shadows crept along the land. Time was passing, although not fast enough to suit him. He wanted it to be a year from now, or five, so he wouldn't have to be adjusting to everything. He wanted that behind him.

Without him wanting it to, his body clenched as if remembering what it felt like to be inside Skye. She'd taken him with a passion he'd never been able to completely forget. She hadn't cared about his missing leg or the years they'd been apart. She'd wanted what he had always been able to give her—what they'd given each other. Then he'd hurt her because she'd deserved it.

Pain had flashed in her eyes and he didn't regret causing it. He could only hope it kept her up nights, that she couldn't breathe for feeling it. He wanted her to have nothing but regret. That might be the first step in evening out the score.

But all the revenge in the world didn't take away the wanting. Even now, not thirty minutes later, he ached for her. Ached to be inside of her, touching her, tasting her. The kissing had been good, but hadn't lasted long enough. He wanted to savor all of her, to lick her between her legs until she screamed and he nearly lost control himself.

He told himself it wouldn't be like that anymore, but he knew he was lying. Whatever happened between them, the fire still burned. It was—

Something moved in the shadows.

He sat up and leaned forward, trying to figure out the shape and speed. A coyote, he thought, disgusted. Scavengers.

Instinctively he reached behind the truck seat, but he hadn't thought to bring a shotgun. Then he saw where the coyote was headed and realized it didn't matter.

The skinny predator moved with a confidence that spoke of experience or extreme hunger. It slipped through a break in the fencing. The hated chickens squawked and tried to get away, but they weren't nearly as fast as the coyote and they were trapped by the fencing. The coyote used that to his advantage. He grabbed one, snapped its neck with a quick, violent shake and retreated, dinner hanging limply from his jaws.

Mitch started the truck's engine and headed back to the house. As he pulled up in front, he saw Arturo standing on the porch, shotgun in hand.

"Did you see what he did?" the older man demanded. "I checked that fence line yesterday but it must have gotten damaged this morning. Damn coyotes are always prowling, always looking for a weak spot. I wish I'd gotten here sooner. I would have shot him."

Mitch hadn't seen Arturo in nearly nine years but, except for a few gray hairs, his manager hadn't changed much. He was still tall and barrel-chested, with a permanent squint as if the sun was always in his eyes. As a kid Mitch had loved watching old

Westerns on TV. He'd thought Arturo was the Latin version of John Wayne—big, brave and able to beat the bad guys, despite any odds.

"It's good to see you, old man," Mitch said.

Arturo dropped the gun onto the bench by the front door and grabbed Mitch by the upper arms. "I'm glad you're back. We missed you. Every night Fidela prayed for your safe return."

"She told me."

"She worried. We both worried."

There was love in the old man's eyes. He had been there for Mitch far more than his own father had ever been. Arturo had taught him all he knew about life.

Carefully, aware of his balance, he hugged the other man. Arturo squeezed him tightly, then slapped him on the back.

"You look good. How do you feel?"

"About what you'd expect."

"Fidela is going to fatten you up. Be prepared to eat. You know how she gets."

"Tell me we're not having chicken," Mitch grumbled, hating the birds.

"We have plenty, even with the one that got away."

"The coyotes can take them all."

Arturo stepped back. "Why would you say that? They're your chickens."

"I don't want 'em. We run beef here. We always have. When did you sell out? Chickens? And organic beef? What's next? Do we all go around saving the spotted owl and hugging trees?"

Arturo frowned, then folded his arms across his big chest. "I told you what I wanted to do seven years ago. I explained everything and said to let me know if you didn't want me to go ahead with the changes."

Which was probably true. "I didn't read any of the reports," Mitch admitted, wishing there was a casual way he could sit down and take the weight off his stump. It felt like it was on fire.

"What about the bank statements?" Arturo asked, sounding more curious than pissed.

"Once in a while." He'd seen enough to know there was plenty of money. The ranch had grown even more profitable in the time he'd been away.

"The cattle industry is changing," Arturo said. "Consumers want things different these days. They worry that their beef isn't safe. They don't want the antibiotics. They want clean poultry that isn't raised in cages. This way we avoid all those problems. Certified, organic beef means…"

Arturo kept talking but Mitch wasn't listening. A hundred years of tradition over in a heartbeat. Nothing was the way he thought it should be. Nothing was right.

He headed for the door. Every step sent pain shooting up his thigh to his hip. His back throbbed.

"You need to know about this," Arturo told him.

"You handle it."

"You're the boss. This is all for you, Mitch. That's why I did it. For you."

Mitch turned slowly. He was sure the old man meant it. That his intentions had been good. "I don't want it," Mitch said slowly. "Any of it. Not the chickens or the organic beef. I want things back the way they were."

What he meant was himself. He knew that. Arturo would know it, too. Nothing about his statement was subtle.

He stepped into the house and stumbled when his prosthesis caught on the threshold. Arturo grabbed him to keep him from going down.

Mitch shook off the help and walked as steadily as he could back to the room Fidela had converted into a bedroom. Once inside, he closed the door, then sat on the bed.

His toes twitched, his ankle moved, his calf tensed. He could feel it. All of it. It was real, as was the pain…and the loss.

Nothing was as it was supposed to be. Everything was screwed up and broken. Even him. Especially him.

SKYE FINISHED rubbing down her horse, then walked back toward the house. For once, the sight of Glory's Gate rising tall and proud against the blue Texas sky didn't lighten her mood. She was battling too many emotions, most of them bad, to appreciate architecture or stately columns. Not when she was torn between the tingles still jolting her body. And shame.

Once in the mudroom, she pulled off her boots and socks and slipped into a pair of sandals. A quick check of the clock told her that casual sex on the ground hadn't put her too far behind schedule.

There was a party that night. A couple hundred of Jed Titan's closest friends would stop by for cocktails between six and eight. A dozen or so of the mighty who attended had been graced with an invitation for dinner, but the meal wasn't her problem. He would take them out for that.

Before then she had to make sure everything was in place. That the party would be perfect. Nothing less was allowed. Titans did things well or they didn't do them at all.

She walked into her downstairs office, the one she used to coordinate the social events that made Glory's Gate sparkle five or six times a month. White dry-erase board covered two of the walls. A grid had been painted in place, allowing her to write in the details for each event. She could look at four different parties at the same time.

Her desk was simple—a long, low surface with a computer and plenty of storage trays for files. She had a Rolodex with the name of every florist, caterer, musician and party planner in a two-hundred-mile radius.

In the closet were hard copies of the details of all the parties she'd given in this house. With an average of five a month over eight years, she was in need of more storage. Because those files contained more than just menus. They listed guests, drinks, decorations, musical selections, the caterer and staff along with any notable particulars—press clippings and even social connections that had been made.

The same information was on her computer and could be sorted by any variation. Two years ago the new White House social secretary had come for a two-day visit and taken continuous notes as Skye explained her process.

It wasn't rocket science, Skye thought as she sank into her chair and turned on her computer. It wasn't even more than mildly interesting. It was just what she did. Skye Titan—master party planner.

"That's not fair," she murmured aloud, knowing that her day job was important. If Jed had remarried, his wife would have taken over, but as he hadn't, it made sense that one of his daughters would step into the breach. Neither Lexi nor Izzy were the least bit interested and there was the tiny fact that Skye had attended Swiss finishing school for nearly two years.

None of this really mattered, she thought, but at least it was a distraction. Because if she didn't think about napkin colors and garnishes she might think about Mitch again.

She knew he'd wanted to hurt her and she even knew why. He'd won that round. So what? She would survive. Eventually the harsh words wouldn't burn so deeply. As for the sex, she would consider that nothing more than a welcome-home present. Slightly more personal than flowers.

She teetered on the knife's edge of emotion. On one side lay cynical humor, on the other, an emotional breakdown. She did her best to fall into sarcastically funny because tears wouldn't solve anything.

Oh, but she'd missed him. She knew he wouldn't believe that and if he did, he wouldn't care. After all, she'd been the one to walk away from him to marry a man she didn't love. She'd been the one to break both their hearts.

"Enough," she said aloud, and pushed to her feet. A quick glance at the clock told her the catering staff should be arriving any second. She returned to the kitchen in time to see three vans pull up.

She welcomed them and chatted with Diane, the catering manager. They'd handled dozens of parties for her and knew what to do. Ten minutes later she climbed the stairs to get ready.

With each step, she felt an ache inside—a physical reminder of what she and Mitch had done.

Sex in the dirt? In the middle of the afternoon? That wasn't her. She was careful and reserved. She was very aware of her position as the head of a charitable foundation and a single mother. She hadn't been on a date since before she'd married Ray. Certainly not since his death. She wouldn't ever allow herself to…

Except she had allowed. She'd done more than

that. She'd taken and given and lost herself in a wave of pleasure she hadn't experienced in nearly nine years. The fire had always burned with Mitch and it still smoldered inside.

"What on earth was I thinking?" she asked herself as she reached the landing. There wasn't an answer, probably because she *hadn't* been thinking.

She walked into her bedroom to find Izzy stretched out on the bed, again watching her TV.

"If you don't like your bedroom, we can find you another one," Skye told her.

Izzy sat up. "There's nothing wrong with my room. I wanted to talk to you before the party."

"The party you're not coming to?"

Izzy grinned. "Not even for money. Come on, Skye. Jed's parties are boring. He expects me to behave."

"Not an area in which you excel."

"Exactly."

Izzy bounced to her feet.

Skye studied her sister. Izzy was the wild child—physically free, emotionally flighty. She feared nothing except getting tied down. Since barely finishing high school, she'd held jobs ranging from ski instructor to underwater welder, the latter being her current position on an oil rig in the Gulf of Mexico.

"I met T.J. last night," Izzy said.

Skye kicked off her sandals. "After you and I talked about what happened?" She groaned. Izzy was very protective and not exactly rational in her approach.

"Tell me you didn't do something that's going to humiliate me."

"Would I do that?"

"Not on purpose."

"I was totally well mannered. You would have been impressed."

"Doubtful," Skye murmured, wondering what part of this conversation was going to make her cringe. "What happened?"

"We talked. He's good-looking. You didn't mention that."

"I guess. Not my type. Not yours, either. He's borderline normal. You know how you hate that."

Izzy crossed to the mirror above the dresser and studied her reflection. "Is he from around here? I get the feeling I've seen him before."

"Yes. He's a couple of years older than Lexi. We all went to the same high school."

"Interesting." Izzy turned to face Skye. "Local rich boy wants to be richer. Jed Titan can help with that. It's an old story, but one I never get tired of hearing. He came on to me."

Skye carefully unzipped her jeans, then pushed them down and stepped out of them. In Izzy's world, every guy came on to her.

"You might want to swing by the kitchen after the party," she said as she headed for the bathroom. "We're having those mini pizza appetizers you like. I'm sure there will be leftovers."

Izzy followed her. "He came on to me, Skye. Seriously. He wants me."

Skye told herself she was too mature to roll her eyes, however much she really wanted to. "Okay. Thanks for the share."

"I'm telling you for your own good. Your sense of duty means you won't blow this guy off on general principle. He's a jerk. Be careful."

Skye's afternoon had been a roller coaster of emotion. The thrill of seeing Mitch again, the pleasure of making love with him, the humiliation of his dismissal. She was tired, confused, ashamed and sick of feeling that everything was her fault.

"Be careful?" she repeated. "Why? Oh, let me guess. Because while T.J. is desperate to have you because you're so amazing, the only reason he could possibly be interested in me is because Jed is offering him money."

Izzy took a step back. "I didn't say that."

"You didn't have to. It's all very clear. I'm no one. A nonsexual being. A man would have to be bribed or desperate to want to get into my bed."

Had Mitch been desperate? Or just angry?

"That's not what I meant," Izzy said loudly, "and you know it. Look, I was mad because he dismissed you and I went to call him on it. We got to talking and he was interested. That's all."

Skye's temper grew. "You went to defend me and

ended up getting a date? Gee, thanks. Your support is overwhelming."

"It's not like you ever date," Izzy snapped. "You're not exactly experienced with guys like him. I'm trying to help."

"I don't need your help."

"Obviously not. Fine. Date him. Play the game. Do what Daddy says. It's what you're good at."

Izzy stalked from the bathroom. Seconds later, the bedroom door slammed.

Skye looked around for something to throw, but she didn't keep anything breakable in the bathroom. Not with a child in the house. She was too sensible for that.

Izzy might be too self-absorbed to understand anyone else's point of view, but she'd gotten one thing right. Skye did do what Daddy said. She was the good mother, the good sister, the good daughter. The good girl. Although if she had sex in the dirt with Mitch a second time, she just might be on her way to blowing her reputation.

And that would be okay with her.

"What an interesting musical choice," the congressman's wife said, staring at the four college kids Skye had hired for the evening. "That kind of music is…"

"Hip-hop," Skye told her. "I read about the group. They're attending Texas A&M and supplementing their scholarships by performing. I went to hear them last month and was impressed."

She'd dropped into a frat party to hear them, but the congressman's wife wouldn't want to know that. Three different guys had hit on Skye in the twenty minutes she'd been in the house. The fact that they were barely out of high school and completely drunk had pretty much diluted any possible compliment.

"Interesting," the other woman said.

Skye was pretty sure she actually meant something more along the lines of "horrifying" but was too polite to say that. Skye didn't care. She liked the guys and their music. She could go the rest of her life without hearing another tasteful quartet.

She excused herself to circulate. There were two hundred people to greet and make feel welcome. The evening seemed more stressful than usual, probably because of her fight with Izzy. She hated arguing with either of her sisters. With their mother gone and Jed being, well, Jed, they only had one another to depend on.

They would talk later, she promised herself. Make things right.

"So far, so good," Jed said as he moved past her.

Skye shook her head. She knew what her father implied—that things were fine now, but the evening wasn't over. There could still be a disaster.

"Have you noticed that every party I've given has been perfect?" she muttered.

"I'm not sure talking to yourself gives a good first impression."

Skye turned toward the speaker and saw T.J. next to her. "Maybe not, but it ensures I have plenty of personal space. How are you? If you're looking for Izzy, this isn't her thing. Or is talking to me going to work, too?"

T.J. winced. "So you did hear."

"News travels fast. Titanville is a small town."

"And the doors at Glory's Gate need to be thicker." He put his hand on her back and guided her to a corner. "I'm sorry. I doubt me saying that makes a difference, but I really am. I was making a point with your father."

He sounded sincere, which meant exactly nothing. "The point being?"

"That when he says jump, I'm not going to ask how high. You're beautiful, Skye. I hope you believe me because I'm telling the truth. You're lovely and intriguing and if I had let Jed know I was the least bit interested in you, he'd have all the power. I can't give that away."

Words she could understand. But could she trust them? Or him? "Not to worry, T.J. We're fine."

One eyebrow lifted. "But you're dismissing me?"

"I'm letting you off the hook."

"We could have dinner together instead. Or have I blown it with you? The fact that your father's pushing us to be together isn't my fault."

She smiled. "I know that. Not dating you because my father would like it is the same as dating someone he wouldn't like just to annoy him."

"Now I'm confused."

"I don't know you well enough to have an opinion of you."

"Let's change that."

His eyes were deep blue and he wore his custom suit with style and ease. He should have been everything she ever wanted.

"Did you come on to Izzy?" she asked.

His gaze never wavered. "We talked last night. Mostly about how she wanted to kick my ass for what I'd said. Did I mention I was sorry?"

"More than once. But you also didn't answer the question. Did you come on to my sister?"

"It's a trick question. If I say yes, I'm a jerk. If I say no, you'll think I don't like her."

She smiled. "Maybe."

He leaned close and whispered in her ear. "You're the one I'm asking out, Skye. Say yes."

He didn't make her heart beat faster, but that wasn't a bad thing. It meant he would probably never break it.

"Please?" he murmured.

She hesitated, then nodded. "Dinner would be nice."

MITCH PULLED the sock over his stump, only to wince as the soft fabric came into contact with the raw and bleeding flesh. He'd been doing too much, too soon, and he was paying the price. His therapist had warned him about pacing himself, not that Mitch had listened.

Ignoring the pain shooting through his leg, he eased it into the prosthesis, then tentatively pushed into a standing position. While it hurt, the soreness was bearable. As the alternative was crutches and an empty pant leg, he told himself he was fine.

He left the makeshift bedroom and walked into the kitchen. He wasn't hungry, but knew if he didn't make an appearance, Fidela would come looking for him. He'd escaped her last night by turning out the lights in his room, guessing she would think he was asleep. But that wasn't going to work for long. Fidela was stubborn and wily. He would rather face her directly. Besides, she was a whole lot easier than the dark.

When it was dark, the past returned, haunting him like a ghost. He remembered what it had been like to be in love with Skye. How happy they'd been. He remembered his pain and disbelief when she'd told him it was over.

In the dark, he remembered the explosion and how Pete had saved him, dragging him, not even slowing when he'd gotten shot himself. Pete had recovered in a couple of weeks and was already back in Afghanistan. Mitch knew the loss of his leg was just one of those things and the sooner he got over it, the sooner the dark would lose its power.

He stepped into the bright, sunny kitchen. Fidela stood at the counter, mixing something in a bowl.

"Morning," he said, then frowned when he saw a young girl sitting at the table. "Who are you?"

She had red hair and big blue eyes. She looked familiar even though he knew he'd never seen her before. Her spoon dropped into her cereal as she sprang to her feet and beamed at him.

"You're here! You're really here. Fiddle said you were coming home and I've been waiting forever." She moved close and reached out a hand, touching his arm as if to make sure he was real. "I've been hoping and praying. Fiddle and I prayed for you every day. And I talked about you in school and we sent cards to the soldiers. Did you get mine? I put your name on the envelope. It was pink. I know that's a girl color, but it's pretty. And you're a hero and I thought you'd like something pretty and Fiddle said you'd come home and you're here!"

"Who the…" He caught himself. "Who are you?"

She grinned. "I'm Erin. Fiddle and Arturo missed you so much. Arturo didn't say anything, but I could tell. He was sad in his eyes. And Fiddle talked about you all the time, so it's like I knew you and then I missed you, too. Are you hungry? Fiddle's making pancakes. I really wanted some, but I waited for you because you're back and it's polite. So do you want pancakes?"

Fidela wiped her hands on a towel. "Good morning," she said, moving behind the girl and putting her hands on Erin's shoulders. "This is Erin."

"I told him that," the girl said happily as she smiled at him.

"Skye's daughter."

He got it then—the red hair, the shape of her eyes, although Skye's were green, not blue. He saw the similarities in the set of her shoulders.

Here it was—living proof of Skye's betrayal. Her child with another man.

The anger that lived inside of him flared again, making him want to raise his fist to the heavens. But then what? Did he plan to call God out? And if he did, what made him think God gave a damn?

"Why are you here?" he snapped.

Fidela glared at him. "Erin comes over most days. She keeps me company."

Some of the brightness faded from the girl's smile. "I wanted to see you," she said, sounding less sure of herself. "I wanted to meet you."

Skye's daughter. The child they were supposed to have together. She'd promised to marry him and then had walked away because her father had told her to. She'd chosen Jed's old friend as a husband, rather than him, and Erin was the result.

"I'm going to make pancakes now," Fidela told the girl. "Why don't you get the plates."

"Okay." Erin looked at him out of the corner of her eye, then turned away.

Fidela was at his side in a heartbeat and dug her fingers into his arm. "She is a little girl," she whispered. "She believes that you're someone special. Do you understand me? She didn't do anything wrong. You have no reason to be angry with her."

He would have ignored the words, except Fidela was right. Erin wasn't to blame for her mother's actions and he hadn't fallen far enough into hell to take out his rage on an innocent child. Not yet, anyway.

He nodded once.

Fidela tightened her grip.

"I'm fine," he told her.

She released him and returned to the stove where she picked up a pot of coffee. Mitch limped to the table. Erin stood there, looking uncertain. He forced himself to smile.

"It's nice to meet you, Erin," he said, feeling stupid but determined to make an effort.

Her smile returned. "Do you want me to get you a mug? I know where they are."

"Sure." He eased into the seat. "Thanks."

She brought back a blue mug and set it in front of him. Fidela poured his coffee.

"I'll get started on the pancakes," she said.

Erin sat across from him. "Are you happy to be home? I would get really sad if I had to go away. Were you sad? Do you have lots of friends where you were? I have friends and I have horses, too. I ride."

"Erin rides over nearly every day all by herself. Very impressive for a little girl."

Erin laughed. "Fiddle, I'm not little. I'm growing like a weed." She smiled at him. "That's what Mom says. Are your friends going to come visit you? Did you fly on a big plane to get home? I was on a plane once. I wasn't scared at all. Mom says I'm fearless. I'm not sure what that means, but it's good, right?"

She kept on talking, apparently not needing anyone to participate. She had an energy he admired. These days it took everything he had just to stay standing. As long as he didn't think about Skye, he could handle Erin sitting across from him, looking at him as if he'd just made her day.

"Fiddle says you're getting more medals. She says you've saved our country."

He glanced at the older woman. "I had help," he said dryly.

"But you're very brave. You're a hero."

He frowned. "I'm not a hero."

Erin's eyes widened. "But you are. Everyone knows that."

He started to argue, then shrugged. Let the kid think what she wanted. Life would teach her hard lessons soon enough.

Fidela slid a plate of pancakes in front of each of them.

Erin picked up her fork. "I told Mom there would

be pancakes, but she didn't want to get up. She said she was tired."

He wondered if Skye hadn't slept well. Had she been haunted, as he had? Had she relived their time together? Had his harsh words wounded her?

He ignored any stirrings of guilt, telling himself she deserved what she got.

The pancakes were better than he remembered. He'd finished three when Erin asked, "Can you ride a horse without your leg? I hope you can because then we could go riding together. Does it hurt? You have a new leg, right? Fiddle told me about it. Can I see?"

Mitch froze, not sure what to say. No one outside the hospital and rehab center had been so open in discussing the amputation. He wasn't sure if he appreciated Erin's attitude or if he wanted her to shut up.

Fidela walked over and touched Erin's shoulder. "Maybe less questions on the first day."

Erin sighed. "I talk too much. Everyone tells me that. Sometimes I don't want to talk about stuff, either."

"We can talk about it later," Mitch said, surprising himself.

Erin brightened. "Okay. And it's my birthday soon. I'm having a party. You can come. You don't even have to bring a present. There's cake. You like cake, don't you?"

A kid's birthday party? "I, ah—"

"It's at my house, which is right next door. You can find it easy." She looked hopeful.

He found himself not wanting to hurt her feelings, but there was no way he wanted to go. "Erin, I—"

"I'm going to be eight and that's a big deal. Mom keeps telling me that. Eight means I'm getting big and everything."

She might have kept talking, but he wasn't sure. The words became a hum that buzzed in the back of his mind.

Eight? Erin was turning eight?

The math was easy. Beyond easy. He knew the exact date of the last time he and Skye had made love. He knew when and where and how they'd held on to each other. They'd been planning on getting married. Laughter had shared space with the moans and cries. There had been so much anticipation.

He looked at Erin, studying the shape of her mouth, the way she held her head. He saw it in her fingers and her movements.

The pancakes he'd eaten sat in his stomach like a rock. He felt both sick and stunned. Reality stared back at him in the form of a nearly eight-year-old girl.

Erin was his. Skye'd had his child and hadn't bothered to tell him.

CHAPTER THREE

SKYE FINISHED her speech to the women's group in Austin. She'd started with a few funny stories and had ended with a couple of case studies about specific children to bring the point home. In the middle, she'd carefully layered in the painful statistics about the over twelve million children who lived in food-insecure households. A statistic her foundation wanted to change.

"I have a few minutes for questions," she said from behind the podium.

One young woman in a red power suit stood. "Why did you pick this issue? You're a Titan. You probably never even knew anyone who went to bed hungry."

Skye had been asked this before and it always annoyed her. Did she have to have cancer to want to donate to that cause? She'd never been in a natural disaster, either. Did that mean the Red Cross was out of luck?

Then she reminded herself of the greater good,

that the person asking the question was probably curious. Cynical, but curious.

"When my daughter was a year old," Skye began, "she fell down the stairs and hit her head on a table. There was blood everywhere and being a good mother, I completely panicked."

The women in the audience laughed.

Skye leaned forward. "We went to the emergency room where she was treated. While we were waiting to fill out the insurance info, I bought a box of animal crackers in the vending machine. A girl about seven or eight walked over and asked me if I was going to eat them."

The audience faded and Skye was back to that moment in the emergency waiting room. The girl had been blond and painfully thin. Her clothes hung on her.

"I gave her the crackers and asked who she was with. She said her mother had been brought in. They lived on the street and she hadn't eaten in three days. I asked my sister to take my daughter home and I took the girl to the cafeteria for dinner. When the social worker arrived, she wasn't surprised by the girl's condition. It happens far too often, in neighborhoods very close to where we live."

Skye drew in a breath. "I went home and took care of my daughter but I couldn't forget about that other little girl. I called the social worker and made an appointment. I wanted to talk about being a foster parent. I knew I had to do something to make a difference. But when I got to the appointment, the woman was tired and busy and told me she didn't have any time for rich people who wanted to play at making a difference. I was a Titan. Why didn't I do something that mattered?"

She shrugged. "I was angry and insulted, but I also thought she might be right. I had an inheritance from my mother, which became the seed money for the foundation. We feed over a million children a year. When I say feed, I don't mean a lunch here or a Christmas dinner there. We provide one to three meals a day to over a million children right here, in this country. Our goal is to make sure no child ever goes hungry again. It's ambitious but I believe it can be done. We can make a difference, one box of animal crackers at a time."

She leaned toward the microphone. "What are you doing to make a difference?"

The woman in the red power suit sat down.

Questions continued for a few minutes. Afterward, Skye chatted with several of the women, took a few checks for contributions before driving to the airport where she caught the shuttle to Dallas. An hour later, she was back in at the foundation.

"You did good," Elsa, her secretary, said as Skye walked into her office. "We've already had three calls from people wanting to be silver-level sponsors. I'm sending out packages today."

Skye passed over the checks. "We're growing," she said. "That's what we want. The more people interested in the problem, the more chance we have to fix it." She shrugged out of her suit jacket and kicked off her heels. Most days she did the business casual thing, but when she was speaking, she wanted to look the part. "What did I miss?"

"Glenna wants to see you," Elsa said. "She says it's important. I cleared you for the next hour. Then you have a phone interview with the *LA Times*."

While the foundation had an excellent PR department, nothing seemed quite so interesting to the press as speaking to an actual Titan. When she wanted to complain about the drain on her time, Skye reminded herself that she was on a mission. So what if she was inconvenienced or tired or pulled in too many directions? She was feeding hungry children. What could matter more?

"Do we have prep answers?" Skye asked.

Elsa produced a folder that would contain all the current statistics on hunger in America, information on how the foundation squeezed every penny until it screamed for mercy, their success at fund-raising and a list of ways the average person could make a difference.

"Great. Thanks. Send Glenna in."

"Will do."

Skye had time to finish nearly two e-mails before her managing director walked in. Glenna was a forty-something professional who knew what it took to run a successful charitable foundation. She'd been courted by every major charity in the country. Skye had been determined to win her.

"I did the lunch thing today," Skye said as Glenna paused to close the door behind her. The other women looked concerned. "I was going to complain about it, but something tells me I shouldn't."

Glenna had short dark hair, sensibly cut, and an easy smile. Only she wasn't smiling today.

"We have a problem," she said, sitting on the opposite side of Skye's desk. "Another one. And it's big."

Skye didn't like the sound of that. A couple of months ago someone had gone to the district attorney, claiming that the foundation was a front for money laundering. Skye and her people had been cleared of all charges, but too much time and money had been spent proving they were innocent.

Glenna passed over several newspaper articles. "I downloaded these from the Internet. Two of them will appear in print over the next few days. They say that our executives are being paid excessive salaries and bonuses. Money that should be going to feed children is funding vacations, cars and parties. Supposedly you make over a million dollars."

Skye wanted to scream. "I don't get a salary at all," she said, deliberately keeping her voice quiet.

"I know, as does everyone who works here. We also don't pay bonuses of any kind. These are all lies. I've contacted the reporters and will be meeting with each of them. I'll try to find out who gave this information and why they wrote about it without checking with us first. One of them claimed he did speak with someone from the foundation."

Skye felt as if someone had hit her on the back of the head with a tire iron. "This is insane."

"I'll take care of it," Glenna said. "I just wanted you to know what was going on."

"I appreciate that. Let me know what happens."

Glenna nodded and left.

Skye reached for the phone and dialed a familiar cell number. "Where are you?" she asked when her sister answered.

"About five minutes away. Why?"

"Can you stop by? I need to talk to you about something."

Lexi Titan was as good as her word. Less than five minutes later she walked into Skye's office.

"What's up?" she asked. Lexi was the cool, blond beauty of the sisters. She owned a day spa and could easily be their spokesmodel. Her clothes were elegant, her skin perfect, her hair a shimmering cascade of ice-blond. Despite being nearly three months' pregnant, she didn't show at all. If they hadn't been sisters, Skye would have found it fairly easy to dislike someone as perfect as Lexi.

But none of that mattered now. Skye stood and hugged her, then led the way to a sofa against the far wall.

"I heard from Garth again," she said.

"Our evil half brother came acalling?"

"In a manner of speaking. Apparently the tip to the D.A. about the foundation laundering money was only the first part of his attack. Now he's got someone telling reporters that we pay excessive salaries and bonuses, not to mention fund staff vacations."

Lexi took the papers Skye held out but didn't read them. "We knew something like this was going to happen. We knew his campaign was just beginning."

A few months ago the sisters had received their first threat from Garth Duncan. At the beginning they couldn't figure out why the successful businessman would care about them. A little digging had produced an unbelievable fact. He was their half brother, and Jed Titan's bastard.

Although Jed claimed Garth and his mother had been given a generous trust fund that should have taken care of them for life, Garth was out for blood. Or at the very least, the destruction of the Titans. He'd waged business and personal attacks on Lexi and Skye, along with Jed. And the hits kept on coming.

"Glenna is looking into this," Skye said. "But these reporters aren't stupid. They would check their facts. Which meant Garth was able to give them the information in such a way that they believed it." She felt sick to her stomach. "Can't he go pick on someone else? Does it have to be us?"

"We're the family he never had," Lexi reminded

her. "He's angry. I just wish I knew what had triggered all this. Why now? Why wait so long to start?"

"He's certainly moving forward with whatever plan he has. This one is especially good. The D.A. won't get involved, but the IRS will. His claims put our nonprofit status at risk. Worse, who will want to donate? Being bad is always front-page news, but the retraction comes much later and on the back page. No one remembers that. They just remember the charges."

Frustration flared inside of her. "I will accept that for some reason Garth hates us. But children will go hungry because of his actions. Doesn't that matter?"

Lexi shook her head. "Not to him."

Skye stood and crossed to the window. "This is beyond frustrating. I have worked my butt off here. I wanted to make a difference and I have. When the rest of my life is in the toilet, the foundation reminds me of what is important. That at the end of the day, I can count the meals we served and the lives we made better. I won't let him take that from me or from those kids."

Lexi stood and moved toward her. "He's not going to win. We won't let him." She hugged Skye. "We're the Titan girls. Nobody screws with us."

"Garth didn't get the memo."

"Then we'll send another one."

"Okay. Just give me a minute and I'll be feisty again."

"We'll get him. One way or another."

"I know."

They returned to the sofas. Lexi sat across from Skye.

"Is there anything else you want to tell me?" she asked. "You don't usually let things get to you. You're as much a fighter as any of us."

Skye leaned back in the cushions. "There's a lot going on right now. I'm a little distracted. It'll get better." She hesitated. "Mitch is back. I've seen him."

Lexi stared at her. "Oh my God! What happened. How is he?"

"I'm not sure. He's different. I know it's been years and he's been through a lot. But I didn't think…" That he would turn mean, she thought, knowing she couldn't say that. She loved her sister and trusted her completely, but she wasn't ready to talk about what had happened.

"He's someone I used to know, right? Just a guy from my past."

"You keep saying that," Lexi said, her voice gentle. "As if you're trying to convince us he doesn't matter. But the fact that he has you rattled means that he does matter. At least a little."

"I don't want him to."

"Maybe you don't get a choice." Lexi smiled. "Look, he was your *first love,* your *first lover.* The relationship didn't end on its own. It was emotionally violent for both of you. You were wrenched apart."

"Because of me," Skye said bitterly. "Mitch sure remembers that."

"You hurt him."

"I didn't have a choice." She glared at Lexi, daring her to say she did. That there were always choices. But it was easy to be critical from far away. Skye had lost her mother when she was only ten; she would have done anything to keep her father—that included giving up Mitch.

"I know," Lexi said. "But Mitch could never understand. There was an intensity between the two of you. It's not surprising you were both hurt."

"When did you get sensible?" Skye grumbled. "I want to be the sensible one."

"You will be. Just not about this. I couldn't be rational about Cruz for a minute."

Just speaking her fiancé's name made Lexi glow. Skye did her best not to be envious, but it was hard. Love should be powerful and compelling—like she'd had with Mitch all those years ago. She'd loved her husband, but it had never been the same all-consuming passion. She had adored Ray, but she'd burned for Mitch...long after she should have. Yet another guilty secret, she thought sadly.

"You were young," Lexi said. "It was a long time ago. Give yourself a break."

"Because you think I made the wrong choice?" Skye asked. "I don't. I did what I had to. What was right."

"I know."

Lexi said the words, but Skye wasn't sure she believed them. Skye had given up love to play it safe. Who did that? Didn't she deserve the consequences of her actions?

"To give up Ray would have meant giving up Erin. She's my daughter. I can't imagine life without her."

"I know," Lexi said. "She's amazing. You're lucky to have her. Isn't that the most important thing?"

"Yes," Skye murmured. A few months ago her life had been boring and familiar. Now there was very little she could count on.

"As for Mitch," Lexi continued. "Why worry about him? It's not as if you're going to be seeing that much of him."

"You're right. I know he's back, we spoke, end of story. It's not as if we're going to be running into each other very often."

IT WAS a little after four when Skye heard yelling just outside her office. She stood to investigate, but before she could cross the room, the door burst open and Mitch stalked inside. Elsa ran alongside him, trying to get in front.

"I'm sorry," she said. "I explained you were busy, but he insisted."

From the angry look on Mitch's face, he'd done more than insist.

"Don't worry about it," Skye told her assistant. "Mitch and I are old friends. I'm happy to see him."

Elsa didn't seem convinced, but nodded and backed out of the room.

"Have a seat," Skye said, pointing to the chair by her desk.

"No, thanks. This won't take long."

He looked good, she thought, taking in the jeans and white shirt. Furious but good. His color was better than the last time she'd seen him and the lines of pain around his eyes had eased.

Despite everything that had happened, despite what he'd said, she was happy to see him. She wanted to go to him and hold him. She wanted to do a whole lot more than that, which probably meant she needed some intensive therapy or at the very least a self-help book with a snappy title.

"You're obviously pissed off," she said, folding her arms across her chest. "Which I find interesting. If anyone has the right to be mad, it's me."

"Do you think I'm stupid?" he asked.

"Is that a trick question?"

He ignored her. "I had an interesting visitor at breakfast Saturday morning. Erin."

Skye opened her mouth, then closed it. She wasn't sure what to say. Erin had breakfast with Fidela most weekends. If Skye was up, they would ride over together. If not, Arturo came and got the little girl. It was a tradition, one that Erin treasured.

"Let me guess," Skye said bitterly. "You object to my daughter being on the ranch. Give it a rest, Mitch.

I know you're adjusting and that you're dealing with an incredibly unfair situation, but Erin has nothing to do with that. She and Fidela adore each other. She's like their granddaughter. They don't have kids of their own. You were like their son, so even you should understand. Don't tell me that Erin can't go over there anymore."

"Is that what you think this is about?" he asked. "Your kid eating pancakes with Fidela?"

"Yes," she said cautiously. "What else is there?"

"Interesting question. Erin invited me to her birthday party. She's turning eight."

"Okay."

He took a step toward her. "Did you think I wouldn't find out? That I wouldn't get it?"

"I have no idea what you're talking about." He looked like he wanted to rip her into tiny pieces. But for what? Her daughter turning eight?

"She told me when her birthday is," he said, his voice filled with rage. "I did the math. When the hell were you going to tell me that Erin is my daughter?"

The room shifted. Had they been in California, Skye would have assumed this was the big one. She couldn't breathe, couldn't think and, even through the wild disbelief, she ached for him. For the pain she was about to cause.

"Don't pretend you're surprised," he told her. "I know the last time we had sex, kid. It was right after I proposed."

"I remember," she said. She remembered everything about that night and the day that followed. "Oh, Mitch. No."

He narrowed his gaze. "Don't bother pretending she's not mine."

"She's not," she whispered.

His expression tightened. "Bullshit. Either she's mine or you're a whore."

She felt as if he'd hit her. "Those are not my only two choices."

"What else is there? If Erin is Ray's kid, then you jumped into bed with that old man, what? Two days later? You putting out on the first date now, Skye?" His mouth twisted. "Maybe you are. These days you don't even require a date. Just a private spot in the sun and a willing guy."

She raised her hand to slap him. He grabbed her by the wrist and held on hard enough to bruise.

"Tell me," he whispered, his eyes blazing. "Did you like fucking the old man?"

Tears burned in her eyes. She pulled free of him and stepped back. Her throat felt tight, as if she would never be able to swallow again.

It hadn't been the first date, but the third and she'd cried the whole time. She'd slept with Ray to find out if she could. He'd held her and told her he'd never meant to hurt her. That he always thought she was special but if the idea of being with him was so disgusting, he would walk away.

He'd been kind and understanding. Sure, he'd wanted an eighteen-year-old bride, but he hadn't been a jerk about it. She'd been tempted to tell Ray that she would never love anyone but Mitch. But Jed had taken her aside and warned her that if she refused Ray, not only would she be dead to him, but that he would destroy the Cassidy Ranch. He would take Mitch's inheritance and erase it from the face of the earth.

She'd believed him but she'd still longed for Mitch. In the end circumstances had made the decision for her. She'd been pregnant with Ray's baby. Just over seven months later, Erin had been born—five weeks premature.

Now she sucked in a breath, wiped away her tears and faced Mitch.

"Erin isn't yours," she said clearly.

"I don't believe you and I'll destroy you for keeping her from me."

"You'll have to prove it first."

"I want a DNA test. If you don't agree, I'm willing to go to court to get it."

A part of her understood. Given their past and the timing of events, it made sense that he thought Erin could be his. A part of her had always wished she was. It was a secret she'd kept from Ray, one that had shamed her. But she'd been unable to let it go.

Mitch's choices were simple. Erin was his or the woman he'd loved had betrayed him.

She thought about explaining that Erin had a birthmark on the small of her back. A tiny half-moon stain that Ray and all his other children shared. She doubted Mitch would believe her.

"I'll agree to a DNA test on the condition that you keep this to yourself," she said quietly. "You won't discuss it with Erin. I don't want her hurt."

"You're not in a position to dictate terms."

She raised her chin. "Erin is my daughter. She's a child and doesn't deserve to be in the middle of this. If you really think she's yours, you shouldn't want her hurt or confused. She can't know until we have the results."

Mitch's dark eyes gave nothing away. "Agreed. I'll call a lab and have someone stop by."

He turned and left without saying anything else. She watched him go. He walked slowly but steadily. If she hadn't known about the prosthesis, she might not have guessed there was anything wrong.

When she was alone, she sank into her chair and closed her eyes. She hadn't expected this. Didn't he know her well enough to believe she wouldn't keep his child from him?

Obviously not, she thought sadly. He believed the worst about her. When he found out the truth about Erin, he would know that she, Skye, hadn't been lying. But she had a bad feeling that wasn't going to make an already difficult situation any better.

MITCH STOOD in the center of the stable. The smell of horse and hay was exactly as he remembered, but he felt completely out of place. What he had once taken for granted now only served to point out everything he *couldn't* do. Ride? He couldn't get on a horse, let alone guide it.

Riding should have been easy. He could use a mount, so he didn't have to push off with his left leg as he swung his right leg over the saddle. But he was unable to balance on his prosthesis. Once on the horse, he wouldn't have the control to use his left heel.

Frustration, never far away, bubbled to the surface. What was he supposed to do with himself now? Ride around in the truck, like an old man?

"I have something for you."

He turned toward the voice and saw Arturo leading a bay into the barn. The gelding was big and moved easily.

Mitch took a step back. His heel caught in the wood floor and he nearly fell into the hay.

"This is Bullet," Arturo said, stroking the horse's nose. "He's been trained so you can mount him on the right side. You also only need to use your right heel. He's strong and fast, with a bit of a temper. I thought you two would have that in common."

Mitch curled his hands into fists. "I don't need your help," he growled.

"Maybe not, but I'm offering it. Besides, I used your money to buy him."

That should have made him smile, but Mitch was beyond humor. He hated everything about the ranch. The chickens, the organic beef with every single thing about their lives documented. He hated how the socks on his stump were soaked with blood every night and how the nightmares kept him from sleeping. He hated that he'd been so grateful to be alive only to find out nothing about his life was how he wanted it.

"You want to ride again," Arturo told him. "I know you do."

"Stay out of my life."

The old man's mouth tightened. "Fine," he said, and dropped the reins. He walked out, leaving Mitch and the horse alone in the barn.

Mitch felt like an ass. He knew Arturo was only trying to help, but there were—

He heard footsteps and was surprised Arturo had returned. But when he looked toward the entrance he saw a different silhouette.

"You're even more of a bastard than I thought," Skye said as she moved into the barn. "Does it make you feel like a man to hurt people who love you?"

She was the last person he wanted to see. Worse, she'd witnessed a part of him he had trouble controlling.

"He loves you," she said. "He wants you to know that." She patted the horse's neck. "Come on, Mitch. Why is that so bad?"

"Arturo is fine. He can take care of himself."

"You're his family. He shouldn't have to."

"Get out," he told her.

She moved closer, until she stood right in front of him. "Are you going to make me? You've pretty much peaked on crappy things to say to me. So what's left?" She raised her chin. "Want to hit me? It seems that you want to hit somebody. Why not me? Don't I deserve it?"

"Do you like it rough these days?" he sneered.

She flushed but held her ground. "I know that certain parts of your life suck, but you got to come home. That counts. You have people who are thrilled you're back. That counts more. What I want to know is, do you have a timetable on the pity party? Or is it playing indefinitely?"

"Right. Because it's so easy for you to judge from your perfect life. Want to trade, Skye? Want to give up a leg or an arm? Live with that for a while and then we'll talk."

"You are so full of crap," she said. "This isn't about your leg. This is about you."

He wanted to crush her. He wanted to take her and make her beg. He wanted her naked and vulnerable and then he wanted to walk away.

She stared into his eyes as if daring him to do everything he was thinking. Finally she drew a breath.

"Erin has provided her DNA sample. Anytime you're ready, you can do the same. Then we'll be done."

"Erin's mine. We're only starting. I'm spending my nights thinking of all the ways I'm going to punish you for what you've done to me."

Sadness invaded her green eyes. "If hating me gives you strength, then go for it. But I will warn you not to get too excited about taking me on. Erin's not yours, Mitch. No matter how much you want her to be, she's not. And if calling me a whore makes that easier to bear, then go for it. Just remember this. That little girl thinks you're a hero. If you give her one reason to believe otherwise, I will make you regret being born."

That made him smile. "You really think you can?"

"Absolutely. You're so far down, you don't care if you live or die. I have something to fight for. My daughter."

She left then, her back straight, her long red hair beckoning. He watched her go, admiring her spirit, however delusional. There would only be one winner in this game and it was going to be him.

CHAPTER FOUR

THE PRIVATE AIRFIELD catered to the rich and adventurous. T. J. Boone qualified for both, Izzy thought as she walked toward him. He'd called the previous afternoon to invite her to join him skydiving. She'd accepted to see how far he would take the game.

As she took in his chiseled features and easy smile she asked herself if that was really her only motive. Was she actually interested in T.J.? He looked good both on paper and in person, which was normally more than enough for her. But this guy was different. This guy might be playing her and Skye in a big way.

She was here to find out who he was and what he wanted. Part of her wanted to prove she was right not to trust him. Part of her wanted to protect Skye, however much her sister might not believe her.

Self-sacrifice was both new and uncomfortable, she thought. She must remember not to do this sort of thing again.

T.J. pushed off his BMW M3 and walked toward her. "Scared?" he asked.

She looked past him to the small plane that would take them skyward before they jumped back to earth.

"I've done this before. It's no big. The real danger isn't from the falling, it's the landing that can kill you." She stared into his blue eyes. "What's the plan? You're going to try to keep up with me? Not likely."

"You say that now," he told her, then smiled. "I'll prove myself."

"And then what? You want to compare me to Skye? Doubling up on your odds? Does Jed not care which of his daughters you take, as long as you claim one of us?"

He continued to smile at her. "You're very cynical."

"I've known Jed a long time. He's not the warm and fuzzy type."

"Neither am I. Isn't that what makes life interesting?" He jerked his shoulder toward the waiting plane. "Come on, Izzy. You know you want to."

She *did* want to jump. It wasn't silent, like everyone said. It was loud, with the air rushing by and the sound of her heart filling her ears. For those few minutes, she was totally free and out of time. She could imagine what it was like to have everything she wanted, to be both connected and alone.

They walked into the flight office and signed the necessary paperwork, then suited up. She half expected T.J. to make a move as she stepped into the jumpsuit, but he left her alone. Then they were on the plane, waiting to take off.

"You do this sort of thing often?" she asked over the roar of the engine. They spoke into microphones, with headphones so they could hear each other and the pilot.

"When I get the chance. I like the rush. What about you?"

"I enjoy it."

"I've heard there's a lot you enjoy. Rock climbing, cave diving."

"Swimming with sharks, mountain climbing, white-water rafting. Want to see my scars?"

His gaze never left her face. "You're going to have to trust me."

"Why? You didn't pack my parachute. You're just a guy, T.J. I haven't figured out your game, but I will. I meant what I said before. Hurt my sister and you'll be in a world of hurt yourself."

"You think you could take me, little girl?"

"I'm a Titan. I have staff to take you."

That made him laugh. "I'm not afraid."

"In the immortal words of Yoda, you will be."

The plane took off and soon they were soaring into the blue sky. She'd jumped in several parts of the country and had done some mountain climbing in the Himalayas but nowhere else was the sky the color that it was in Texas.

"Maybe I like you," he said, his voice coming over the headphones.

She looked at him. "You don't know me well enough to like me. Are you dating my sister?"

"No."

She'd been around powerful men enough to recognize that she'd asked the wrong question. "Do you and Skye have a date planned."

He barely hesitated. "Yes."

"May the best woman win?"

He shrugged. "Like you said. I don't know you. Yet."

"So you're going to see which one you like best before picking?"

"I already have an idea about that."

She supposed she was supposed to infer that he was leaning toward her. Big whoop. For all her success with her foundation and as a single mom, Skye was a baby when it came to the real dating world. She didn't understand that men like T.J. would do whatever it took to get ahead. And she wasn't going to listen to Izzy on the topic.

Unless Izzy had proof of T.J.'s sliminess.

The problem was she didn't dislike him—she just didn't trust him. Which left her confused. She was once again forced to ask if she was doing this to save her sister or to help herself to some good-looking guy.

Izzy hated self-awareness nearly as much as she hated sitting still. Fortunately the plane had reached the right altitude. They stood and adjusted their parachutes, then got into position, leaving their headsets behind.

"You really going to do this?" T.J. yelled.

"Of course." She elbowed him out of the way,

walked to the open door, waited for the thumbs-up and jumped.

The sensation of plummeting toward the earth thrilled every part of her. The air rushed by so fast, she had trouble breathing, but that didn't bother her at all. It was just her and the day and invisible forces of gravity pulling her steadily down and down and down.

She laughed from the joy of the moment, from the pleasure of being exactly where she wanted to be. Right now she didn't care about T.J. or his motives or anything else. She spread her arms and turned in the air, pumped on the adrenaline rush.

Seconds later, reluctantly, she braced herself and the parachute popped open. The free fall ended in a quick upward jerk, followed by an easy back and forth drifting to the landing spot.

As the ground raced toward her, she bent her knees and relaxed so the impact wouldn't hurt, then settled on a spot of brown grass.

T.J. landed a few feet away. He laughed as he unfastened his parachute, then stalked over, grabbed her and kissed her.

His mouth was firm and sensual, taking as much as offering. "What a rush," he said when he released her. "Nothing beats it."

She stayed where she was, trying to gauge her reaction to the kiss. It had been fast but nice. She wouldn't say no to another one, but she wasn't dying to repeat the process.

"Some things beat it," she said. "You're obviously doing them wrong."

It was an automatic response. She flirted with available men. She measured interest and frequently took advantage of the situation because it was fun. She didn't get involved so there was never a boyfriend to worry about. Life was too short for commitments.

"Is that a challenge?" he asked.

"Do you want it to be?"

He grabbed her by the shoulders and pulled her against him. She was a lot shorter than him and he had to bend over to kiss her again.

She put her hands on his shoulders, as much to feel the strength of him as to hang on. She was in no danger of falling.

While the feel of his lips on hers was nice enough, she couldn't seem to emotionally detach enough to enjoy the moment. She was thinking too much—about her sister and T.J., about who he was and how much or little she should trust him. His mouth moved against hers, then he nipped her bottom lip. She nipped back, biting hard enough that he drew away.

"You like it rough?" he asked, sounding a little surprised.

"Not at all. I'm making a point. I give as good as I get. You might want to remember that when you take Skye to dinner."

"No kissing?"

"I don't care if you kiss. Just don't hurt her."

He touched her cheek with the back of his knuckles. "What about you, Izzy? Do you ever get hurt?"

She smiled. Her? Getting hurt would mean giving her heart. Like that was ever going to happen. "I can take care of myself."

"Maybe you need someone to take care of you."

The smile turned into a chuckle. "Are you volunteering? Then you don't know me at all. Take care of me? Right. Say that to my father and he'll laugh you out of the building."

She unhooked her parachute and headed to the waiting truck. Once she'd gotten out of her flight suit, she walked to her car and climbed inside.

T. J. Boone remained a mystery. Her gut told her that Skye was in danger, but the problem was Skye wasn't in the mood to listen to well-meaning advice. Izzy knew the smart thing was to walk away. Skye was a big girl and could handle her own life. Except letting her step into danger wasn't an option. They were sisters and Izzy loved her. That meant learning more about T.J. and very possibly pissing off Skye when she told her the truth.

"YOU'RE NEW," Mitch said as he stared at the older man in front of him. "I don't want anybody new."

He also didn't want to be in physical therapy but that wasn't an option. He wasn't progressing as well as he could and he knew the reason. He wasn't doing what he was supposed to. Not only wasn't he interested, he didn't remember half of what the other therapist had told him.

"I'm not new," the guy told him. "You haven't met me before. There's a difference. I see you still have your chip on your shoulder. I hope it's not on the left one. The extra weight will make learning to walk a real bitch. I'm Joss."

Joss was a fifty-something, muscle-bound bald man with piercing blue eyes and an impressive jungle tattoo running down both arms.

"Mitch."

"Oh, I know who you are. You have an interesting file."

"What's interesting about it?"

Joss grinned. "Word has it you're a pain in the ass. That's why you're seeing me. I'm good with hard-assed cases. You could have had a pretty girl feeling you up. But you skipped out on your appointments and you haven't been working out at home. So now you've got me. Welcome."

Mitch refused to feel uneasy. "I'm busy. I can't come in twice a week."

Joss led the way back to the therapy room where specialized exercise equipment lined the walls. The center of the room had open space and several areas for patients to practice walking between two rails. Mitch remembered his first shaky steps on his prosthesis in this very room. He'd felt a combination of relief to know that he would be mobile and fury that his leg had been lost in the first place.

Now a half-dozen guys and one woman worked with therapists on various pieces of equipment. They were all sweating from the effort, but each looked determined. As if they expected the therapy to make a difference.

"You come in when I say come in or you don't get a permanent prosthesis," Joss said easily. "You piss me off and I'll take the one you have."

"I used to be a SEAL. How are you going to take it?"

"Special Forces," Joss told him. "And you're the gimp here, kid. Not me. Let's go in an examining room and see what you've done to your stump."

Mitch hesitated. Joss narrowed his gaze.

"What?" he demanded. "Are you still bleeding? I swear to God, if you're bleeding, I'm going to beat the shit out of you. What about 'take it easy' was hard for you to understand? You want to get back to normal? You want to be able to live your life without coming here all the time? You want to go more than fifteen minutes without fire shooting up your leg? Then you'll goddamn listen to me."

Mitch turned and walked toward the door. He didn't need this. He didn't need any of it. He was doing fine and if this jerk wouldn't fit him for his permanent prosthesis, he'd find someone else who would.

"You think Pete risked his life to save yours so you could act like this?" Joss asked.

He didn't shout the words. Mitch doubted any of the other patients had heard them. Still, they cut through him like glass, ripping into his gut and slicing his heart to shreds.

Pete was a friend. A good friend. They'd gone through BUD/S training together and had been assigned to the same SEAL team. Mitch knew about Pete's devotion to his young wife and how excited he'd been when he'd found out he was going to be a father. Pete knew about Skye and how many nights Mitch had lain awake that first year, unable to believe she'd really left him.

Pete who had faced enemy fire to drag a wounded and possibly dying Mitch to safety. Pete who'd taken a bullet for him. Pete who was already back in Afghanistan, facing it all again because it was his job.

Joss had spoken the only possible words to make Mitch stay.

He straightened and squared his shoulders. "I've got blood in my sock nearly every day. It's not the scar opening. There are a few raw spots."

"How much are you resting your leg?" Joss asked, then sighed. "Let me put that another way? Are you too stupid to rest your leg during the day?"

"Apparently."

"Admitting you have a problem is the first step, kid. Let's take a look."

Joss led him into an examining room. Mitch settled on the exam table, rolled up his jeans, then removed the prosthesis and the sock.

"You gotta massage the stump a couple of times a day," Joss said as he sat on a stool and flipped on a light that he adjusted. "You doing that?"

"Sometimes."

"Let me guess. You're not getting enough rest, or eating right, either." He pressed down on the stump. "That hurt?"

Mitch clenched his teeth as fire raced through him. "A little."

"Getting a lot of phantom pain?"

"Some."

"Doing the energy work?"

If Mitch had still been a teenager, he would have rolled his eyes. "It's total crap."

Joss straightened. "Right. The idea that the body has an electrical system is crap. We'll ignore the fact that brain waves are electrical or what an EKG is measuring. If you can't see it or touch it, it doesn't exist. Typical."

He stood and folded his arms across his chest. "Just once I want someone to come in here ready and willing to do the work. Just one time. Is that too much to ask? But does it happen? No. We always gotta go through the steps. Fine. Where are you? I'm guessing anger. Maybe some denial. Why did this happen to you? How can you get your life back.

Here's a tip. You're not the first guy to go through this. We've done it before and we know what works. So listen. Make your life easier."

If Mitch could have walked out, he would have. As it was, all he could do was turn his head.

"You need to be doing the massage," Joss told him. "Energy sweeps. The exercises we gave you. Get sleep, come in for group sessions."

Mitch stopped listening. Group sessions. Right. Because he wanted to sit around in a circle with a bunch of people he didn't know and talk about his feelings. Not that he wanted to do it with people he *did* know, either.

"I'm running late," he said. "Can we hurry this along?"

He glanced back at Joss, who surprised him by shrugging. "Sure. Whatever."

Mitch had expected more of a fight. "That's it? You're giving up?"

"Why not? You have. I got plenty of guys who are begging me for help. One day you'll be one of 'em."

"Not likely."

Joss surprised him by smiling. "You've got dark days ahead of you, kid. Bad times. But you'll get through them. When you figure out you can't do it alone, come back. I'll be here. But until then, I'm not wasting my time on an idiot." He handed him back his prosthesis. "Good luck."

Then he turned and walked out, leaving Mitch alone in the examination room, feeling very much like the idiot Joss had called him.

MITCH DROVE BACK to Titanville fighting the anger burning inside of him. He knew it wasn't helping, but it seemed anger was the only safe feeling. He'd expected to be sore from his session with Joss, but there hadn't been any therapy. He knew in his head he only had himself to blame—he needed the therapy to adjust to his prosthesis. The problem was he didn't want to do it. Didn't want to practice some energy sweep over a part of his body that wasn't there anymore. Didn't want to attend sessions with other amputees. Didn't want to have to deal with any of it. He wanted what he didn't have anymore.

He drove through town. When he stopped at the red light, he saw Skye walking into Bronco Billy's. Not sure of his plan, he pulled into the next open parking space and followed her.

He hadn't been inside the restaurant in nearly a decade but little about it had changed. TV screens played a Dirty Harry movie. The sound was off but the closed captions told the story. There were posters and movie memorabilia everywhere. Bronco Billy's was Clint Eastwood in all his glory.

Skye was already seated at a table, studying a menu. Mitch walked over and pulled out a chair before she realized he was there.

"Mind if I join you?" he asked, already taking a seat. "Am I getting in the way of something important?"

He hoped he was. He hoped he was pissing her off and that she would take him on. A fight, even with Skye, would feel good right about now.

"Not in the least," she said, her expression more sad than annoyed. "I know that's disappointing for you, but there it is. I'm here because I've had a bad day and I need a sugar fix. You might want to rethink staying. After all, you'll be a distraction, which would be a good thing for me. You wouldn't want that."

The waitress arrived before he could answer.

"Know what you want?" she asked.

"An Oreo milk shake," Skye said, handing her the menu. "The really big one."

"Make it two," Mitch told her.

Skye wrinkled her nose. "Don't you want your own table? Won't it be more satisfying to glare at me from across the room?"

"Not really."

He wasn't budging. Skye could tell. He wanted to bug her and she would guess he thought he could do that better up close. The problem was he did get to her, but not in the way he thought. She wasn't fighting guilt over keeping a nonexistent secret. The problem of being around him was much more about her reaction to seeing him again.

Despite his anger, despite the things he said and how he acted, she'd missed him. Buried under the bastard he was pretending to be was a good guy who had loved her with a devotion that made her head spin. He'd been her world and she'd walked away from him.

All these years later, she couldn't help wondering what-if. The wonderings were complicated by the knowledge that she knew she'd made the right decision…even if it was for the wrong reasons.

"We should get to know each other," he said, surprising her.

"Why? You hate me."

"I don't hate you."

She managed a slight smile. "Very touching. And convincing. If the ranch thing doesn't work out, you could go into advertising."

"We have a child together, Skye. Whether we like it or not, we're stuck together."

She wanted to bang her head against the table. Erin wasn't his. She knew that, but he wasn't going to believe her. She had a bad feeling that there was a part of him that *needed* Erin to be his. What would happen when he found out the truth?

"I don't want to argue about that," she said.

"Then let's argue about something else. You're dressed all fancy."

She glanced down at her black suit. "I had an emergency board meeting this morning. I find it helpful to dress the part of a powerful woman. I'm faking, of course, but they don't seem to notice."

He frowned. "You're on a board?"

"I run a foundation that feeds hungry children in this country. I started it six years ago with the money my mother left me. We've grown a lot and now feed over a million children a day." She leaned back in her chair.

"Go ahead," she told him. "Make fun of the rich bitch playing at saving the world."

"Why would I do that? You're doing a good thing. Kids shouldn't go hungry."

She opened her mouth, then closed it. "Okay. I thought there would be something more than that."

The waitress arrived with their milk shakes. Skye pulled out the whole cookie on top and took a bite, then drank some of the creamy milk shake.

The ice cream slid down her throat and sugar flowed into her bloodstream. She would swear she could feel it lifting her mood already.

"Better?" he asked when she'd swallowed.

"Some."

"What's Izzy doing with her half of the inheritance? I can't see her running anything."

"She's not the type." Skye hesitated. "Pru didn't put Izzy in her will. I don't know why. Maybe she didn't think to change it." There hadn't been any hint of the reasoning. When their mother died, she left her considerable fortune only to Skye. "I gave Izzy half in a trust fund. She can't touch it until she's thirty."

"But you got yours at twenty?" he asked, raising his eyebrows.

"I'm very responsible."

"Izzy must hate your guts."

Skye thought about their recent fight over T. J. Boone and Izzy's claims that he wasn't actually interested in Skye as a person. "We've had our moments. She wasn't happy about the trust. But she's totally wild and crazy. I didn't want her blowing through the money. I wanted it there to keep her safe."

"Does she see it that way?"

"She didn't at first, but she does now. She knows I love her."

"As long as you get to be in control."

The dig hurt, although she did her best not to show it. "You don't know me anymore, Mitch. It's been a long time."

"You're right. There have been a lot of other relationships between then and now."

Something she didn't want to talk about. The other women in his life. He would have attracted plenty of attention wherever he went. He was just that kind of guy.

"Did you enjoy being a SEAL?" she asked. "Taking on the world with a Q-tip."

He frowned. "What?"

"I thought you had all kinds of specialized training. Like how to kill someone with a Q-tip."

He grinned. "I didn't take the Q-tip killing class, but I learned a few things along the way. And yeah, I liked it. I liked working with my team, making a difference."

"Erin thinks you're personally responsible for saving the world."

"She mentioned that. I think Fidela talks too much."

"She loves you and is proud of you. Why wouldn't she talk?"

He shifted in his chair, almost as if he was uncomfortable. Good. He'd earned a little squirm time.

"What's it like being back?" she asked.

"Different. Arturo made a lot changes I didn't expect."

She felt her lips twitch. "Are we talking about the certified organic beef or the free-range poultry."

"Damn chickens."

She tried not to laugh. "On your family's grazing land. How the ancestors must be feeling."

"I know. It's humiliating. I'm sure there's good money in it, but still. What's worth that? Chickens." He swore under his breath. "Do you know there's documentation on every cow. From conception to their last breath, he has to keep track of every single thing that happens to them. And if they get sick or hurt and need antibiotics, they're no longer organic. They get pulled from the herd. It's insane."

"Welcome to the new organic world."

"I told Fidela if I found tofu in our refrigerator, I was throwing her out of the house. Or soy milk. I'm not drinking soy milk."

Skye laughed. "Big, tough, old cowboy. That's what you are."

He glared at her. "Very funny."

Their gazes locked. The room seemed to fade away until there was just the two of them. Her heart pounded so fast, she thought it might jump out onto the table and flop around. The image was enough to break the spell. She looked away.

"So, um, you're adjusting to being back," she said, feeling awkward. "If you hadn't gotten hurt, would you have come home?"

"No."

"Don't you want to think about the question?"

"There's nothing to think about. I didn't miss the ranch. There was nothing keeping me here."

Not even her? Which was a stupid question. Of course he hadn't missed her. It had been years. She'd broken his heart and that wasn't something he would easily forgive.

"Why don't you ask what you mean?" Mitch pushed away his milk shake. "How long it took me to get over you. Because that's what you want to know, isn't it? Fine. I'll answer that question but first you answer mine. How long did it take for you to stop thinking about me when you screwed your husband?"

Skye had had a really bad week already. Despite her need for sugar, she stood, grabbed her milk shake and threw it directly at Mitch. It hit him in the center of the chest and splashed up onto his face.

"You want to hear that my late husband was a total

bastard and that I cried for you every day because that gives you the right to punish me? Well, I didn't. I loved him. Ray was a good man. A decent man. You know what? You would have liked him. That's just the kind of guy he was."

She grabbed her purse and stalked out, leaving Mitch alone at the table, ice cream dripping onto his lap.

CHAPTER FIVE

THE RESTAURANT WAS trendy—an upscale Tex-Mex with comfortable seating and great margaritas. Skye clutched hers in an effort to keep from downing it in a single gulp.

"You all right?" T.J. asked.

"Not really," she admitted. "I don't think this was a good idea."

"The restaurant?"

"The date."

"Oh. Because I've already bored you so much you're ready to chew your arm off in an effort to escape?"

Three hours ago, she'd had the hideous run-in with Mitch. She was dealing with her half brother trying to destroy her life's work, her ex-boyfriend thinking he was the father of her child, and lots of unresolved feelings for said ex-boyfriend. While a perfectly nice man had asked her to dinner, all she could think was that she wanted him to be someone else.

"You haven't bored me."

"Give it time."

She tried to smile. "It's not you. I'm not ready for this. The whole boy-girl thing."

"Dating?"

"Yeah. Dating."

"It's been a couple of years since your husband died."

"Meaning I should be ready to move on? I know. I am. Ray isn't what makes this awkward. My life is…complicated."

"You have a crush on a woman?"

She laughed. "No, but thanks for asking."

He leaned forward. "Then what? I've told you I think you're beautiful. God knows I'm a hell of a guy. Rich, handsome, charming. What's not to like?"

"Modest. You left out modest."

"I like to leave people with something to discover on their own."

She looked into his blue eyes and wished she felt something. A spark. A whisper. Anything. He was as handsome as he'd claimed, so why couldn't she seem to notice?

"If you're worried about getting back into dating, don't sweat it," he said. "It's like riding a bike. We ask each other questions, have a conversation, I pay for dinner, you let me kiss you, we call it a night."

Kissing? She wasn't ready for that. At least not with anyone who wasn't Mitch. "You make it sound simple."

"It is. Tell you what. If you start to lose your way, let me know and I'll help you find it."

Why couldn't Mitch be like this? Fun. Easy to be with. He had been, all those years ago. Everything was different now.

"Stay," he said, lightly touching the back of her hand. "At least through appetizers. I want to get the avocado egg rolls and if the plate comes with just me sitting here, everyone will feel sorry for me."

"Okay. I'll stay."

"Good. Just so you know. No matter how much you pressure me, we're not having sex tonight. I'm serious. Even if you beg, I'm not giving in. It's just the kind of guy I am."

Some of her tension eased. "I can live with that."

He winced. "Couldn't you at least pretend to be disappointed?"

"I am, on the inside."

"I wish that were true. Now, let's begin that conversation. We'll talk about me because it's one of my favorite topics."

"I'm dying to know everything."

"I grew up in the area. In fact I went to high school with your sister Lexi."

"I think I knew that."

"We dated. Twice. I tried to get to first base and she tried to make me a eunuch."

Skye laughed. "She's a Titan. You have to respect that."

"I did. I played football where I was so good I was practically a god. We probably know a lot of the same people." He named a few. She recognized some, not others.

"Oh, yeah, Mitch Cassidy. Isn't his place next to Glory's Gate? He was in my class."

She did her best not to react to the words. "I knew Mitch. We, ah, dated for a while. Years ago. Before I got married. Obviously it was before. Dating during would have been so awkward."

T.J. leaned back in his chair. "The ex, huh? Was it serious?"

Skye took a drink of her margarita and hoped she could pull off sounding casual. "At the time, but we were both really young."

T.J.'s gaze didn't waver. "It must have been right before he went into the navy."

"It was."

"You know he's back."

She forced a smile. "Yes. We've run into each other. He was wounded but he seems to be doing better now."

"Anything I should know about you and Mitch?" he asked.

"Not at all. That was over a long time ago."

"Good. Because I'd like you to give me a chance, Skye. I think we could have fun together."

Her stomach lurched and not in a good way. The tequila sat uneasily and she couldn't imagine keeping food down. Still, none of her reaction was T.J.'s fault. If Mitch hadn't come back she would be enjoying her date. So she was going to fake it until it was real. Or something like that.

"I think we could, too," she said, and raised her glass. "Here's to finding out."

MITCH HAD NEVER been inside Glory's Gate before. He'd been in the barns—they'd been a favorite place for Skye and him to meet when they'd been dating. He knew how to ride in by darkness and escape undetected. But he'd never walked up the front steps like someone who had been invited.

Too little too late, he thought, pausing at the bottom of the stairs.

"Are you all right?" Fidela asked, hovering at his side. She held a brightly colored bag in one hand— a bag containing birthday gifts for Erin.

He could see Fidela wanted to offer help but didn't dare. It hadn't taken her long to figure out his temper was something to be avoided and all too close to the surface these days. There were moments, flashes in time, when he saw what he'd become and didn't like the result. But mostly he was pissed at the world and didn't care who knew.

"I'll be fine," he said, clenching his teeth and taking the first step.

The pain was manageable, but it promised to grow. He worked steadily, climbing the stairs, focusing only on the step in front of him, ignoring those left and those behind. By the time he reached the top, he'd broken out into a sweat and felt nauseous. He knew the latter was the result of the fire burning in his leg and that it would soon fade.

What mattered was showing up. His last encounter with Skye—when she'd thrown the milk shake at him—had reminded him of his purpose. To take her down in every way possible. Being at Erin's birthday party was the next step in his plan.

They moved toward the big front door. Fidela stayed by his side, not touching, but willing him along. He could feel her love and concern and took strength from it. Then the door opened and Erin rushed out.

She wore jeans and a pink shirt. A tiara proclaiming Birthday Princess sat on her head. A purple boa was draped around her shoulders.

"You came!" she crowed in delight. "I knew you would and you did, you came!"

She rushed at Fidela and hugged her tight, then turned on him and did the same.

She was small and slight and possibly his child. Emotions rushed through him, moving too fast for him to identify them. Still, he knew having a daughter would change everything. It would define him and give him purpose. Being her father mattered.

But before he could get caught up in the moment, Erin stepped back and grinned.

"There's lots of food. All my favorites and some stuff Mom said we had to have for the grown-ups. And the cake is so big!" She clapped her hands together. "Come see." She hugged him again. "You came."

"I wouldn't have missed it."

She gazed up at him. "You're my hero."

His throat tightened. "Yeah, well, um, happy birthday, kid."

She grabbed his hand and Fidela's, and pulled them both into the house. They moved through a foyer the size of a grocery store. He had a brief impression of soaring ceilings, a circular staircase and a grand piano before Erin led them into a nearly normal-size space with a few couches, a Happy Birthday, *Erin* sign on one wall and balloons tied to nearly everything that didn't move.

There were probably thirty people in the room, but Mitch had no trouble spotting Skye. It was as if everyone else was in black and white and she was the only one in color.

She stood talking to her sisters. The Titan girls, he thought, remembering how guys had talked about them in high school. They had been considered the ideal women, then—something to be achieved—yet they were all different. Lexi, the cool blond beauty. Izzy, the wild one with a smile that warned she didn't take prisoners, and Skye. Skye who radiated sex with every move, every word. Even now, despite everything, he wanted to drag her into some dark room and have his way with her. He wanted it so hot and so fast that neither of them could catch their breath. He wanted to take her and make her beg. He wanted—

A tall, blond man walked up to the sisters. He was familiar enough for Mitch to realize he knew him.

It took a second for the memory to fall into place. T. J. Boone. They'd gone to high school together, played football on the same team. Until he saw T.J. put his hand on the small of Skye's back, Mitch had always liked the guy.

Now Skye looked at T.J. and smiled. The smile burned in Mitch's gut. Lexi said something then excused herself. Izzy watched the two of them before shaking her head and walking away. Before Mitch could decide what he was going to do, someone joined him.

"You've spent a lot of your life wanting what you can't have."

Mitch turned and saw Jed Titan.

"I'll welcome the soldier but warn the man that Skye isn't for him." Jed shrugged. "It's just the way it is around here. She's a Titan. However much you want her, you couldn't have her before and you sure as hell can't now. Not with that." He jerked his head toward Mitch's missing leg.

The insults didn't matter. Mitch had never been afraid of Jed Titan, had never felt his power the way others had.

"I see you're still a pompous old man with delusions of influence and intimidation. But guess what? I know fifty ways to kill you and not leave a mark."

Jed sipped his drink. "Probably, but that's the difference between us, Mitch. You wouldn't kill me because I haven't done anything to deserve it. I prefer to take care of my opponents *before* they cross the line. It ensures I win."

"Well-meaning advice? That's not like you."

Jed smiled. "Despite you trying to marry my daughter before, I've always liked you, Mitch. You have backbone and guts. You weren't well-connected enough to be a contender but so few are. I heard you served our country well. Let me be clear though. You stand in the way of what I want and I'll reduce you and everything you love to a pile of rocks."

Mitch chuckled for the first time in days. "You don't scare me."

"I don't have to. Look around. I have it all, Mitch. Money, power, three beautiful daughters. Skye married Ray for me nine years ago and she's going to marry T.J. now. They'll make beautiful babies, don't you think?"

Mitch couldn't help looking at Skye, who still stood talking to T.J. "She wouldn't do that," he said, but even he didn't believe the words.

"Oh, I think she will and if you know her at all, you'll think so, too. Skye's a very dutiful daughter. She'll do what I say. You know I'm right." Jed patted him on the shoulder. "Welcome home, son. Welcome home."

Mitch watched the old man walk away. He told

himself that Jed was wrong about all of it. That Skye was stronger than that and could make decisions for herself. Then he returned his gaze to her and T.J. and knew he was fooling himself.

THE PARTY WENT well into the evening. Erin fell asleep on the sofa around eight-thirty and the last of the adults left shortly after ten.

Skye stood in the center of the kitchen and told herself she would tackle the mess in the morning. It wasn't going anywhere and what she didn't get cleared up would be handled by the daily staff who would return to work on Monday morning.

Izzy appeared with a bowl of tortilla chips in one hand and salsa in the other. "You have got to give me this recipe," she said as she set the bowls on the coffee table and dipped a chip. "It's my favorite."

"You plan to make salsa?" Skye asked with a laugh. "Oh, please."

"There's no cooking involved. Just chopping and stirring. I can chop and stir."

"With someone supervising."

"It could happen."

Skye shook her head. "Right. I'll get the recipe and you can fix it for us."

"Deal."

Skye collected a few glasses. Now that Izzy had come into the room, she felt the need to keep busy. Things still weren't totally right between them.

"T.J. had fun," her sister said, dipping a second chip.

"Yes, he did. I was surprised that he came," Skye admitted. She hadn't invited him, so it must have been Jed's doing. "Erin likes him." Not as much as she liked Mitch, but then T.J. didn't have hero status.

"T.J. can be charming," Izzy said, following Skye into the kitchen. "How was your date?"

"Nice."

"Nice bad or nice I'm-going-to-see-him-again."

"We're going to keep seeing each other." She set the glasses on the counter, then turned to face her sister. "Let me guess. You want to warn me that he's just in it for what he can get. That he's asked you out as well and you're the one he's really interested in. You're fun and I'm duty. The only way I can get a guy is if my father buys him."

Izzy pressed her lips together. "I'm not saying a man wouldn't want you," she began.

Skye groaned. "Izzy, come on. Isn't it possible T.J. likes me?"

"Do you like him?"

"I don't know. He's...fun. I enjoyed being with him more than I thought." He wasn't complicated. She could look at him without wanting to take her clothes off. She could look at him without feeling an emotional longing that left her weak.

"And it doesn't bother you that he's dating both of us?"

Skye squared her shoulders. "No," she lied.

"You don't think he's in any way playing us?"

"I think you're upset that he wants to go out with me. I think you can't believe he could possibly be interested in me so you're throwing yourself in the middle of this. You have to be the special one all the time. It's all about you."

Izzy folded her arms over her chest. "I was trying to be nice," she said, obviously angry and hurt. "I was worried about you because I care about you. You don't date a lot and I do. I have more experience at this. But fine. Think I'm so truly horrible that I can't let my own sister be happy with a guy. Think that I need it to be all about me. But when I'm right about T.J., and I will be, you'll be the one apologizing to me."

Izzy stalked out of the kitchen.

Skye stood by the sink, feeling sick to her stomach. She didn't want to fight with her sister. It wasn't right. But Izzy had always been the one guys went for. Her appeal to men defined her. So to have Skye steal some of the spotlight, even on such a tiny scale, had to bother her.

She left the kitchen and started toward the stairs. Her father called her.

"The party went well," Jed said, coming out of his study. "You and T.J. got along."

"Not even subtle, Dad," she said. "He's a nice man and we've been on one date. We're not engaged." Nor were they likely to be, she thought, knowing she didn't need any more heartache in her life. There had been enough already. And falling in love was only an invitation for more.

"No one's talking about you getting engaged," he said.

"Not in public, but we all know you have big plans to sell me again."

"Harsh language, baby girl. I'm only looking out for you."

If only that were true, she thought.

"Are you?" she asked. "Then you won't mind telling me what T.J. has that you want so badly?"

Her father's easy smile faded and his expression tightened. "Be careful, Skye. There are consequences for screwing with me."

His cold voice combined with the threatening words drained all the strength and will from her. She could barely remain standing. Even after he returned to his study, she felt weak and afraid.

Without wanting to, she remembered being ten years old. It had been a good day, a happy day. The sun was bright. That's what she recalled. The play of sunlight on the bathroom tiles.

Every day when she got home from school, she raced upstairs to her mother's rooms. Only her. Izzy stayed in the kitchen with the housekeeper, but Skye flew into Pru's room.

"I'm home, Mom," she called. "Did you miss me?"

Pru would be on the bed or in the chair in the corner. She would always look up and smile and say she'd missed Skye more than anything. Even on the dark days when the smiles didn't seem right, she said the words as if she meant them. As if she loved Skye more than anything.

But on that last day, Pru hadn't been in her usual places. And deep inside, Skye had known something was scary wrong.

She'd walked into the bathroom. The first thing she saw was light on the tiles. Then she saw the letter...addressed to her. She'd picked it up and read.

He doesn't love me, Skye. Jed doesn't love me. No matter what I do or how I try, he doesn't love me at all.

That was it. Those few words. Skye had read them again and again, not understanding but getting more scared by the minute.

It was only then she noticed the sweet sickly smell of blood in the room. Terrified but unable not to look, she approached the bathtub.

Pru lay inside, fully dressed and covered with blood. She'd slit both her wrists. Her face was so peaceful—that had been Skye's last thought before she'd started to scream.

CHAPTER SIX

AFTER GETTING Erin on the bus for school, Skye walked back to the house for a last cup of coffee before leaving for work. When she returned to the kitchen, she found Izzy standing there, holding the paper. As the two of them weren't exactly speaking, Skye wasn't sure how to act.

Izzy solved the problem by putting the newspaper on the table and pointing to the headline—Titan Cattle Tainted With Mad Cow.

Skye felt her knees give way and grabbed the counter to keep from falling.

"Oh, no," she breathed. "This is bad."

"There's an understatement," Izzy said with a sigh. "You know what this means."

Skye nodded. No Texas cattle ranch could survive even a whisper of the feared disease. Prices would plummet. Thousands of pounds of beef would be returned. Cattle would be tested and retested and in the end, even if there wasn't a problem, people would remember the charge.

"Jed isn't stupid," Skye said, scanning the article. "His ranch manager knows high standards are required. Jed eats that beef, as do his guests. He would never risk himself or them. Just as important, he wouldn't treat his cattle that badly."

"They eat vegetarian diets." Izzy walked over and poured herself a cup of coffee. "They have for years."

"This is Garth," Skye said, frustrated that he was still a problem. "How are we going to stop him?"

"I don't know, but Lexi's coming over. She called while you and Erin were waiting for the bus."

Five minutes later Lexi arrived looking angry and frustrated.

"Our jerk of a half brother is taking this too far," Lexi said as she tossed her purse on the counter and walked to the coffeepot. Halfway there, she paused, swore and detoured to the refrigerator where she pulled out a jug of juice.

Despite everything, Skye smiled. "Still missing the caffeine, huh?"

"Every day." Lexi sat at the table with her juice.

"I called Jed on the way over," she said. "Or at least I tried. He was busy and couldn't be disturbed. He can't be happy."

"He'll handle it," Izzy said confidently. "That's what Jed does."

"What I want to know is how the story got out there," Skye said, remembering the false leaks about her foundation. "Somehow Garth is able to convince the press he has the real story and they don't bother to check with us. How can he do that?"

"Money," Lexi said. "Influence. We'll figure it out."

They talked more about the "Garth problem" then Lexi picked up Skye's mug of coffee and inhaled the aroma.

"Nice party for Erin," she said.

Skye eyed her sister. "She had a good time."

"Mitch was there."

If Skye and Izzy had been getting along better she would have tried to get her sister to help distract Lexi. But under the circumstances, she was on her own.

"Yes, he was. He and Erin have met. She adores him and asked him to come, so he did." She took back her coffee and gulped it. "Nothing more."

"Uh-huh." Lexi looked at Izzy and raised her eyebrows. "There was plenty of smoldering going on."

Skye wanted to be anywhere but here. "In your imagination."

"I think it was more than that, but you were only hanging with the other guy. What's his name?"

"T. J. Boone," Izzy told her. "He's Jed's latest pick for Skye. They're going to get married soon."

Skye clutched her mug. "That is neither true nor fair. Yes, Jed wants me to consider him, but I'll be making my own decisions."

"The way you did with Ray?"

Skye stiffened.

Lexi stared at Izzy. "Okay, what's going on with you two? Izzy, that was just plain mean."

"She won't listen to me," Izzy grumbled, looking uncomfortable but not apologizing.

"Right," Skye snapped. "Make this my fault. God forbid you should take responsibility for anything."

"I'm taking responsibility for this and you won't listen." Izzy flipped her long, dark curly hair over her shoulder. "I told her T. J. Boone is just messing with both of us. The first night he was here, he came on to me. I tried to warn Skye, but she's not interested in that."

Skye stood. "You didn't try to warn me. You told me he couldn't possibly be interested in me, that he was just doing what Jed told him and the only one who got him hot was you. That the only way I would get a guy was if Jed bought me one."

"I never said that."

"You implied it. You also implied I'm too feeble to figure out a guy's intentions on my own."

Izzy sprang to her feet. "You're taking it all wrong. I'm trying to protect you. T.J. asked me out. There's something going on. I can tell. I just want to help."

"By telling me he's going to totally fall for you because what man could look at the two of us and want me?"

Izzy hesitated just long enough to make Skye want to slap her.

Lexi got to her feet and rubbed her forehead. "You

two both need therapy. Skye, do you really care enough about this guy to fight with Izzy about him?"

"Of course not. But it's not about T.J." She looked at Izzy. "I'm really hurt that you think I'm such a spaz that I can't get a date on my own. And yes, you're fun and beautiful, but somewhere on the planet there has to be at least one guy who could possibly be interested in me even after he meets you."

Izzy shifted uncomfortably. "I didn't say there wasn't. I'm not all that."

"Sometimes you act like you are."

"I'm just afraid of what T.J. is up to."

"I'm a big girl. I can take care of myself."

Izzy looked like she wanted to say more, but she appeared to think better of it. "Okay. I'll stay out of it."

Lexi glanced between the two of them. "Better?" she asked. "Are we all happy?"

"Sure," Izzy told her. "I need to go shower." She left the kitchen.

Lexi and Skye both sat back down.

"We have enough trouble with Garth," Lexi said. "We don't need the two of you fighting."

"I know. I should be more mature." Skye finished her coffee. "She just bugs me sometimes. She's not all that."

Lexi raised an eyebrow.

Skye laughed. "Okay. She *is* all that, but I can be all that, too. At least a little."

"We all need a goal." Lexi leaned forward. "At

the risk of us fighting, too, have you talked to Mitch much?"

Skye didn't know how to answer that question. They'd had sex, they'd fought, but had they actually talked? As in just having a conversation?

"Some," she said. "He's...he's having trouble adjusting."

"Not a big surprise."

"I know. Things are complicated." She hesitated. "He thinks Erin is his."

Lexi winced. "You're kidding. She's not...is she?"

"No. How could you ask me that?"

"You got pregnant pretty fast."

Not something Skye was proud of. "Erin is Ray's. She has a birthmark that comes from his side of the family. I've told Mitch Erin isn't his, but he doesn't want to listen. He basically told me either she was his or I was a whore for sleeping with Ray."

"Ouch."

"My reaction was a little stronger." Skye didn't want to think about their fight.

"It makes sense," Lexi said. "While you two haven't been together in a long time, coming back home probably brings everything to the surface. He's angry and hurt. After all, you dumped him the day after you accepted his proposal. That's going to piss off anyone."

"Thank you so much for taking my side."

"I'm sorry."

Skye shook her head. "Don't be. You're simply

telling the truth. I acted badly and Mitch wants me punished. I can handle that. I just want to make sure he doesn't also hurt Erin. She hasn't done anything wrong."

MITCH WALKED into the barn expecting to find it empty. Instead he saw Erin grooming Bullet. As soon as she heard his footsteps, she turned and tucked the brush behind her back.

"Hi," she said, looking guilty. "I, um. Hi."

"What are you doing?" His voice came out more harshly than he'd planned and she flinched.

"Bullet's lonely," she said, her shoulders hunching as she seemed to shrink. "I didn't want him to be sad because you're not riding him."

Mitch was willing to take on just about anyone, but he didn't want to hurt Erin.

He crossed to her and touched her arm. "Thank you," he said quietly.

She looked up, her big eyes wide and apprehensive. "You're not mad?"

"No. You're right. Bullet is in a strange barn and I haven't been paying attention to him. It was nice of you to think of him."

Erin smiled and he would swear it lit the whole barn. "He's a really nice horse. He's been specially trained, you know. So you can mount him from the other side. I think he's really smart. Maybe after you get to know him and everything maybe I could ride him sometime."

"Sure," Mitch said absently, thinking he would never ride the horse. What was the point? There wasn't anywhere to go.

Erin handed him a brush, then grabbed a second one for herself. She stepped up to Bullet and went to work.

"You're not scared, are you?" she asked, not looking at him.

He studied the horse. "No. I'm not scared."

"Then why aren't you riding him?"

"I'm not that man anymore."

"What man?"

"Someone who rides."

She wrinkled her nose. "You think you forgot? I could help you remember. It's really easy. You gotta get back on the horse. It tells people who you are."

"You hear that from your grandfather?" he asked.

"Uh-huh, and Mom, too."

"What about your dad?"

The question popped out before he could stop it. Erin continued brushing the horse.

"He's been gone a long time." She pushed her bangs off her forehead and sighed. "I don't remember him much. I try really a lot. Sometimes at night before I go to sleep I think about something we did. Like going to Disney World, or Christmas. But it's hard." She leaned against Bullet. "I have a lot of half brothers and sisters. They're really old. Older than Mom. It's hard to explain."

Maybe for an eight-year-old, but it wasn't hard to

understand. Ray had been significantly older than Skye. He had children from his first marriage. Erin was probably aunt to adults in their thirties.

"He loved us," Erin continued. "He would tell me every night when he put me to bed. I remember that."

She smiled and he could only smile back. Because to do otherwise was to be more of a bastard than even he was comfortable with.

Arturo walked into the barn. "I don't know about this," he grumbled when he saw Erin.

She dropped the brush and ran to him. "Please? You promised. Mom said it was okay. She's coming by. I'm ready. I'm really, really ready."

Arturo looked over her head at Mitch. "She wants to start jumping."

Mitch frowned. "Isn't she a little young?"

"That's what I've been saying. But she's determined."

"No, I'm not," Erin said, sounding a lot like her mother when Skye got stubborn. "I'm not scared and I can do it."

"Which sounds a lot like determined to me," Arturo said and ruffled her hair. "I'll set up the jumps, but you're going to listen to everything I say. Promise?"

She threw her arms around him. "I promise and cross my heart." She ran down the length of the barn calling for her horse.

"I hope I'm not going to regret this," Arturo muttered. "You taking Bullet out?"

"No."

"He needs some exercise."

"You should have thought of that before you bought him."

Arturo stared at him for a long time, then turned away. Mitch ignored the twinge of guilt and led Bullet to his stall.

Nearly a half hour later Erin proved she was more than ready. She easily took the low jumps Arturo had set up in the corral. She rode like she'd been born to the saddle. His genes at work, he thought as he leaned against the fence, watching her.

Familiar anger built up inside of him, battling with pride. Everything would have been different, he thought furiously. If he'd known about Erin, he would have come home. He would have been a part of her life. He wouldn't have missed so much.

A car pulled up but he didn't turn around. Seconds later he knew Skye was next to him. He could sense her, not to mention smell her perfume. Just a whiff of the floral fragrance was enough to make him want her again. They could do it in the barn, like they had when they were kids.

Back when life hadn't been so damn complicated, he thought. Before he'd gone away and she'd betrayed him.

"We need to talk, Mitch," she said, standing next to him.

He sensed her gaze on him but didn't turn. "So talk."

"Not here."

"Why not? You have somewhere better in mind?"

"Somewhere private. The barn or your office or wherever. Just not in front of Erin."

He glanced at her, saw the worry in her eyes and something else. Something that made his gut tighten.

"My office," he said, and led the way.

His office was off the main barn and wasn't a place he'd been to since his return. He half expected the door to be locked, but the handle turned easily.

Inside everything was as he remembered. The same desk in the same place. The computer looked new. Maybe Arturo had replaced the old one when he'd found out Mitch was coming home. There were files, pictures and a small refrigerator humming in the corner.

At one time he'd thought this would be his life. That he would grow old on this ranch. Then he'd lost Skye and everything had changed.

Mitch ignored it all. He faced her. "What?"

She pulled a slim envelope out of her purse and handed it to him. The return address was the lab in Dallas.

"You reading my mail?" he asked as he took it.

"Fidela saw me driving by and asked me to give it to you. I think she knows what's inside."

The envelope was still sealed. Anticipation tightened his gut. "Do you?"

She nodded. Worry darkened her green eyes. "Mitch, I'm sorry," she began.

He leaned against the desk and prepared for her to grovel. He planned to enjoy every minute of it and then he was going to crush her.

"I didn't sleep with Ray on the first date," she said. "It was the third and I cried the whole time. I hated being with him more than I can say. There was nothing wrong with him except he wasn't you and I was so in love with you."

Her words made him sick to his stomach. "I don't want to hear this."

"I know, but let me say it anyway. Ray felt badly and I was devastated. I couldn't do it. I couldn't marry him. I realized it that night. I was going to find you and tell you. I was hoping you would forgive me. Jed figured all that out and I knew he was going to threaten me or you or both of us. Which he did. He also pointed out that I'd better be sure I wasn't pregnant before running back to you."

Tears filled her eyes. "I was. I found out a few days later. I knew I couldn't show up, carrying another man's baby. I knew you'd never forgive me. I also couldn't keep Ray from his child. Marrying him was the best choice."

"That's all bullshit," he growled. "It wasn't the best choice, it was the easiest one. You got everything you wanted, including keeping Erin from me."

Only speaking the words no longer felt right and the certainty in her eyes made him doubt himself.

"He was a good man, but he wasn't you," she said.

"We all have guilty secrets. That's mine. I grew to love him, but it wasn't enough. He never got my whole heart. Erin was born five weeks early. She's his. I'm sorry. Not for that but for everything else."

Tears spilled onto her cheeks. She turned and walked out, leaving him alone, holding the letter.

He didn't have to open it because he already knew. She wasn't lying. Erin wasn't his. She never had been. He'd come home to nothing.

He left the office, not bothering to close the door behind him. He had no idea where he was going, he just knew it was away from here. In the distance he heard Erin's laughter. The sound cut through him, reminding him of all he'd lost. Even the anger seemed gone. There was nothing inside of him anymore. Nothing but useless space.

He walked and walked until his leg ached so bad he began to stumble. He could feel the blood soaking the sock on his stump and still he kept moving. He reached a rise in the land and stood staring at everything he owned.

In the distance, the cattle moved—dark shadows on the land. He could see the goddamn chickens and the horizon in the distance. All his. And he didn't care about any of it.

He would swear he could still hear Erin's laughter, that the sound carried to him on the wind. He could feel her surprisingly strong hug, feel her bony arms holding on to him. His daughter.

He'd been so sure. He'd convinced himself that she was what he'd had to come home for. But it had all been wishful thinking.

He opened the envelope and stared at the typed words. Skye had spoken the truth. Erin wasn't his.

He crumpled the paper and let it fall to the ground. Then his leg gave way and he sprawled onto the dirt, broken and worthless.

Sometime later, when the sun had burned his skin and his lips had crackled from dryness, he heard a truck engine. Arturo parked next to him and got out. Mitch tried to get up but couldn't. He had to wait and let the old man half drag him into the passenger seat.

His stump ached more than it had since the initial surgery. He could feel the blood, the raw flesh and knew he'd probably done some serious damage, but he didn't care.

Arturo was silent and Mitch didn't bother speaking. What was there to say?

Arturo drove past the ranch and headed to Dallas.

"Where do you think you're going?" Mitch asked.

His ranch manager pointed to the front of Mitch's jeans. "The hospital."

Mitch glanced down and saw bloodstains. He swore under his breath, then leaned back and closed his eyes. There wasn't a single part of him that could imagine giving a damn about anything ever again.

"YOU'RE MORE STUPID than I thought."

The words came clearly, despite the haze of pain-killers. Mitch opened his eyes and saw Joss standing over him.

It took him a second to figure out where he was and what had brought him here. The E.R. doctor had taken one look at his bleeding stump and admitted him. Apparently Mitch had lost more blood than he'd realized because now he'd been given a transfusion, put on an IV, drugged up and scolded by nearly every medical person he came in contact with.

"They're transferring you to the VA in a couple of hours," Joss went on. "When I heard what had happened, I came by to see if it was true. You're a real idiot."

"You mentioned that."

The physical therapist stared at him. "You trying to kill yourself or are you thinking that's just a happy by-product of all this?"

"I got distracted. I didn't pay attention to what I was doing."

"Uh-huh. Anyone here believe that?" Joss picked up the prosthesis from the chair in the corner. "They had to cut this off you, which means you need a new socket. Imagine how fast I'm going to be ordering that."

That brought Mitch to a sitting position. "You can't keep me on crutches."

"Sure I can. I'm mean and vindictive. I'm also

the boss of you, so I can do anything I want." Joss grinned. "I sound like one of my grandkids."

Mitch collapsed back on the pillows. He hurt all over and the medication had left him sick to his stomach. Or maybe that was more about the thought of being on crutches.

"You need to heal," Joss told him. "You wouldn't do it on your own. Now I'm going to make it happen. You're not getting this back for at least two weeks." He put a business card on the tray by the bed. "Your next appointment, where you'll get this back. Don't be late."

Then he was gone.

Frustration and rage built up in Mitch. He wanted to go after Joss, grab him and pound him into the ground. But he couldn't get up, couldn't walk without some kind of help.

Worthless, he thought as he lay there hurting everywhere. So fucking worthless.

A man in an expensive suit knocked on his open door.

"Mitch Cassidy?" he asked as he entered.

Mitch frowned. "Who are you?"

"Garth Duncan. Does that name mean anything to you?"

"No. Now get out."

"I will, in a minute. I would like to discuss a little business with you."

Mitch wasn't interested. "Unless you want to buy

a whole lot of free-range poultry, this conversation is going nowhere."

"I understand you used to date Skye Titan."

Mitch looked at the other man. There was something familiar about him, although he didn't think they'd met.

"What business is that of yours?"

"None, really." The man pulled up a chair and sat down. "I'm Jed Titan's bastard."

The last of the drug-induced fogginess faded. Mitch pushed the button to raise the bed and he stared at Garth. Now he realized why Garth looked familiar. There was plenty of Jed in him, at least physically.

"I never heard about you," he said.

"No one has, although it's a pretty common story. Jed knocked up my mother and bought her off. Now I want payback." Garth leaned back in his chair. "I thought you might like a piece of the action."

"You want to bring down Jed?"

"I want to bring down all of them, Mitch. Every last Titan." Garth tugged at the sleeve of his jacket. "Not the kid. Erin doesn't interest me. But the sisters and their father? I want them ground to dust."

He spoke casually but there was intensity in his words.

Mitch felt a flicker of interest. "What makes you think you can do it? The girls might be softer targets but Jed's another matter. He's a mean old son of a bitch and he doesn't care who he hurts."

"Like father like son," Garth said. "I have unlimited resources. I have people in places that would turn Jed Titan's hair white. I'm going to win this and when I do, I'll be the one sleeping at Glory's Gate. I'm offering you a chance to get even."

Mitch was less sure about that. "Why would I need to get even?"

Garth shrugged. "Skye dumped you."

"That was a long time ago."

"Jed screwed over my mother before I was born and I'm still pissed. It's your call. If you're not interested, so be it."

"I could tell them all you've been here."

"You could. It wouldn't change anything."

Mitch had to admit Garth had a pair on him.

Hurt the Titans. He'd never considered it an option, but he sure could warm to the idea. Not so much the rest of them, but bringing down Skye had a certain appeal. She was in the middle of all this, he thought grimly. He wanted her to feel as helpless as he did, as angry, as unable to make things right. Screwing Jed would be a nice by-product.

"What would you want from me?" he asked.

Garth gave him a slow smile. "Just listen, pay attention and report back to me. I want to know vulnerabilities. What makes them bleed. Information is power."

Mitch knew Skye's greatest vulnerability was Erin, but he wasn't going to say that to Garth. Despite everything, the little girl still mattered to him.

"I'll pay you," Garth began.

Mitch's gaze narrowed. "Don't make me kill you."

Garth held up both hands. "Sorry. I have people who are only in on this because of the money."

"I'm not one of them."

"Fair enough. I'll be in touch." He stood and crossed to the bed, then offered his hand.

Mitch hesitated a second before shaking it.

"Good to meet you, Mitch."

Garth left.

Mitch turned away from the door and told himself he should feel better about finally having a plan. He was going to help destroy the Titans.

But as he lowered the back of the bed and tried to find a more comfortable position he found himself wondering if he'd lost more than a part of his leg in Afghanistan. Had he also lost part of himself?

CHAPTER SEVEN

IF THIS WAS a family dinner, Skye thought, it certainly wasn't greeting-card material. The table in the dining room groaned with food, but no one was eating. She and Izzy still weren't exactly friends. Jed was distracted and Lexi and Cruz only had eyes for each other. Erin alone was normal, chatting about how school was almost over, the things she wanted to do on her summer break and how high she could jump now.

"You should come see me jump, Grandpa," she said cheerfully.

Jed managed to look up and frown. "You win any medals?"

"I'm just starting, but I will."

Jed grinned. "That's my girl. You're going to be the best. Bring home an Olympic medal and we'll put it front and center."

Erin looked pleased and attacked her mashed potatoes.

"I was a barrel racer in high school," Izzy told

Erin. "It was a lot of fun. We could practice together sometime."

"Okay," Erin said, always happy to spend time with her aunt.

Lexi whispered something to Cruz, who grinned. They were crazy about each other, Skye thought, trying not to be bitter. She didn't begrudge her sister her happiness—she just wanted a little of the same for herself. Someone to lean on. Someone to share with. Someone to help and laugh with and smile at for the rest of her life.

Even knowing it was stupid, her brain turned immediately to Mitch. She hadn't seen him since he'd found out the truth about Erin. Fidela had told her he'd landed in the hospital and was now on crutches. Apparently he hadn't been ready for all the walking he'd done.

She wondered how he was and wanted to go see him. Not that she would. He would only try to beat up on her again. She shouldn't think about him at all.

He wasn't her ideal man. He was just some guy she used to know…and couldn't stop thinking about. But who needed lust? She had loved her husband. Maybe their relationship hadn't been all fire and passion, but it had been strong and admirable. She winced inwardly knowing no one who wanted to be in love was looking for "admirable."

People wanted the fire, although in her opinion it was highly overrated. She burned for Mitch and what did that get her? A giant pain in her butt, that's what.

"The teacher at school said you have mad cows, Grandpa," Erin said into the silence. "I said our cows are very happy."

Jed looked up, his expression furious. "What stupid bi—"

"Dad," Skye said sharply. "She was just expressing an opinion and she's Erin's teacher."

Jed glanced at Erin. "She's an idiot."

Erin put down her fork. "She knows a lot. She's a good teacher, Grandpa. She just doesn't know our cows."

Izzy's mouth twitched. "Perhaps we should invite her over. They could have tea."

Skye ignored that. "She's not saying the cows are unhappy. Mad cow is a kind of sickness cows get. If people eat the cows, then they can get sick, too."

Erin chewed on her steak. She'd been raised on a working ranch. She knew where dinner came from. "But our cows aren't sick, are they?"

"No. They're fine. But people get confused."

"Mostly grown-ups," Erin muttered under her breath.

"You got that right," Izzy said, looking at Skye.

Dinner limped painfully along. When they were finished and the table cleared, Lexi and Cruz took Erin out for ice cream. Skye paced restlessly in her bedroom before grabbing her car keys and running downstairs. She was probably going to get her head chewed off, but she had to see him. Had to know if he was okay.

At the Cassidy Ranch Fidela answered the door immediately.

"He's in the barn. In his office," she said, looking worried. "He's been in there every day since he got out of the hospital. He won't talk to me or eat. He just drinks. I don't know what to do. You'll go talk to him? You'll make him feel better?"

"Let's not get carried away," Skye murmured. "I'll check on him."

"Good. He needs something." She spoke softly in Spanish, her words almost like a prayer.

Skye drove around to the barn and got out of her car.

It was early evening. The air was still warm, with a hint of coolness. The bugs were loud, the horses quiet and she had the sense of being the last person alive. That lasted until she heard the crash of glass breaking.

Stuffing her keys in her jeans pocket, she hurried toward Mitch's office. She found him standing by his desk, supported by one crutch. His left pant leg hung empty. A Scotch bottle lay in shatters by the wall, another sat on his desk.

"Well, lookee here," he said, his words slurring. "Skye Titan. Is it your day to make calls on the local cripples? You gonna check on the widows and orphans after you see me?"

His skin was pale, his eyes bloodshot, but his hand was steady as he poured himself another drink from the fresh bottle.

"I wouldn't want to be you when you wake up in the morning," she said.

"You wouldn't want to be me anytime," he told her. "God knows, I don't want to be." He sank heavily into his chair and pushed the bottle toward her. "Help yourself. Sorry I don't have another glass. You can drink out of the bottle. I don't care."

She ignored the invitation. "I wanted to see how you were."

He waved the crutch at her. "Never better. How 'bout yourself? You're looking particularly sexy tonight, Skye. Why don't you take your shirt off so I can see those pretty breasts of yours." He raised the glass toward her. "To your breasts, darling, and every man they've brought to his knees."

He was beyond drunk. She eyed the bottle and wondered if he was in any kind of danger from alcohol poisoning.

She picked up the bottle of Scotch, walked over to the sink in the corner and poured it out.

"I've got five more just like that one," he said.

She turned to face him and set the empty bottle on the counter. "Maybe, but you're going to have to get up to find them and I doubt you'll make it halfway across the room."

His gaze centered on her chest. "That depends on my motivation."

She ignored that. "Have you done anything since you got out of the hospital?" she asked. "Other than drink? Or are you just sitting around feeling sorry for yourself."

He drained his glass. "You don't get to play this game with me."

"Why not? Someone has to. Look at yourself, Mitch. This isn't who you are. I know you had a rough time, but you're alive. You have a home and people who care about you."

"Not a kid, though. Right? No kid."

"You came home," she said, determined to get through to him. "What about the guys who didn't? What about the guys who don't have a home or a family? I think they get first shot at the pity trough. You're hogging way more than your share."

He glared at her. "Don't push me, little girl," he growled. "I can still take you."

"Not tonight, you can't."

"I can try and I promise that will hurt."

She approached the desk and stared down at him. "Is that what you want? To hurt me? Will that make it all better? Fine. Give it your best shot. I dumped you, Mitch. I walked out on our relationship. Start the punishment."

He slammed the glass back on the desk. "That's just it, Skye. You didn't dump me. You accepted my proposal. You told me you loved me and wanted to be with me forever and then you changed your mind because your daddy told you to."

He was right. About all of it. "I was scared," she

admitted, her defiance gone. "Jed was going to turn his back on me. I couldn't stand that. I'd already lost my mom. He was all I had left."

"You were all *I* had," he yelled. "I'd lost both my parents that summer, Skye. I thought we were going to be there for each other."

She hung her head. "I know. I'm sorry."

"Sorry isn't good enough."

She straightened. "Fine. Then what do you want?"

"I want you to bleed the way I've bled. I want you to feel all of it."

His anger and pain were living creatures in the room. They sucked out the air and made her want to bolt for the outside.

Then she finally understood.

"You think this is my fault," she whispered. "You blame me for everything. If I hadn't broken up with you, you wouldn't have gone away. You wouldn't have become a SEAL or lost your leg."

He didn't say anything.

She couldn't believe it. "Are you sorry for what you did? The lives you saved? The difference you made?"

"That's not the point."

"Then what is? You made a choice. We both did, and now we have to live with the consequences."

"Must be tough for you," he said, his voice thick with anger. "Living in your big house with your kid and all. Does the pain and suffering keep you up nights? Do you regret marrying Ray?"

Which was what it all came down to, she thought sadly.

She stared into the eyes of the man she had loved more than anything, but not enough to defy her father.

"No," she whispered. "I don't. He gave me Erin and I would never wish her away. It's done, Mitch. This is where we are."

"This is where *you* are. I'm somewhere else."

"I don't know you anymore."

"Too bad. I'm a helluva guy."

"You used to be. Now you're just a man who wants the whole world to feel sorry for him."

MITCH HADN'T KNOWN it was possible to feel this bad and not be dead. He'd passed out in his office some time the previous night and had woken up on the floor shortly before dawn. It had taken him the better part of an hour to limp to the house. The crutches had been as much a hindrance as a help.

Showering, a pot of coffee and a handful of aspirin did nothing to ease the hammering in his head and the sour rock in the pit of his stomach. Nearly as bad was the fact that he didn't remember much about what had happened, except he was pretty sure Skye had visited and he'd treated her badly.

The devil on his shoulder told him that she deserved whatever he'd said, but the rest of him wasn't so sure. There were some lines he wasn't willing to cross. It was a bitch not knowing if he already had.

Fidela fussed over him until he couldn't take it anymore so he jammed a hat on his head and made his way back to the barn. If he remembered correctly, he had a mess to clean up in his office. Later, he would deal with Skye.

The dim quiet of the barn eased the pressure in his head. For about eight seconds.

"Mitch! Hi. Are you going riding? You haven't been riding yet and you really need to ride Bullet. He's very sad. I can tell."

Her shrill, eight-year-old, high-pitched voice cut through him like broken glass. He winced and wished he was anywhere but here. At this point, physical therapy was looking good.

"Erin," he said, speaking softly. "I'm not feeling too good today. Could you keep your voice down?"

"Why? Does my talking make your head hurt? Why are you sick? Do you have a cold?"

He wanted to groan. Yelling at her wasn't an option. She might not be his kid, but he couldn't be mean to her. It wasn't much but right now that was the only bright spot on his otherwise tarnished character.

"Everything makes my head hurt," he told her.

"I know what will make it better." She put her small hands on her skinny little hips. "If you get on Bullet and ride with me I'll be really quiet."

"I will not be manipulated by an eight-year-old."

She grinned. "Want to hear me scream?"

"Erin." He growled her name in warning.

The grin widened. "Or I could sing. Come on, Mitch. Let's go riding."

Bouncing around on a horse was a particular brand of hell he didn't want to experience. There was no way, he told himself. No way at all.

But he found himself looking into her eyes and seeing the hope there.

"It'll make you feel better," she whispered. "I promise. I won't talk at all." She looked at his left leg—or where it used to be. "I know you're hurt. Fiddle told me you'd done too much. She said that your pros-y thing can hurt."

She bit her lower lip and touched her own thigh. "I'd be scared if I lost my leg. I'd be so scared and hugs from my mom might not even help. It's really sad." She raised her gaze to his and he saw tears there. "I'm sorry you're hurt now and that you got hurt before in the war."

A single tear slipped down her cheek. "Would it hurt you if I hugged you?"

His throat got real tight and he had to swallow. When he shook his head, she rushed forward and wrapped her arms around his waist, then hung on as if she was never going to let go.

She could have been his, he thought sadly. She should have been. He and Skye were supposed to get married. They'd have a family by now. Maybe a daughter like Erin.

Instead her father was some old guy who'd stolen

Skye. No, he reminded himself. It wasn't Ray's fault. He'd only taken what had been offered. The real villains here were Skye and Jed. And he was going to get both of them.

"Say yes," Erin said, looking up at him. "I won't scream or yell or sing. Just come riding with me."

"Okay. I will."

She jumped back and hooted with excitement, then slapped her hand over her mouth. "Sorry. I'll be real quiet now."

"That would be good."

He walked to Bullet's stall, then held the door open while she led out the horse. Using crutches meant Mitch couldn't help gather equipment, but Erin knew what she was doing and quickly had the saddle pad in place. The saddle was big and heavy. She half dragged, half carried it to him. He balanced on one leg, handed her his crutches and managed to swing the saddle in place.

Ten minutes later her horse was ready, as well. Mitch led Bullet over to the mounting block and hesitated.

"I haven't been on a horse in nearly ten years," he muttered. "And that was with two legs."

He also wasn't used to getting on the right side, but without a prosthesis, he didn't have much choice.

"You can do it," Erin said, standing in front of Bullet and stroking his face. "I'll hold him. But I don't think he'll move. He's special."

Trained for a cripple, Mitch thought bitterly. He

leaned his crutches against a post, then hopped up the three stairs, holding on to the railing to stay upright. When he was on the mounting block he gripped the railing and half lifted, half threw his left leg over the saddle. He shifted his weight, pushed off with his right leg and found himself in the saddle.

"You did it," Erin crowed, the sound ripping his head from the inside.

But he didn't remind her to be quiet, mostly because it felt pretty good to be on a horse again. She passed him the reins. He urged Bullet forward and the horse moved.

Erin climbed on her horse like a little monkey and joined him as he rode outside.

The sun was bright and hot and made his head throb, but he ignored it. Bullet's movements were familiar, making him wish he hadn't been so stubborn about riding. This felt good. Almost normal.

"I knew you could do it," Erin told him.

"Yes, you did and you were right."

She grinned at him and he smiled back.

They rode toward the cattle and circled around the herd. To their right was the fencing for the chickens.

Erin pointed. "There's a break in the fence. We need to tell Arturo so the coyotes don't get them."

The coyotes could have them all, he thought. Damn chickens.

"You tell him," he grumbled.

"Don't you like the chickens?"

"No."

"Why?"

"This is a cattle ranch."

"Diversification is important."

He looked at her and laughed. "How do you know that word?"

She pressed her lips together and looked smug. "Sometimes Arturo and I talk. He's teaching me about the ranch. He said you can't just depend on having one thing. Like cows. You need more. So if something bad happens, you're safe. It's like bringing your raincoat if it looks cloudy. If you don't, you might get wet."

"You're saying chickens are a raincoat?"

She wrinkled her nose. "I guess. Arturo said it, not me."

"My family has run cattle on this land for nearly a hundred years. No Cassidy ever kept chickens."

"They didn't use computers, either, but you do."

He glanced at her. "You're very smart."

"I know. And it's not their fault they're chickens. You shouldn't be mad at them."

"I'm not mad."

"You look mad when you talk about them. They're really good chickens. They eat coconut."

He reined in Bullet. "What?"

"Maybe not a whole one, but part. It's in their food."

Coconut? "Do they get piña coladas, too?"

"I don't know."

He shook his head. "Never mind."

"It's so they don't eat soy. You'll have to ask Arturo. I don't know what it all means."

Coconut? Sure. And they were probably served dinner on silver trays, with champagne.

"Where's your mom and dad?" Erin asked.

"They died nearly ten years ago."

Her mouth twisted. "That's sad."

"Yes, it is. They liked to travel a lot. They were in Europe, taking a small plane from Italy to a resort on the Black Sea. The plane crashed."

"Do you remember them?"

He nodded. They hadn't been around much. His father had grown up hating the ranch, feeling he was trapped by the land and the cattle. He'd married and had Mitch, but inside he'd been waiting until *his* father died so he could escape.

Mitch had been nearly ten when his grandfather had passed on, leaving Mitch's parents free to travel the world. They'd been gone within a month. Arturo and Fidela had stepped into the emptiness, giving him the stability he needed.

He hadn't missed his parents that much, although he'd found himself feeling lost when they died. Maybe it had been the realization that he had no other family. Skye had been there for him and at the time, it had been enough.

"You want to go fast?" Erin asked, looking eager.

Mitch found himself wanting to see what he and Bullet could do.

"Sure," he said.

She leaned over her horse and whispered something. The animal shot ahead. Mitch tightened his muscles and Bullet raced after her. The wind blew in his face. Despite his amputation, he stayed on the horse without a problem.

Freedom, he thought, grateful for the chance to experience this again. He owed Erin for pushing. Owed and would find a way to pay her back. He would also pay back Skye, but for very different reasons.

CHAPTER EIGHT

SKYE WALKED into the Calico Café and found both Lexi and Dana, their friend and Titanville deputy, already waiting.

"Where's Izzy?" Lexi asked, then slapped her menu on the table. "Don't tell me you two still aren't speaking. What's going on there?"

Dana picked up her coffee. "Let me guess. It's a man."

"Sort of," Skye said, feeling defensive. "I told her about breakfast. She's the one who said she didn't want to come."

"Who's the guy?" Dana asked.

"He's not important."

"But you're fighting over him?"

"I know." Skye slid into her seat and nodded when the waitress brought over a pot of coffee. She waited until hers had been poured to say, "I'm tired of Izzy assuming she's the only guy magnet in the family. I could be one if I wanted."

Lexi and Dana glanced at each other, then at her.

"Do you want to be one?" Lexi asked.

"That's not the point."

"I'm thinking therapy or medication," Dana said. "Maybe both."

Skye managed a smile. "I know it sounds crazy. I can't really explain it. T. J. Boone is—"

"I know T.J.," Lexi said, looking confused. "I went to high school with him. He lives in Dallas." She turned to Dana. "You remember him, don't you?"

"Uh-huh. He's pretty enough, if you're into blond guys."

"This isn't about his appearance," Skye said primly. "It's about principle."

"The principle of being right?" Dana asked.

Being in law enforcement and basically sensible to her bones, Dana could be counted on to get to the heart of a matter. Normally Skye appreciated that in her friend. Just not this morning.

"Jed is trying to hook up T.J. and me," Skye said. "Izzy talked to him and then informed me that there's no way he's actually interested in me as a person. And that T.J. is wild about her because who wouldn't be. The way she tells it is that she's dating him to protect me and, I guess, to save me from myself." She took a sip of the coffee. "I'm a big girl. I can take care of myself."

Lexi shifted in her chair. "There is a chance that Izzy's intentions are good and that she really is worried about you."

"Maybe."

"She's your sister."

"I know that."

Dana leaned forward. "What she's trying to say is maybe you should be the mature one in all this."

"Not what I want to hear."

"Do you even like the guy?" Lexi asked.

"He's charming and funny and making a serious effort to win me over. I should like him."

"But?" Dana asked.

"Can we change the subject? Let's talk about something easier to define, like our evil half brother. Any luck finding out Garth's source with the media?"

"Not yet," Lexi said. "Cruz has hired a detective who's digging around, but so far we're not even close. If we could just find a way to link him to something, anything illegal, we could call in the police."

"Speaking for Titanville's finest," Dana said. "I'm ready to be called."

"I've spoken with that woman who filed the lawsuit against my spa," Lexi said. "She later withdrew it. She's moved away and despite the fact that she's not working for Garth anymore, she won't testify against him. She won't even admit she filed the suit on his request. It's so frustrating."

"But he's good," Dana said. "You have to give him that."

"Yeah, good at destroying us," Skye said. "Why couldn't we have a normal half brother? One who wanted to bring us flowers and eat fried chicken? Instead we have someone who is plotting our destruction. It's like being in a James Bond movie but without all the cool gadgets."

"Or James Bond," Dana said.

"That, too."

"I want to get my hands on him," Dana said.

Lexi looked confused. "James Bond?"

"Garth."

"He's not your type," Skye teased.

"Tell me about it."

"And speaking of types." Lexi eyed Skye's coffee but reached for her juice, then turned to Dana. "Are you seeing anyone?"

A few weeks ago they'd had a girls' night helping Dana recover from being dumped. At the time she'd made it clear she was far more upset about the guy leaving *her* rather than the pain of being left.

"I'm between men," Dana said. "I'm going to keep it that way for a while."

"What about you?" Lexi asked Skye. "Are you still going to see T.J.?"

"I don't know. He's very nice."

"Words every man longs to hear," Dana muttered. "*Nice* is the death of hope in a relationship. If he's not making you all tingly, you should leave him for Izzy to play with."

"Maybe," she said, knowing she couldn't tell them the truth. If Jed was serious about her getting together with T.J. then he would pressure her in ways her sister and her friend couldn't begin to understand. That even now, as a mother herself and a woman with a relatively successful life, she was still afraid of losing her father's affection.

No matter how many times she told herself she wasn't that ten-year-old little girl standing over her mother's dead body, she couldn't shake the fear of being abandoned yet again. She hated the part of herself that feared Jed, but she also couldn't ignore it.

"SO, YOU'RE THE JACKASS Joss told me about."

Mitch looked up from the computer to see a tall man standing in the doorway of his office. The guy was probably in his mid-forties, fit and tanned.

"Who are you?" he asked, already suspecting the truth. Joss wouldn't be happy just taking away his prosthesis. He would want to make a point, as well.

"I'm Alex." The guy walked into the office and took a seat without being asked. "Joss asked me to stop by and talk to you."

Mitch could see both the guy's hands, so he must have lost a leg. "Which one?" he asked.

"Right. Makes it a bitch to drive. Mid-thigh. I was a kid, driving drunk." Alex shrugged. "It happens. At least I had the excuse of being a teenager. What's yours?"

"I fell on a bomb."

"I don't mean for losing your leg. I mean for

acting like a jerk. From what I hear, you beat yourself up pretty bad last week. No matter how hard you push yourself, you're not going to grow back your leg."

Mitch's mild interest turned into annoyance. "Thanks for the greeting card's worth of advice. I'm busy."

"Too bad. I'm not leaving until I've said what I came here to say."

Mitch crossed his arms over his chest. "You think you can make me listen?"

"Probably, but think about it. Two cripples wrestling on the floor, prostheses and crutches flying. Do you really want people to see you like that?"

The image was so clear, Mitch found himself fighting a smile. "It might damage my tough-guy image."

"You think?"

"So why are you here?" he asked, although he already had a good idea.

"To talk to you about what it's really like, long term. To tell you that it's going to get better, but not until you accept that your life has changed. Beating yourself up, mentally and physically, won't make it go away. You've got to be smart about the prosthesis."

"Assuming Joss gives it back to me."

"He will. But take it slow this time. You have to adjust."

"Slow isn't my favorite speed."

"It won't have to be for long. You have sex yet?"

The question surprised Mitch. "Yes."

"Good. Some guys put it off. You need to get back on the horse, so to speak."

Mitch thought about Skye and the way she'd lost herself in the moment. "It wasn't with a horse."

Alex laughed. "I didn't think so. Did you get on top?"

Mitch hesitated. "No. I wasn't sure…"

"You'll have to practice. If you're not in a relationship, wait until you're comfortable with the lady. It takes a bit to get the leverage right." Alex grinned. "But it's worth it."

Mitch's imagination went back to Skye, but instead of picturing them outside, on the ground, he imagined a bed and her below him, breathing hard, her eyes sinking closed. It didn't seem to matter how angry he was with her, he still wanted her.

"You're not the only one going through this," Alex said, pulling Mitch back from his fantasy. "Everyone around you is adjusting, too. Your friends and family don't know what to expect or how to act. Should they help? Get out of the way? Ask how you feel? Most people want to do the right thing but don't want to push. Help them by being honest. If you don't want help, say so. If you want assistance, make that clear. If you expect them to guess right every time, you will be losing a whole lot more than a few toes."

Mitch looked at the other man. "It's hard for me

to consider that the people around me are going through something, too."

"They are. It's a big change, but it doesn't have to be a bad one. It's all up to you. Take control."

"That I can do," Mitch told him.

IZZY LACED UP her climbing shoes. T.J. waited until she was done to hand her a harness. She grabbed it from him, feeling crabby and not sure why. He'd called and asked her to go rock climbing. She'd accepted the invitation. So why did she want to snap at him?

There were a lot of complicated reasons, she thought, tightening the harness. Most of them revolved around her sister, but it was a lot easier to be pissed at T.J.

She wanted to yell at him, but couldn't think of a good reason. Maybe she could complain about the date. She was good enough to sweat with but not good enough for dinner and a movie? Except she wasn't the dinner and a movie type. If they were going to have fun, they should have fun. If the night was about sex, why waste a lot of time eating a meal she probably didn't want or seeing a movie? They should get to the sex.

But what was rock climbing? It was the kind of afternoon you could spend with a relative.

"You look like you want to take me on," he said. "Are you mad at me?"

"No." The word came out sharper than she intended. "You're dating my sister."

"Skye and I have been to dinner."

"That's a date."

"I didn't say it wasn't."

"You can't be interested in both of us. We're totally different."

"I'm a guy with varied interests."

Not a good enough answer. "If you have a sister sex fantasy, let me be clear. Yuck. And no way in hell."

He grinned. "I hadn't thought about it but now that you mention it…"

She glanced around for something to throw at him. "I'm serious."

"Then I guess I have to be. Do you want to get exclusive?"

She blinked at him. "Excuse me?"

"Should we get serious, be boyfriend and girlfriend, only see each other and no one else?"

Izzy took three steps back and had to resist the need to make the sign of the cross. "No way. Why would you even ask that? We've been out twice. I barely know you."

He tightened his own harness. "I'm going to bask in the boost you just gave my ego. After that endorsement, I can die a happy man."

He was slick, she would give him that. And smart. But what else was he? "Okay, I get your point. We've only been out a couple of times. Why should I care that you're seeing anyone else when I don't feel the need to avoid other men."

"You have other men?" he asked.

"Not the issue. I don't care who else you see." Except for Skye, she thought, the crabby feeling coming back. But why should she sweat any of it? She did though and that complicated everything.

"I don't care who else you see, unless it's my sister. You should make things easy and just pick one of us to pursue."

"Any suggestions as to which one would work out best?"

If she said herself, then Skye could get hurt. She would certainly think Izzy was trying to make a point. But Izzy wasn't ready to back out, either. Mostly to see how far T.J. would take things.

"You two could decide between you," he told her.

"You're not that much of a prize."

He clutched his chest. "Wait for it. Ego boost number two. I'm not sure I'm going to get my head through the door when we're done here."

"This is stupid," she said, and walked to the wall. After hooking her harness to the line, she reached for the first handhold.

T.J. came up behind her and put his hands on her waist. He moved close, so they were touching—his front to her back. He was warm and strong and masculine and she liked the feel of him next to her.

"Don't walk away," he murmured into her ear. "Please."

"Give me one good reason why I shouldn't."

He turned her until they were facing, then bent down and kissed her.

This wasn't like the first kiss where all he did was claim and take. This time he kissed her gently, pressing his lips to hers lightly enough to promise but not enough to push. He moved slowly, as if giving her time.

She liked his mouth on hers. Liked the way he rubbed and teased before touching his tongue to her lower lip. Which asked a question. Did she want to take this to the next level?

She parted her lips, as much because she was curious as because she was enjoying the contact. His tongue swept inside, claiming her. Unexpected passion shot through her, making her catch her breath. Not that she wanted him to know.

He tasted of coffee and mint. His fingers were warm, barely touching her waist. Their tongues tangled and danced. Surprising heat poured through her, making her go wet and weak in all the right places.

The sound of people approaching made her pull back.

She stared into T.J.'s blue eyes. Wanting flared there. He looked like a man who needed to get laid. But was she the right woman to satisfy that itch?

If he'd been anyone else, she would have suggested blowing off rock climbing and adjourning to whoever's place was closest. But that wasn't an option. Not with Skye in the picture.

"Don't walk away," he repeated, still staring into her eyes.

"All right."

The words were pulled from her. They came from deep inside and she hadn't known she was going to say them. He rubbed her lips with his thumb.

She turned back to the wall and started to climb. She wanted to go as high as she could, up the steepest wall, so all she had to think about was hanging on. After all, the alternative was to fall.

ARTURO KNOCKED on Mitch's open office door.

"I'm going to drive the fence lines," his manager said. "Want to come with me?"

Anytime up to two days ago, Mitch would have refused and he guessed Arturo expected him to. But Alex's point had been a good one—Fidela and Arturo had to adjust to the changes nearly as much as he did. This wasn't easy on them, either.

"Sure," he said, and saved his work, then grabbed his crutches.

"You feeling better?" Arturo asked as they made their way to the truck parked behind the barn.

"I'm healing. I need to call about my temporary prosthesis." Assuming Joss was ready to give it back to him. Mitch had a feeling the new socket had come in fairly quickly, but Joss wouldn't tell him that. He would wait for Mitch to make the first move.

"How's the temporary one different?" Arturo asked, then held up a hand. "Sorry. I shouldn't have asked."

"You can ask," Mitch told him. He waited for his friend to open the truck door, then slid onto the passenger seat. When Arturo was behind the wheel, Mitch continued.

"The temporary prosthesis has a different kind of foot on it. It's easier to learn to walk with it. The permanent leg will have a spring-loaded foot, which will ultimately give me more endurance and a more natural walk, but it takes getting used to."

"Makes sense."

"I was walking too much on an incision that wasn't completely healed. I got a few raw spots that I didn't take care of."

"You're okay now, though, right?"

Mitch smiled. "Let's say I've learned my lesson. I don't like being on crutches and will do what I have to so I can stay off them."

"Fidela worries about you."

"I know." Arturo worried, too, but he wouldn't admit that.

They rode in silence to the fence line. Mitch stared out at the cattle, grazing in the warm sun.

"This is better," Arturo said. "The cattle are healthier."

"If you're trying to convince me about going organic, I'm starting to see your point," Mitch admitted. "I've been looking over the books. We're averaging two dollars a pound more than regular beef. And the cattle don't get sick, which is a cost savings."

"It's more than that," the other man said, driving slowly by the fence. "We respect the land. All those chemicals and pesticides weren't good. We contract with three small farms for organic feed to supplement the grass. They had to be certified, as well. Now they're growing more vegetables that they're selling. The grasslands are coming back. We breed the cows later, so the calves are born closer to summer. The weather's better and they can eat grass."

He stopped the truck and climbed out to inspect a post, then returned to the truck.

"To stay organic, the land around us has to avoid chemicals. The groundwater is better quality."

"I swear if Fidela starts serving tofu for dinner, I'm firing you both."

Arturo grinned. "No tofu. I hate the stuff. She keeps saying she's going to put it in a burrito and I won't know the difference, but she wouldn't do more than threaten."

"She's a good woman."

"Yes, she is. You know, she checks on you in the night sometimes."

Mitch hadn't known that. "Why?"

"To see that you're really there."

He wondered if there was more to it than that. He wondered if she heard him screaming. "Sometimes I have nightmares."

Arturo glanced at him, then returned his attention to the dirt road. "About the explosion?"

"Mostly right after." He wasn't sure if he remembered the explosion or had heard about it enough that he thought he did. "There are missions I dream about." Mostly ones where someone he cared about died.

"You were gone a long time. You did things. Saw things."

Mitch nodded.

"You could have come home."

Mitch looked at his friend. "I was—" He didn't have an excuse.

"We're your family. We raised you, loved you. You don't have our name, but you are as much our child as any we could have had. Fidela prayed for you every night. Not a day went by that she didn't speak of you. But you never came home to see her."

Or him, Mitch thought, waiting for the anger. It was the familiar response, the easy one. But for once, it wasn't there. Instead he felt regret and sadness.

"I'm sorry," he said quietly. "I didn't want to come back."

"Because of Skye."

It wasn't a question.

"Because I didn't belong here."

"You have always belonged."

"Because I didn't want to be here. I didn't want to see..." Everything he'd lost. Everything that wasn't his. "I'm sorry," he repeated.

"I know."

Arturo did know and he probably understood, which only made Mitch feel worse. "I'll talk to Fidela."

"She would like that. She's making a baby blanket for your friend Pete. His wife called after…to say what a hero you were to them. She mentioned she was pregnant."

"That's nice of her," he said, knowing both Pete and his wife would appreciate it. They didn't have a lot of family around.

Without wanting to, he remembered the noise and chaos right after the explosion. Pete had been dragging him, yelling at him to hang on. At first Mitch hadn't felt anything but stunned and confused. Then he looked down and saw blood, bone and muscle where his leg had been.

His first instinct had been to run so far and so fast, he could go back in time before any of it had happened. But he couldn't move, could barely keep breathing as Pete dragged him behind an over-turned truck.

He remembered the blood on Pete's jacket, but hadn't known where it had come from. Himself, Pete or someone else.

"Stay here," Pete had yelled over the gunfire. "I'm going to find a medic."

After talking to the doctors, Mitch knew he'd been in shock from the explosion and the blood loss. He'd been unable to speak, but when his friend had disappeared, he'd managed to grab his gun, turn over and lay down some cover.

The pain had come then. Dark and alive, it had sucked the strength from him. He'd wanted to curl up and scream. Instead he'd searched for the snipers pinning them down and had picked off at least two of them.

He'd fired until he was out of ammo, then he'd crawled to a fallen enemy, had taken his rifle and used it until Pete returned.

"Pete saved my life," he said. "He dragged me to safety and got a medic to stop the bleeding. He was wounded himself, but didn't stop to get help until later."

"The way his wife tells it, you saved his life," Arturo told him. "You saved everyone. You're getting a medal."

"I don't want it." What would it prove or change?

"You should take it. People like to say thank you."

"Good point." He wanted to thank Pete for saving him. He'd tried but his friend had brushed off the words. They were a team. They took care of each other.

They crested a small rise. Arturo stopped the truck and watched a couple of calves running around their mothers. It was a perfect scene, Mitch thought. Far from war and pain and anything ugly.

"Maybe you should talk to someone," Arturo said without looking at him. "A professional. I know you won't tell me everything. I can't understand and you wouldn't want to burden me. But you need to talk, Mitch. It starts the healing."

"I'm doing okay." He rubbed his leg. "It barely hurts anymore." Which was almost true.

"I'm not talking about the outside. You need to talk to someone."

"I'll think about it," he said, and wondered if they both knew he was lying.

CHAPTER NINE

TRISHA, THE FOUNDATION'S chief financial officer, had requested a meeting. Skye found herself dreading it, knowing there was unlikely to be good news.

Garth's attacks came from every direction and without warning. He was smart, determined and apparently unconcerned about the consequences of his actions. He wanted every Titan taken down. She was starting to wonder if he would get his wish.

Trisha arrived at her office exactly on time and closed the door behind her. The knot in Skye's stomach doubled in size, then hardened into an uncomfortable rock.

"You don't look happy," she said, studying Trisha's concerned expression. "I guess we should sit down."

Trisha moved to the small round table in the corner and spread out several sheets of paper. Skye joined her.

"It's bad," Trisha said bluntly. "Our internal investigation shows many members of the senior staff were paid huge bonuses. In a few cases, the amount given them exceeds their annual salary."

Skye felt her mouth drop open. She had to consciously close it. "That's not possible. We don't do that. You know we don't do that."

"I agree," Trisha told her, "Nonprofits are held to extremely high standards. There are regulations in place. There is also an unwritten code of ethics."

Her tone sounded a little preachy, which Skye didn't like. "Trisha, you know me. You've worked for me from the beginning. You know how I feel about the foundation. I've poured myself into it and I would never do anything to jeopardize our mission. We don't pay bonuses. Ever. That's a very clear policy."

"I know, but they're in the system." Trisha pointed to several columns. "I'm very angry and upset about this. As CFO, I have tremendous exposure on this. I'm ultimately responsible for the money. These payments didn't come through my department. I've been over the accounting books and I can't find their origin, but they're there. It's almost as if there were a second set of books this entire time and they've somehow merged."

A second set of books? Is that what people were going to think? Skye wanted to pick up a chair and toss it through the window.

"That's not possible," she said.

"Then how do you explain what's happening?"

Garth, she thought grimly. This was so him. But how had he done it? How had he hacked into the foundation's computer system and screwed around?

"How secure are our electronic records?" Skye asked.

"Very. The firewall is state-of-the-art. If you're suggesting someone broke in…"

"It's the only thing that makes sense. We have to be able to trace these entries, work backward and figure out when they were first put in the system."

Trisha looked doubtful. "I'll have to work with the IT guys and see if that's even possible. You're talking about finding a few dozen data entries in a list of possibly millions. All our records are on computer."

"I think it's more than a few dozen entries," Skye told her. "I think there are probably a few hundred. I think someone hacked into our system and planted a lot of false information."

Trisha nodded. "There are checks made out to you. Lots of them, in huge amounts."

Skye hadn't thought it could get worse, but she'd been wrong. "What?"

"Nearly a million dollars."

"No. That's not true. I don't even take a salary. I'm the one who put in the money to start the foundation. I don't take a penny."

Trisha wouldn't look at her. "A few people have hinted that you've been having investment trouble. That you needed the cash to cover some debts."

"That's not possible," Skye said, getting angry and having nowhere to put her temper. "My portfolio is extremely healthy. I live at Glory's Gate, where

I have virtually no expenses. My car is two years old, I don't buy jewelry or horses or even take vacations beyond Erin and I going to Disney World."

She shouldn't have to explain herself. Not that it would matter. Once the rumors started, people would believe what they wanted to believe.

"I'm just sharing the talk I hear." Trisha finally looked at her. "This is getting out of hand."

"I know," Skye said, wishing she had an answer. "We're risking our tax-exempt status. Worse, we'll have to divert money from the food programs to deal with this. I want the IT guys on this for however long it takes. I want to find out how this happened. I want proof that we're being set up by someone with a personal vendetta."

"We're a nonprofit. Why would someone want to hurt us?"

Skye wasn't willing to tell her just yet. So far only her sisters and Dana knew about Garth and his plans for revenge against the family. While she was desperate for advice, she needed it to come from someone who wasn't closely tied to her business. Someone who could look at all sides of things.

"We have to solve the problem," Skye said.

"All right. I'll get on it. I'll do what I can from my end." Trisha collected her paperwork. "You're going to lose some people over this. Not just supporters, but staff."

Not exactly news, Skye thought sadly. "Will I lose you?"

"No. I was there when it started. I understand the dream, and I know you, Skye. I know you wouldn't do this."

"Thanks for that."

She appreciated the support but wondered how long it would be until Garth turned everyone away from her.

SKYE WAS STILL UPSET when she left for home that afternoon. She hated problems with no solutions and so far she hadn't figured out how to fix this one. About two miles before the turnoff to Glory's Gate, she saw a truck coming in the opposite direction.

She recognized the vehicle and the driver. Mitch.

They hadn't seen each other since the night he'd been drunk in the barn, when he'd infuriated and disappointed her in equal measures. She knew the changes in him were because of what had happened to him. What she didn't know was if they were permanent. Would the man she'd known and loved ever make an appearance or was the bitter bully the new and not-improved Mitch?

As her car drew closer, she saw him slow. Instinctively she did the same, rolling down her window as they came to a stop in the middle of the quiet road.

"Hey," he said through his open window. "You're home early."

He looked good, she thought, taking in the dark

hair and eyes and wishing nothing about his appearance got to her.

"It was a really bad day," she said. "I needed to get away."

"What happened?"

She eyed his concerned expression suspiciously. "Why do you want to know? Are we speaking now? Or is this just some trick to get me to open up to you so you can use it against me later?" She held up her left hand. "You know what? I don't care. I'm tired of being your emotional punching bag. You've turned into a real bastard, Mitch Cassidy, and I'm done feeling bad about what happened before. Yes, we had a relationship. Yes, it ended badly and while I take responsibility for that, I refuse to spend the rest of my life being punished. You're not the judge and jury in this. You're just one voting member on a committee of two."

She thought he'd take off, dust flying, wheels spinning. Or that he might get cold and sarcastic. He surprised her by smiling.

"You do have a burr up your butt, don't you?"

She pressed her lips together. "Yes, I do. And for good reason."

He rested one arm on the door. "I'm sorry for my part in it."

"You're just saying that."

"No, I really mean it. I don't remember what all happened the last time we were together. I was pretty drunk. But I'm sure I was a jerk and I'm sorry."

She wanted to believe him. She wanted things to be good between them. Not romantically—she wasn't foolish enough to think they could go there anymore—but as friends. She'd missed him for nearly nine years. It was horrible having him back and being so distant.

"You've tricked me before," she told him. "You've acted all nice and then turned on me."

"I want to keep you guessing."

"You're doing a good job of it."

He reached across the space between his truck and her car. If she'd stretched out her arm, they might have touched. "Want to talk about whatever is bothering you?" he asked. "I promise to listen and not trick you in any way."

There was so much going on lately. So much that she couldn't control and that scared her. "I could lose the foundation," she said.

"What? Why? Are you running out of money?"

"No. That would be easy to fix. We have funding. At least for now. It's worse than that. It looks like someone is planting evidence that we're spending millions on bonuses and vacations. It's not true, but even the rumor could shut us down."

He drew back his arm. "Come on. Follow me back to my place. We'll talk and figure out how to make this better."

She stared at him, wishing she knew if he really meant it.

"Give me a chance, Skye. Not because I deserve it but because you want to."

She wanted a lot of things where he was concerned. "That's not playing fair," she whispered.

"I'm not playing. I mean it. Come on. We'll find a solution together."

He drove past her, turned around and waited until she put her car in Drive and continued down the road to the entrance to the Cassidy spread. She parked next to him and waited while he got his crutches.

"How bad was the hangover?" she asked as they walked toward his office in the barn.

"I've never felt that crappy in my life," he told her. "Not even after the surgery removing my leg."

"Good. Maybe you'll learn something."

He opened the door to his office and grinned at her. "You're assuming I'm that smart."

"You can be."

"On a good day."

There was a worn cloth sofa against the wall opposite the desk. Skye set her purse on the coffee table and settled in a corner. After kicking off her shoes, she angled toward him.

"It's a mess," she said. "Everything is confusing and complicated."

"It wouldn't be a quality problem if it wasn't."

"You're not taking this seriously."

He sat down and put his crutches on the floor. "Tell me more about what's going on."

Trisha had asked nearly the same question, but Skye hadn't felt right telling her. Mitch was different—they'd known each other nearly all their lives and they were connected in a way that time and distance couldn't break.

"Jed has a bastard son none of us knew about."

Mitch reminded himself that he wasn't supposed to know about Garth Duncan or his relationship with the Titans.

"When did you find this out?"

"A few months ago. Apparently all this happened before Jed married Lexi's mother. The woman he got involved with is named Kathy. She works in the pet store in town. She's…" Skye looked at him. "Something happened to her. She's mentally challenged. We don't know if it was a car accident or what and it must have happened after their affair. But we don't have any details. Jed swears he set her and Garth up with plenty of money, but people get angry for all sorts of reasons."

Mitch hadn't known about Garth's mother. Was that the reason the man was out for revenge? Did the reason matter?

"How did you find out about him?" he asked.

"Lexi's fiancé Cruz first made the connection. Lexi had borrowed money to expand her spa business. It was a great loan with excellent terms and only one tiny detail. The note was callable. At any time, Lexi could have to repay it back with only a few weeks' notice. Garth was the lender and he called the note."

Skye leaned her head against the back of the sofa. Her long, wavy auburn hair tumbled down the ratty fabric, making it difficult for him to pay attention to what she was saying.

"Next a couple of Jed's racehorses tested positive for drugs."

"No way," Mitch said, drawn back into the conversation. "Your old man thinks he runs the world, but he would never dope a horse."

"I know. Then the D.A. got a tip that we were using the foundation to launder money, so that was a mess. Lexi managed to fix her business and Jed can't be hurt by very much. The D.A. investigated and we were cleared of all charges. Still, it was a lot of negative publicity."

Garth had game, Mitch thought, both respecting the other man's thoroughness and feeling guilty for agreeing to spy for him. It didn't sound like Garth needed any help. Plus, this was Skye. Did Mitch really want to hurt her?

Not on a good day.

"There have been other things," Skye said, sounding defeated. "A former client sued Lexi. It turned out she'd been working for Garth and had a huge crush on him. When Lexi pointed out that filing a lawsuit under false pretenses was illegal, the woman disappeared."

Mitch remembered the recent headlines. "The rumors about mad cow?"

"We're guessing that's Garth. Now he's after the

foundation again. Somehow, someone got into our computer program. Financial records have been changed. They're showing big bonuses paid to senior staff, but we don't pay bonuses. They're also showing that I wrote a lot of checks to myself and someone's started rumors that I'm covering some bad investments." She cleared her throat. "None of it's true, but no one will care about that. Successful nonprofits survive because of their reputations. If we lose that, we could lose everything."

He felt even worse than before. "Are you sure this is all Garth?"

"Yes. He said he was going to take us down. What we don't know is why now. Did something happen to trigger him? Does he just now have enough influence and money? He's thought this through. He has connections, money, means and plenty of motivation. We don't know where the next blow will come from or how to stop him."

"What does Jed say?"

"Nothing. Lexi tried to talk to him, but he blew her off. He says he's handling it. Cruz suspects that Jed might even be proud of what Garth is doing. After all, Garth is Jed's son. I don't understand that. If Garth is angry, he should talk to us directly. I run a foundation that feeds hungry children. That's all we do. Every dollar we have to spend on legal fees or an investigation over false charges is a dollar not going to a kid's dinner."

Okay, now Mitch knew he was officially jerk of the month. He'd thought Garth had some mild interest in screwing with Jed. But this was different. This bordered on evil.

"Are you sure there's no way someone at the foundation has been playing fast and loose with the money?" he asked.

"We'll find out soon enough," she said with a sigh. "I'm starting an internal investigation. My CFO is bringing in some of the computer guys to pinpoint the charges in the system. Once we have that, we'll figure out where it came from. I'm guessing Garth has paid someone to hack into our system. We have the usual protections, but they obviously weren't enough."

Mitch had seen Skye in nearly every mood possible, but he'd never heard her sound defeated before.

"Once you have that, you'll go after him?" he asked.

"Maybe. If we can take it to the authorities. So far we haven't been able to pin anything on him. The woman he used to file the lawsuit won't talk. The loan to Lexi, while ruthless, isn't illegal. When someone tipped off the D.A. about the money laundering at the foundation, it was untraceable. This is our first real chance to get hard evidence. At least I hope it is. Part of me thinks it's another dead end. That it will just lead to some poor kid in a basement somewhere, working on a contract without having ever met Garth."

Mitch had to fight to keep from squirming. He wasn't used to being the bad guy. He'd thought Skye deserved whatever happened, but she didn't deserve this.

"How can I help?" he asked before he could stop himself. Help? He was supposed to be on Garth's side.

She looked surprised. "I thought you hated me."

"I don't hate you."

"Then you should be in Hollywood making movies because you had me convinced."

He didn't want to talk about that, either. "I had a lot on my mind."

"You called me names. You acted like a total jerk."

"I was drunk."

"It wasn't the one time."

He didn't know what to say. His anger, always so accessible, seemed to have faded away. "You need to give me a break. I have a lot going on."

She looked away from him and sighed. "It doesn't matter. You can hate me if you want. I probably deserve it."

He didn't want to hear her say that. This wasn't the Skye he knew. His Skye gave back as good as she got. She stood up to him and flung milk shakes at him. She called him names, took him on and came back for another round.

"I'll help you with Garth," he said, willing to commit to anything to see a little fire in her.

She sat up. "Really? You mean it? Jed's having

one of his cocktail parties in a couple of days and Garth is going to be there. Would you come, too? You could keep an eye on him, maybe size him up. I'd like your take on the situation."

Mitch bit back an oath. He was a lousy spy to begin with—he wouldn't be much of a double agent. Besides, he was having his doubts about his agreement with Garth.

A cocktail party at Glory's Gate? He couldn't imagine a worse night. But he couldn't refuse Skye. Not when she looked so hopeful.

"I'll be there."

"Really?"

She smiled at him as if he'd just handed her the sun, then threw her arms around him.

"Izzy and I are in the most ridiculous fight," she murmured, her face pressed into his shoulder. "Lexi is busy with Cruz and I've been feeling really alone in all this. It means so much that I can count on you."

His self-worth meter hit an all-time low. Unfamiliar guilt made him feel like an eight-year-old who just knocked a baby bird out of a nest.

"Skye, I don't know if I can find out anything."

She pulled back enough to stare into his eyes. "I know. No pressure, I promise. It's enough to know that you're willing to try. Despite everything, I've always known I could trust you."

He held in a groan. Not knowing what else to do, he leaned in and kissed her.

MITCH'S MOUTH was warm and familiar. Skye told herself that giving in to him wasn't a smart idea. That she would probably regret it later, but right now she couldn't seem to care. With all the confusion in her life, it felt good to have something solid around and today that was Mitch.

She shifted closer, wanting to feel all of him, even as she parted her mouth to admit him.

She'd expected the kiss to be enticing—she'd always loved kissing Mitch. She hadn't expected the wave of heat that crashed through her, making it tough to breathe.

Wanting exploded from nowhere. It was as if her insecurities, her fears and all her worries faded into the background. The only thing that mattered this second was never letting go.

He wrapped his arms around her, as if to hold her in place. If she'd been able to speak, she would have told him she wasn't going anywhere. Not while they were touching and every nerve in her body danced in anticipation.

His mouth claimed hers with a certainty that made her want to give in more. She ran her hands across his shoulders, feeling his strength beneath the soft cotton of his shirt. His tongue played with hers, each stroke sending need rippling through her.

It was like the last time, she thought hazily. Desperate and fast, but without the anger. This time there was only passion.

He drew back a little and kissed his way along her jaw. She went to work on the buttons holding her blouse together. She found herself fumbling a little as he licked his way down her neck.

Sensual shivers caused her skin to pucker. Between her legs she felt heat and swelling. Every part of her wanted to be with him again, to feel him inside of her. She ached for what only he could give her.

She pulled her blouse free of her slacks. He'd already reached behind her and unfastened her bra. The second it came off, he leaned in and took her right nipple in his mouth.

The warm dampness of his mouth made her sigh. The flick of his tongue against her sensitive skin made her gasp. She wanted to take off the rest of her clothes, but she could only hang on as he sucked deeply, pulling her into his mouth.

Fire shot through her, burning down to her belly, making her squirm. Now, she thought frantically. She needed him now.

She didn't remember it being like this—fast and uncontrolled. Making love with Mitch had always been about connecting. There had been pleasure, but they were just as intent on being together. Now, she wanted what he could do to her and what she could do to him. She wanted him hard, filling her, losing control. She wanted him desperate.

There was no time to analyze the change. Even as he moved to her other breast, she reached for the belt at his waist and worked it free. Then his hands were unfastening her slacks.

She stood so she could push them, and her bikini panties, down. She stepped out of her clothes, completely naked. His gaze roamed her body, and desire darkened his eyes. But instead of unzipping his jeans, he slouched down on the sofa and drew her closer.

"Kneel," he told her.

She looked from him to the couch, understanding dawning. The shy part of her hesitated, while the rest of her sent up a quiet cheer. Before she could pick a side, he reached out and slid a single finger between her legs. He moved through her waiting heat, finding that one spot and rubbing it.

"Now," he whispered.

She knelt on the sofa, her knees on either side of his hips. She grabbed the back of the couch for support while he shifted until he could press his mouth against the very center of her. His hands rubbed her bare legs, his thumbs moving closer and closer and then she felt his tongue lightly stroke her most sensitive spot.

She gasped at the contact, then closed her eyes. He licked her slowly, thoroughly, as if rediscovering everything she liked. Pleasurable sensations poured through her, making her groan.

There was nothing for her to do but let him have his way with her. She arched her body as he licked her over and over again, moving just fast enough to make it impossible for her to catch her breath.

She'd never done anything like this before, she thought hazily. Not in this position, not with her body so exposed. He had total control, moving faster, bringing her closer, then slowing down until she was panting with need.

She got lost in all of the various sensations, the feel of gentle stroking, the scrape of his teeth and the play of his lips on her body. Tension filled her, pushing her toward the end. Her body quivered and clenched, anticipating. She rocked slightly, holding in the need to beg.

And through it all he kept pushing her toward her release, closer and closer.

She clutched the sofa back and pressed down, needing more. There was sound and movement beneath her, but she didn't know what and didn't care.

More, she thought desperately as he moved faster. More and more and…

She came with an unexpected shudder. Her orgasm rushed through her body, filling every cell, making her cry out. It went on and on, thrilling her, satisfying her, muscles shuddering, skin quivering. And when it was nearly over, he shifted on the cushion, straightening, then he lowered her onto him.

She let him guide her down until she settled on his erection. The unexpected fullness as he pushed inside shocked her back into climax. This time she came from the inside.

Even as the pleasure staggered her, she opened her eyes and found him watching her.

It was too intimate, she told herself. He shouldn't be seeing this. But she couldn't seem to close her eyes. Then she was moving up and down and he was coming and they were lost in each other.

She saw him tense, saw the moment his orgasm took over, knew that for those few seconds, he was hers.

She rode him until he was done, then she was still.

When their breathing returned to normal, Skye braced herself for what would happen next. Last time she'd felt ashamed and Mitch had become cruel. Now she was more vulnerable than before. She felt naked and raw, but she couldn't seem to pull up any emotional protection.

Instead of lashing out at her, he stared into her eyes, then tucked her hair behind her ears.

"You okay?" he asked.

A simple question. Nothing fancy or special, but still she found herself fighting tears.

"I'm good."

"Me, too." He smiled, his expression one of a very satisfied male.

She moved off of him and stood. Once again she found herself the one who had undressed while he had little to do except straighten his jeans and pull up a zipper.

But this time he grabbed a crutch and stood, then reached for her panties and passed them to her.

"I'd offer to help," he said, his gaze lingering on her breasts. "But that would only slow you down."

She pulled on her bikini panties, then picked up her bra.

"Wait," he said, and carefully pulled her against him.

She went willingly into his arms. Although they touched, she didn't lean against him. That might throw him off balance.

How was he adjusting? What did he miss the most? Was there still pain? All questions she wasn't comfortable asking. She wasn't a part of the healing process. She wasn't sure what, if any, part she had in Mitch's life.

He kissed her, the movement of his mouth making her want him again.

Long locked-away feelings woke and stretched. They pushed against the walls of her heart, as if seeking light and a chance to grow.

Care about Mitch again? Risk it all?

The thought was as exciting as it was terrifying. That road was a dangerous one. There was Erin to consider and everything else going on in her life. She couldn't be sure where his heart was and they were both very different people now.

She drew back and fastened her bra, then quickly finished dressing.

"I'll see you at the party," he told her.

Party? What…oh. The one she'd asked him to attend. Because he was helping her. He was on her side.

"I'll be the one making sure it all flows smoothly," she said with a smile. As if her insides weren't shaking. As if she wasn't more scared than she'd been in forever.

She couldn't give her heart back to Mitch. It had taken her nearly all this time to get over him. If she fell in love with him again and got hurt, she might never figure out how to be whole.

MITCH STOOD in the center of the physical therapy center and watched the other patients work on their problems. There was plenty of sweat and cursing, not to mention a few tears. But everyone there was making progress.

Three weeks ago, he'd been walking around on a prosthesis. Now he was stuck on crutches and he hated every minute of it. Hated it enough to do what he was told.

The receptionist, a young woman in a bright shirt covered with dancing teddy bears, smiled. "Mitch Cassidy?" she asked. "Joss is expecting you." She picked up a chart. "If you'll follow me to exam room one."

He limped along behind her on the smooth floor. She held open the door and waited until he was inside before flashing him a smile and retreating.

Less than two minutes later, Joss entered, flipping through the chart. "You can't be here without a note from your doctor," he said, not looking up from the pages.

Mitch pulled it out of his back pocket and passed it over.

"How do I know it's not faked?" Joss asked.

Mitch laughed. "Because I'm not that stupid. You'll call and check."

"You bet your ass I will. He'd better tell me you're cleared to be back on your prosthesis, or I'll break your other leg."

Mitch settled on the examining table, drawing his crutches up next to him before unrolling his pant leg.

"Having much pain?"

Mitch desperately wanted his prosthesis back, but knew he had to change if he wanted to stay healthy. "Some," he admitted. "More an ache than a sharp pain."

"Uh-huh." Joss massaged the stump. "You doing the exercises I e-mailed you?"

"Twice a day."

"Ready to come back to therapy as often as I tell you?"

Mitch knew he didn't have a choice. "Yes."

Joss straightened. "What about group therapy? Want to get all touchy-feely with a bunch of strangers, then go hug a tree?"

Mitch managed a weak smile. "Do I have to hug a tree?"

"Is that a yes?"

He nodded. "It's a yes."

"Smart answer."

Joss left the examining room and returned a few minutes later carrying the prosthesis. The new socket looked different.

"I made some modifications," Joss told him, handing over the leg. "It should be more comfortable. I want you to go easy, too. No more than a half hour at a time the first couple of days, with at least an hour off. Ease into it. You screw this up, Mitch, and I swear I'll beat the shit out of you myself."

The anger was still there, Mitch thought, as the feeling surged over him. The difference was he no longer felt the need to react to it. Yeah, he was pissed. So what? Being pissed hadn't gotten him anything but in the hospital and back on crutches. The past few weeks had taught him he wanted to walk more than he wanted to be mad.

If nothing else, it was a start.

CHAPTER TEN

SKYE DRESSED carefully for the cocktail party. She'd hosted a hundred more just like it, but this one was different. At least it was from her perspective... mostly because Mitch was coming.

Craziness, she told herself. She'd asked for help and he'd agreed. So he wasn't being a jackass anymore. He was adjusting, that was it. Nothing significant had happened between them.

Her mind immediately flashed to them making love. While she wanted to get all girly about the event, she knew she shouldn't read too much into it. If she did, she might be the only one. Mitch likely wasn't getting all gooey inside when he thought about them doing it.

She slipped on her shoes and made her way downstairs to her party office. The catering staff had already set up in the kitchen. She reviewed the menus before checking the food they'd brought.

Next she went over the selection of music. Tonight she'd be using CDs rather than anything live. It was a more informal gathering. Only about a hundred people. Including Garth.

Her father walked into her office. He might be well into his sixties, but he was still a handsome man. His hand-tailored suit hid any weight he'd put on over the past few years. He wore power as easily as his custom shirts.

"The food looks good," he said as he checked out the lists on the boards. "What's the theme tonight?"

"A good old-fashioned barbecue. Appetizers based on barbecue favorites. It's nearly summer. I thought this would be a fun kickoff."

Jed looked at her. He was tall, with dark hair that had only begun to go gray.

"You're good at this sort of thing, Skye. You need to get married again."

"To T. J. Boone. You've mentioned that before."

"Well, how's that coming? Any progress? T.J. didn't strike me as the kind of guy to drag his feet. Was I wrong about him?"

"We've only been out once."

"Then call him yourself and set something up."

She picked up the wine list. "I don't think so. I'm a Titan, Daddy. I don't call men, they call me." Which was a total lie. Men didn't call her. Not counting the single dinner with T.J., she hadn't been on a date since before she'd gotten married. But the comment had the intended effect—Jed laughed.

"That's my girl," he said.

"Why'd you invite Garth to the party?" she asked. "I didn't put his name on the guest list."

"I thought it would be interesting to have him around."

"See how your boy turned out?"

His expression hardened. "What's your point, Skye?"

"He's dangerous. I know Lexi already tried to talk to you about this and you refused to listen. I don't know if you're secretly proud of him or if this is all some twisted game that only the boys can play. But I will tell you this isn't going to end well for any of us. Garth wants revenge and he wants it bad."

Jed didn't look impressed. "What has your panties all in a bunch?"

"He's coming after my foundation again. He's hacked into the computer system and is making a lot of trouble."

"Then you should do a better job of taking care of what's yours."

"We're yours, Daddy. We're your daughters and you're not doing a very good job of taking care of us."

"You're always telling me you three can do it on your own. You can't have it both ways, Skye. Either you can handle things on your own or you can't. If the foundation is too much, then get rid of it. I always thought it was a ridiculous waste of your time and money."

She stiffened. "We feed hungry children right here

in this country. Most of the time we're the only steady source of food they have."

"If their parents can't provide for them, they shouldn't be breeding," Jed said, with a typical callousness. "Besides, I know all this. I've read your brochures, Skye. You're playing at making a difference. If you want to be like everyone else, go out and get a job." He glanced at the boards on the wall and poked at the wine list she held. "A real one. Say what you want about Garth, he's made something of himself. I can respect that."

As opposed to his daughters, she thought bitterly. By his definition, they'd done nothing.

Jed left her office. She stood in the center of the room fighting the sense of defeat that had haunted her for days. Doubts crowded in. What if she couldn't do it? What if she couldn't protect the foundation? What if Garth won?

"I won't let him," she said aloud. She couldn't. There was too much at stake.

Nothing Jed had said was news. He'd never understood why she'd wanted to start a foundation with her mother's money. He thought it was all a waste of time. He made his own rules, then he expected everyone to live by them. If people didn't agree, he dismissed them.

That's what had happened to her mother, she thought sadly. He'd married her and given her everything she wanted...except his heart. And that had pushed Pru over the edge.

Skye thought about something Izzy had said a while ago. That Jed could no longer father children. Was that what had gone wrong with his marriage to Pru? That she hadn't been able to give him more children? Jed wouldn't have cared it was his fault— he would have found a way to blame her. Or was it that she hadn't given him a son?

Thinking about all this was a lot easier than dealing with the truth of what Jed thought about her. Maybe she was stupid to stay here, at Glory's Gate. While she'd always loved the house and considered it her real home, what price did she pay to be its mistress? How much pride and self-respect could she lose before she started to lose herself?

The sound of running footsteps brought a smile to her face. She put down the wine list and braced herself.

Sure enough Erin rounded the corner at top speed and threw herself into her arms.

"Hi, Mommy," she said as she hugged Skye tight. "I wanted to see you again before the party started." Erin looked up at her and grinned. "The food smells really, really good."

Skye kissed the top of her daughter's head. "In about fifteen minutes a tray will be delivered to the media room," she promised.

"With enough for Amber, too?"

"When have I ever let Amber starve?"

"Never. Not even one time!"

Amber had been Erin's kindergarten teacher. She

had a fiancé in the military and was desperate to wear Vera Wang at her wedding, so she was open to all the babysitting Skye needed.

"Okay, then."

Erin hugged her again. "I love you, Mommy."

"I love you, too, Bunny Face."

Erin giggled. "You'll come see me after the party?"

"I will."

"Okay." Erin smiled at her, then skipped out of the office.

Her daughter had lost her father two years ago. Would she now lose her home because of Skye's pride? Erin loved everything about Glory's Gate.

On the other hand, maybe it was time for them to be on their own.

"Not the moment to make a decision," Skye told herself. But one would have to be made eventually. She was beginning to realize she couldn't stay here forever.

But first she had a party to deal with.

Skye heard the music start and checked her watch. The first of the guests would be arriving any minute. She went through the kitchen but as always, the catering staff had everything under control. She headed for the front door, only to meet up with Izzy at the foot of the stairs.

"You look great," she said, taking in her baby sister's halter-style dress in a shimmering silver fabric. Izzy's dark hair was a curly cloud that tumbled down her bare back. She wore impossibly high sandals and a dozen or so thin bangles on one arm.

"I'm here to dazzle," Izzy said as she turned in a slow circle so Skye could take it all in.

"T.J. isn't going to be here," Skye snapped, wondering how far Izzy was going to play the game. Yes, she was beautiful, yes, she could get any man she wanted. Yes, Skye was the most unfortunate looking of the sisters. Let's all move on.

"Not him," Izzy said, dismissing T.J. with a wave of her fingers. "Garth. I thought I'd do my best to make him uncomfortable."

"You think the fact that you look amazing will make him uncomfortable?"

"There he is. Let's go find out."

Izzy grabbed her hand and led her across the foyer. There were already forty or so guests circulating. Skye knew she would have to greet every one of them but first there was Garth to deal with.

She had no idea what Izzy had planned, but was curious to see how their half brother would stand up to the force of nature that was Izzy. As they approached, Skye tried to figure out if she could see his true evil from across the room. Were there clues?

Garth saw them and held his ground. Izzy released Skye, walked up to Garth, threw both arms around his neck and kissed his cheek.

"Finally," she said, sounding relieved. "I thought we'd never meet. Why is that? You've known about us forever. But do you call or write? Nothing. I'm waiting for a desperately clever excuse. You've had long enough to think up one."

Garth raised his eyebrows as he disentangled himself. "Izzy," he said, easing her away. "Have you been drinking?"

"Not yet, but I will. My time off is nearly over."

"Time off?" he asked.

"Oh, please. Don't pretend you don't know everything about us." She winked. "But I'll go along with it for now. I work on an oil rig. I'm an underwater welder. I work long hours with no time off for weeks at a time. When we're finally cut loose, we get all our days off in a row. I've been enjoying myself. Kind of like you."

Skye watched the exchange, not sure where Izzy was going.

She leaned against Garth. "So tell us," she murmured. "What's your end game? Total annihilation of all Titans?"

Garth's expression didn't change. "No. Just the gradual disintegration of wealth and privilege that has made all of the Titans entitled sons of bitches."

Skye's breath got caught in her chest but Izzy didn't blink. "Sort of the opposite of those bombs that kill people but not buildings? You want to leave the people standing."

"As long as they have nothing."

That was clear, Skye thought, losing her fear in her

anger. "Why?" she demanded. "What did my sisters and I ever do to you?"

"You'll have to take that up with your father."

"So this is about Jed?"

"It's about all of you."

"How much of it is about your mother?"

Garth's dark eyes hardened. "Please excuse me. I see someone I need to talk to."

He walked away before they could stop him.

Izzy fanned herself with her fingers. "If looks could kill, we'd both be stains on the carpet right now. So it *is* about Kathy. What do you think Jed did to her?"

"I don't know, but we're going to have to find out." Even though there was a part of Skye that didn't want to know.

"I need a drink," Izzy said. "Want one?"

"Go ahead. I need to circulate."

Skye walked into the crowd, careful to keep track of Garth as she went. She greeted guests, made sure everyone was eating the food, and tried to ignore the sense of dread inside. Fifteen minutes later she saw Mitch and felt her knees go weak with relief.

"You're here," she said as she rushed over. "I'm so glad."

He smiled at her. "Do you welcome all your guests that way? Because if you do, I can see why you get such a crowd."

"I probably should, but I don't. Tonight has been stressful."

He looked at his watch. "It's only seven-thirty."

"I know. We peaked early. It's been a mess. Jed and I had our usual fight about the foundation."

"What fight?"

"He thinks it's a waste of time and money."

"What do you think?"

She looked at him. He'd always had the power to take her breath away and that hadn't changed. She wanted to touch the new scar on his jaw, trace the line of his mouth, kiss him until they both forgot everything but each other. Maybe not the best plan in the middle of a party at her father's house.

"I think I can make a difference," she said.

"Then screw Jed Titan."

That made her laugh. "I think there's a club by that name. Garth would be the president."

Mitch glanced around. "He's here?"

Skye found him and pointed him out. "Izzy decided on direct confrontation. He basically said he was going to destroy everything we had and leave us with nothing. It was a tense few minutes that pretty much confirmed everything we'd been thinking." She touched her stomach. "Too much stress. Let's talk about something else. You pick the topic."

"I have my leg back."

She glanced down. "You're right. You're not on crutches. Sorry, I should have noticed."

He looked at her curiously.

"What?" she asked.

"I'm missing a leg."

"I know that."

He gave her a slow, heart-stopping smile. "Maybe I'm the only one defining myself in those terms."

"Maybe you are." She grabbed a glass of champagne from a passing server. "Okay, second subject change. We have the weather, a perennial favorite, and politics, which can be dangerous. Are you enjoying being back home." She tilted her head. "I know. Where did you live while you were gone? Were you stationed somewhere?"

"San Diego."

"It's supposed to be lovely there."

"It is. Great weather."

"Beautiful women," Skye teased. "So was there someone special?"

Mitch hesitated just long enough for her to realize she didn't want him to answer the question.

"I shouldn't have asked," she said quickly, wishing she'd stuck to politics as a conversational topic. "Of course you got involved. You were gone nearly nine years. So, what was she like? Did you..." Her brain froze. "Were you married?"

He could have married someone and then gotten a divorce. Or maybe she'd died horribly, leaving him with perfect memories of a young woman who would never screw up and abandon him.

"You're taking things a little far," Mitch told her. "I dated. There was someone I was seeing for a while. She wanted to take things to the next level and I didn't."

Meaning she loved him and he didn't love her back? Or he didn't love her enough? So many questions and Skye wasn't sure she could handle the answers.

Lexi and Cruz walked up, providing a welcome diversion.

"Hi," she said. "Lexi, you remember Mitch."

"Of course." Lexi smiled at him, then turned to Cruz. "A guy I knew in high school. You should be worried."

"I am," Cruz teased, their love an obvious and welcome third party.

"Hey, Lexi," Mitch said as he leaned forward and kissed her on the cheek. "You look beautiful."

Lexi was perfect, as always, her long blond hair flowing down her back. She wore navy, which brought out her blue eyes and she glowed, as every woman with her first baby should.

Cruz reached for Skye's hand. "May I have this dance?"

The invitation surprised her, but then she realized Lexi had probably seen her distress and, without knowing the cause, had arranged a rescue.

"Of course," she said, and allowed Cruz to lead her away.

Mitch watched Skye go.

"Looks like you're stuck with me," Lexi said. She nudged him to the dance floor.

"I can't," he said, still focused on Skye.

"How do you know?"

That he couldn't dance? "I don't," he admitted. He'd just assumed. But the music was slow. "Keep your expectations low," he said as he took Lexi's hand and they joined the crowd.

Once they were in position, Mitch concentrated on keeping his weight centered. He'd been off the prosthesis most of the day so he wouldn't overtire himself being on it tonight. Now he moved self-consciously, holding Lexi lightly, keeping them in time with the music.

"Not bad," she said. "Can you dance *and* have a conversation?"

"We can try it."

"Where the hell do you get off hurting my sister?"

She smiled as she spoke and her tone was pleasant, so it took him a second to hear what she'd said. Not that it mattered. Lexi kept talking.

"I understand you're in a world of pain so you get a partial pass for that. But you have been nothing but a total shit since you got back home. Apparently that trend is continuing, based on the look I saw on her face five minutes ago."

He stiffened. "You don't know what you're talking about."

"I don't know all of it," she admitted. "I'm sure Skye has kept the really bad stuff from me. Because despite everything, she still defends you. Amazing, isn't it? Not that you deserve it."

He glared at Lexi. "What about what she did to me?"

"You mean nine years ago when she wouldn't marry you?"

"She chose her father over me."

"Oh, I get it," Lexi told him, her blue eyes flashing with annoyance. "She should have picked you because you're her one true love. Well, this isn't the movies. This is real life and things don't always work out the way we want. Yes, Skye chose Jed. She chose her father because he was all she had."

"She had me."

"Did she? You got mad and left."

The unfairness of that statement made him come to a stop. "She married someone else."

"Did you bother to find out why?"

He already knew. "She was pregnant with his kid."

"Before that," Lexi said, pulling him to the side of the room. "Before she went out with Ray."

"Screwed him, you mean."

"So you're still having the pity party," Lexi said. "I should have known. Does it occur to you that this is about more than who she married? That it might be about why Jed's opinion matters so damn much? Jed is the only parent Skye has left."

"You're preaching to the choir. I lost my parents,

SUSAN MALLERY   197

too. It was the year Skye and I fell in love. So when I lost her, I had nothing left."

"Right. Nothing except Fidela and Arturo, who were as much like parents to you as your own. Skye, on the other hand, found her mother's body. Did you know that? Pru couldn't handle the fact that Jed didn't love her so she killed herself. She got in the bathtub and cut her wrists, but not before leaving a note."

Mitch hadn't known the details. Skye didn't talk about them.

Lexi continued. "She addressed the note to Skye because Skye always came to her room after school. Pru knew her ten-year-old daughter would find her body and she didn't have a problem with that. The note told Skye that Pru had to kill herself because Jed didn't love her. What do you think Skye took from all that? Just picture it, Mitch. A kid two years older than Erin finding her mother's dead body and reading that note. Is it possible she believes, somewhere deep inside, that if her father doesn't love her, she'll die, too? Is there even a remote chance that at all of eighteen and in love for the first time in her life, she couldn't think straight? That she could only panic? Or is this all about you?"

Lexi walked away.

Mitch stood in the corner, feeling small and wrong and wondering how it was possible for a mother to act that way. He'd heard rumors that Pru was a little crazy and self-absorbed, but now he knew those were more than rumors.

He looked around the room, searching for Skye. When he caught sight of her, he didn't know what to do. Telling her he knew about her mother wasn't going to help anyone. What it came down to was whether or not knowing this changed anything at all.

SKYE KNEW something was wrong. She couldn't figure out what it was, exactly. The guests were still talking, but the overall noise level wasn't right. There was a slight hush she couldn't explain.

There was plenty of food. She saw the servers circulating and the guests eating. They hadn't run out of liquor. From what she could hear, Jed hadn't said anything that had offended twenty or thirty people. So what was it?

She was about to tell herself she was imagining things, when one of the servers hurried up to her.

"There's a problem," the woman said. "A couple of people are sick. It came on really fast. I hate to think it's the food, but maybe it is."

Skye's body tensed. "Where are the guests who aren't feeling well?"

"In both downstairs' bathrooms."

She hurried in that direction, only to have a local banker go rushing past, his hand covering his mouth. She heard a gagging sound and saw a well-dressed woman suddenly vomit.

Horror rushed through her. What was going on? Had the caterer brought something tainted? Was it food poisoning? Didn't that usually take—

She turned toward the kitchen and saw Garth standing by the bar. He raised his glass toward her. All around her people started rushing for the door.

She walked to Garth. "What the hell did you do?"

He smiled. "Something seems to be wrong with your party. It can't be the food, can it?"

"You poisoned my guests?"

"*Poison* is a strong word. It's more of a prank. But you might want to call nine-one-one just in case."

"Bastard."

He took another sip of his drink. "Yes, but you already knew that."

Two hours later everyone had left. Whatever had caused the sickness faded as quickly as it started. The paramedics took a few older people to the hospital to be checked out.

"This is going to ruin me," Mary, the caterer, said. "I don't know what happened. I've never heard of anything like this before."

Skye didn't know what to say to reassure her. The truth was Mary hadn't done anything wrong.

"If you need a reference," Skye began.

Mary wiped away tears. "Like that will help," she whispered, then walked away.

A few minutes later Dana arrived.

"I got your message," her friend said. "What happened?"

Skye told her about people getting sick and what Garth had said. "One of the paramedics said there were only a few things that could cause instant vomiting."

Dana shook her head. "Are you sure it's Garth?"

"I know it's Garth. He practically told me he did it. But when I explained that to the police, they wouldn't listen. Why would a guy like that do something like this?" Skye was beyond frustrated. "At least that's their reasoning. Oh, they'll do an investigation, but they're assuming it's somebody's kid playing a stupid game. Maybe a fraternity initiation. Garth is too smart to get caught. I'm sure he's covered up his involvement. Jed's no help. He disappeared at the first sign of trouble."

"Can I make you feel better by saying you've never loved throwing Jed's parties. Maybe now you won't have to."

"Small comfort," Skye said, knowing Jed would blame her for this and equally aware that right now she didn't care.

"I'll ask around. See if I can find out anything. Garth is one busy guy. Eventually he'll make a mistake and we'll be there to catch him."

"I hope so. I don't want to think about what he might do next or who might get hurt."

MITCH HATED to waste the time on his prosthesis, but he couldn't stop pacing. He was angry, which wasn't news, but for once it wasn't at the world in general. This time his temper had a specific focus—Garth Duncan.

Last night had been a disaster for Skye. Nearly everyone at the party had gotten violently sick. While the illness had passed as quickly as it had come on, it had been bad for anyone who'd experienced it. People would be talking for months about what had happened.

Mitch hadn't realized Garth was behind the illnesses until Skye had called him that morning. Now he was going to confront Garth and put a stop to what was going on.

He heard a car pull up and walked out of his office. Garth got out of his Mercedes.

"Do we have a problem?" the other man asked.

Without thinking, Mitch hauled off and punched him. Garth staggered a step, then steadied himself.

"I take it you got sick last night," Garth said, rubbing his jaw. "Sorry. I should have warned you."

"I didn't eat anything, you bastard."

"People are calling me that a lot these days. Word must be getting out."

"What the hell is wrong with you? Why would you do something like that?" Mitch demanded.

"I told you I was going to take down Jed and his daughters. Last I heard, you liked the idea. You wanted to help." He touched his jaw. "I take it this means you're not working for me anymore?" He shrugged. "Don't worry about it. I've got my bases covered."

Mitch clenched his fists. "I never worked for you."

"I didn't pay you," Garth corrected. "That doesn't mean you weren't spying for me."

"Whatever," Mitch muttered, not sure why Garth was being so pointed. "You're wrong about all of it. Take down Jed if you want, but his daughters aren't a part of it."

"They are for me. Besides, you only care about Skye. Unfortunately, it's a little too late for that."

Mitch didn't know what he meant, at first. Then he heard a sound and knew.

Dammit all to hell, he thought as he turned and saw Skye standing behind him. She looked horrified and beyond hurt.

"You were working for him?" she asked, her eyes wide, her skin pale.

Mitch would have given his other leg to have the past five minutes to play over.

"Skye, no."

She ignored him and ran. Ran hard and fast, probably knowing there was no way he could go after her.

CHAPTER ELEVEN

"I'M FINE," Skye insisted as Dana foamed milk at the espresso machine on the counter and Lexi and Izzy both hovered close by. "You don't need to worry about me."

She didn't have to look up to know her sisters and Dana were exchanging looks of disbelief. It was her own fault, she thought grimly. All of this. Getting involved with Mitch. Believing him, trusting him. He'd shown her his true self the first day he'd come home. He'd made everything clear and she hadn't listened. She'd wanted him to be more and he'd been willing to play along, but he hadn't changed. He still resented her and wanted her punished. Now he was not only angry about the past, but about Erin. She'd brought this on herself and only she was to blame.

Dana poured the steamed milk into a mug and handed it to her. "Want some whiskey for that?" she asked.

Skye looked at the clock. It was barely noon. "No. I'll be okay. I just need a minute."

"What you need is Mitch's head on a platter," Izzy said, sounding furious.

They were in the big kitchen at Glory's Gate. It was a beautiful sunny Saturday. Sunlight pooled on the floor. A warm breeze whispered. Normally that was enough to brighten Skye's mood, but not today.

"I can't believe it." Lexi took the second mug Dana offered. "He seemed like he was really happy to be back. He was so…nice."

"When did you talk to him?" Dana asked.

"Last night, at the party. I thought he still cared about you." She looked at Skye. "I'm sorry."

"He played us all," Skye told her, trying to keep the bitterness from her voice. "We all fell for it. Me more than most. I was so worried about him, about how he was healing and fitting in. I felt awful when he thought Erin was his. I ached for him when he found out the truth. Now I think it was just more of Garth's games. Mitch probably never thought anything about Erin. It was just one more way to suck me in."

"Do you know how long he was working for Garth?" Izzy asked.

"Does it matter?"

"It might," Lexi said. "If this is a recent development, then maybe it's not so bad."

Skye raised her eyebrows.

"At least he wasn't lying before," Dana added, then shook her head. "Sorry. I'm trying to be supportive, but I'm just too cynical. Mitch turned into a real jerk and I'm sorry about that. He used to be one of the good ones."

Before, Skye thought angrily. She would bet that if they were to talk, Mitch would blame all this on her. He would say she'd earned it.

She could accept that he'd slept with her to lead her on and punish her. She could accept a lot of things. But she'd gone to him and asked for help. He'd agreed, the whole time knowing he was going to betray her. He'd set her up.

"He's not the man I thought," she whispered. "That's what gets me the most. I was wrong about who he is on the inside."

He used to be so honorable, she thought sadly. So earnest.

"I really don't like this," Izzy grumbled. "I had a crush on him and now he's an asshole."

"Because it's all about you?" Dana asked.

"Well, yeah."

Lexi chuckled. Skye tried to smile and failed. Then she reached into her jeans pocket and pulled out the ring she'd dug out of her jewelry box that morning. She tossed the ring onto the kitchen table.

The diamonds glittered in the overhead light. The gold still gleamed. All four women stared at the ring.

"It's beautiful," Lexi said.

"It was." Skye sipped her coffee. "The one Ray gave me was bigger, but this is the one that mattered.

Mitch and I were outside. We'd been riding and the clouds had come in. I said it was going to rain and we should get back. He teased me about not wanting to get my hair wet and while we were laughing, he pulled out the ring and dropped to his knees."

The image was so clear. She could smell the cut grass, see Mitch's dark eyes, his gaze so intense. She'd stopped breathing and all she could hear was the pounding of her heart.

"He told me loved me and wanted to spend the rest of his life with me. He said that I was the best thing that ever happened to him, then he asked me to marry him."

Tears trickled down her cheeks as she remembered how much she'd loved him. How she'd known they would be together forever.

"When I told him I couldn't marry him, I gave him back the ring," she continued, her voice shaking. "He took it and threw it in the dirt. I was horrified. We fought and he walked off. I was crying so hard, I could barely see, but I was determined to find the ring. I clawed at the dirt until I saw it." She touched it with the tip of her finger. "I thought it meant something."

Dana crouched down next to her. "Do you want me to beat him up for you? I could take him."

Despite everything, Skye laughed. "That's really sweet of you, but I don't want you to hurt him." Skye wiped her face. "Is that stupid or what? After all this time and everything that's happened, I don't want him hurt. Stupid, stupid me."

"You didn't know," Lexi said. "You couldn't have known."

"He betrayed me."

"He's not over you," Izzy said. "He can't be. These aren't the actions of a man who doesn't care. He's really pissed off."

"He blames me for the loss of his leg. If I hadn't dumped him, he wouldn't have gone into the navy and so on. It's my fault."

Yesterday she would have said there might still be something between them. A chance, maybe. But now? Today? There was only anger and treachery.

"What if he's sorry?" Izzy asked.

"What if he's not," Dana said, then swore. "Why did it have to be Mitch? I could handle someone else, but not him. Not like this."

Skye stood and wiped the last of her tears. "We're not going to fix this. It happened and we'll deal. Mitch isn't one of the good guys anymore. End of story."

She sounded strong, she thought, pleased she was faking it so well. She left the kitchen and found Erin sitting on the stairs. Her daughter had pulled her knees to her chest. The girl looked sad and scared.

"What's wrong?" Skye asked, sitting next to her and smoothing her hair.

"You're mad at Mitch."

Skye winced silently. "You were listening."

Erin looked at her. "Not on purpose. I just heard a little and then I left." Her daughter leaned against her. "You were crying, Mommy."

"I'm done now."

"I don't feel good."

It was the tears, Skye thought. They reminded her of when Ray had died. Skye had cried for weeks.

"Does your tummy hurt?"

Erin nodded.

"It will get better. You want to go riding? We could go for a long ride and that will help."

"I'm supposed to practice my jumps with Arturo."

Which put her on the Cassidy Ranch. Skye didn't know what to say. While she didn't want her daughter coming into contact with Mitch anytime soon, she didn't want to forbid her from visiting with Fidela and Arturo. They both meant a lot to her and she needed them in her life.

"I'll drive you over," Skye said. "Go get your boots."

Fifteen minutes later she pulled up to the barn. She didn't see Mitch anywhere, which was a good thing. She didn't feel strong enough to face him right now.

Arturo was waiting. He opened the car door for Erin. "You have a horse to saddle," he told Erin. "Then we're jumping."

Her daughter grinned. "I'm ready," she yelled as she hurried to the barn.

Arturo bent down and looked at Skye. "You okay?"

The simple question told her he knew what had

happened. Maybe not the specifics, but enough that he was concerned about her.

"I will be," she said.

"I'm sorry. That's not who he is."

"Apparently it is."

Arturo sighed. "I'll bring Erin home when she's done. She'll want to see Fidela so it will be a couple of hours."

"That's fine. Thanks for bringing her back."

"No problem."

He stood and closed the passenger door, then turned toward the barn. Skye put the car in Drive and headed back home. She saw movement out of the corner of her eye but didn't turn or look back. There was nothing there for her to care about anymore. The sooner she realized that, the better for everyone.

MITCH KNEW it was going to be bad when he walked into the kitchen for lunch and found a can of tuna sitting on the counter. Fidela was nowhere around, but the message was clear. He was to get his own lunch.

He couldn't remember her ever not cooking for him, no matter what he'd done.

She'd seen him talking to Garth that morning, had seen Skye run away and had asked questions. When he'd told her the truth, she stared at him as if she didn't know him anymore, then had gone back inside. Apparently she was still angry.

He wanted to find her and tell her it wasn't as bad

as she thought. He'd never actually given Garth any information. He'd been a halfhearted accomplice at best. But did any of that matter? Wasn't it all about intent?

He'd been so angry, he thought now as he searched the refrigerator for something to eat. Angry because he'd been forced to come back. Angry at the loss of his leg and angry at Skye for a list of transgressions, some of which she'd even done. Finding out Erin *wasn't* his had pushed him over the edge.

An explanation, he thought grimly. Not an excuse.

He gave up on lunch and went outside. He followed the sound of hoofbeats and laughter until he stood at the edge of the corral where Arturo worked with Erin.

The girl took the practice jumps easily, then begged for them to be higher. Arturo was patient with her, pointing out what she should do differently, praising her when she got it right. Mitch was sure they'd both seen him, but neither of them acknowledged his presence.

Arturo made sense. Fidela would have told him about Garth. But Erin? What did she have to be mad about? Had Skye said something to her about him? He didn't want to believe it, but what else could it be?

Mitch left them and went into his office. Okay— so he'd blown it. He was sorry. Didn't that count for anything?

He spent the next half hour feeling sorry for himself, then Erin walked into his office.

She was four feet of eight-year-old fury as she stalked up to his desk and glared at him.

"You made my mom cry," she said, obviously outraged. "I wasn't supposed to be listening but I was and she was crying because of you. Heroes aren't supposed to be mean. You're supposed to take care of us."

It was as if the strength suddenly left her and she sagged a little. Tears filled her eyes and poured down her cheeks. "You made her cry," she whispered.

Watching her was the worst thing he'd ever been through. The sense of guilt and helplessness drove him to his feet. He circled around the desk and tried to reach for her, but she backed up.

"Don't," she yelled, wiping her face.

"I'm sorry," he told her. "I didn't mean to hurt your mom."

"But you did hurt her." She sounded shocked by the concept. As if she hadn't known he was capable of that sort of thing. "You're a bad man."

"I'm not. I made a bad choice. They're not the same."

"Yes, they are."

He knew in his head she felt betrayed by someone she hadn't known could betray her. But he didn't know how to make it better.

"I'm sorry, Erin."

She shoved him, as if trying to push him off balance. As if trying to make him fall. He didn't go down but he was stunned she would do that. Which was maybe a little of what she was feeling.

The tears came faster now. She covered her face with her hands. He bent down and grabbed her around the waist and set her on his desk. She sobbed and kicked her feet against the wood.

He waited until she'd quieted some before speaking. "You can't stay mad at me forever."

"I can," she said, and wiped her face.

"I'll make it right with Skye."

Erin looked doubtful. "You're a hero," she murmured. "You're special. But you're not. You're just…"

She jumped down and glared at him. "You're just mean and I don't like you anymore."

In Erin's world, it was probably the worst thing she could say. She left him. Sitting there alone, he knew he'd lost something very precious. Something that wouldn't easily be replaced or mended.

The hell of it was, he hadn't had to do anything for Garth. The other man had won the round without even trying. Mitch had played right into his hands. Now Skye was feeling more isolated and Garth was that much closer to getting everything he wanted.

SKYE SPENT a terrible weekend pretending to be strong for Erin and feeling as if she'd been sucker punched in her heart. By dawn Monday morning, she'd given up trying to sleep and was grateful she had work to deal with. At least going into the office would be a distraction.

She showered and dressed and was just about to go down for coffee when Izzy came into her room.

"You'll want to see this," her sister said, handing her the morning paper.

The headline made Skye's head spin—Titan Executives Charged With Smuggling.

"This isn't happening," she whispered as she began to read.

The article was light on facts, but heavy on speculation. Apparently the shipping division of Titan World Enterprises was under investigation. Not only had company employees been charged with bribing foreign officials, they'd brought in ships with illegal cargo.

Manifests had been forged. What was supposed to be simple manufacturing parts turned out to be guns and ammunition. Jed Titan was being accused of being a gunrunner.

"This is bad," Izzy said. "They're hinting at treason."

"It's bad," Skye agreed, knowing Garth was behind this. She'd worried about what the next attack would be and here it was.

"Jed could go to jail," Izzy said.

Skye put down the paper. "If he's charged with treason, there's no way he's getting out of this one, and going to jail will be the least of his problems."

CHAPTER TWELVE

MITCH WAITED THREE days before trying to see Skye. He knew she was feeling hurt and betrayed, but as much he wanted to make things right with her, he knew first he had to give her time. There was no excuse for what he'd done but there was an explanation. One he would have to tell her—not that he could make her listen.

Even though Garth had come to see him and had asked Mitch to spy on the family, he hadn't fully understood how serious the other man was about his campaign. Garth would do anything to bring down the Titans. Hurt anyone. Even Skye and Erin. Mitch had to make sure that didn't happen.

He waited until he knew the school bus had been by. He still had to come to terms with Erin, but dealing with her would be a whole lot easier after he'd talked to Skye. At least that was the theory.

He drove over to Glory's Gate and was relieved to see her car by the back door. He got out of his truck and started toward the house. The back door banged open and Skye appeared at the top of the stairs, a shotgun in her arms.

"Don't even think about it," she called as she walked down the two stairs and approached him. "You're not welcome here."

She looked amazing, her long red hair blowing in the breeze. She'd dressed for work in a skirt and fancy blouse. He assumed there was a suit jacket somewhere but she hadn't put it on yet. Still, the combination of conservative clothes and the shotgun was more of a turn-on than he would have expected.

"We have to talk," he told her.

"We don't have to do anything. You're not welcome here."

"Skye, I know you're pissed."

She shifted the gun and raised it to her shoulder, then sighted down the barrel. "Pissed doesn't come close, Mitch. I trusted you. I came to you as a friend and you were working for Garth the whole time."

"It was more like fifteen minutes. I didn't tell him anything."

"And that makes it okay? The fact that you didn't do actual damage? I don't think so."

He could feel her fury and see the fire in her eyes. She was incredibly beautiful—that hadn't changed but every now and then he got a reminder.

"Get your butt off my land," she said forcefully.

"This isn't 1840 and I'm not here to rustle cattle."

"That doesn't make you any less a criminal."

He looked at her. "I'm sorry. I was wrong. Garth showed up right after I found out about Erin. I was angry and I wanted you punished."

"For not keeping a child who wasn't yours from you?"

"Yeah, I know. When you put it like that, it doesn't make sense."

"It never made sense." She set down the rifle. "Dammit, Mitch, I wouldn't have kept your kid from me. You should know that and me. You should have trusted me."

She was softening. "I needed an attitude adjustment."

"You needed a lot more than that."

He moved a little closer. She raised her hand.

"Stay back," she said.

"I was confused," he told her, knowing it was the truth. "I'd just lost my leg, I was angry and I needed..."

"Someone to punish."

He nodded. "I'm not proud of what I did. It's not who I am. You know that, Skye."

She swallowed. "Why didn't you know I wouldn't keep Erin from you?"

"Because it wasn't about that. I wanted her to be mine because I wanted something good in my life."

"You have the ranch and Fidela and Arturo."

"It didn't seem like enough. If she was mine, then I had something to live for."

He walked toward her. He kept moving until her hand was pressed against his chest.

"You're going to have to shoot me," he told her. "I'm not leaving."

He looked into her eyes. "Please let me in, Skye."

She turned and went into the house. He followed her.

"I'm sorry about Garth," he said as she sat at the round table and picked up a cup of coffee. "I didn't know he was that serious. I saw the article in the paper."

"Jed could be charged with treason. This *is* serious. Not that I have any idea if my father has figured that out yet. He won't talk to any of us about it. He's never here. I'm not sure he's even sleeping here. Maybe he has a place in Dallas. Or a girlfriend."

Mitch poured himself a cup of coffee and settled across from her. "Garth is playing hardball. I'm sorry about the party. I didn't know he was going to pull something like that."

She sighed. "Honestly, in comparison to finding out you were working with him the fallout from the party was nearly manageable. I've spoken with some press people. I can't tell them the truth, so we're saying it was a frat stunt. The police are investigating, but because I told them it was Garth and he's such a powerhouse in the community, they now think I'm hysterical. Or that I want him punished because he wouldn't go out with me or something. Dana's trying to find out something on her own, but Garth is good. I doubt he left anything for her to find."

"I could ask around."

"Uh-huh. Because I'd believe you."

"I'm not working for Garth."

"You were."

"I didn't do anything." He leaned toward her. "You have to accept my apology."

"Number one, I don't. Number two, you haven't apologized."

"I'm sorry."

"Great."

"You're not going to forgive me?"

"Not anytime soon."

This tough Skye was more like the woman he knew. "Want to punch me in the arm?"

"Can I use a hammer?"

"No."

"Then I'm not that interested. Maybe later."

"Can I do anything to help?"

She hesitated. He could see she wanted to say yes, and for now, that was enough.

"I'll ask again later," he told her.

Her mouth twisted. "Don't be nice, Mitch. It's more than I can deal with right now."

"You'd rather I was mean and surly?"

"It's easier to handle."

Easier to keep her distance? Mitch wasn't sure why he wanted her closer, but he did.

"Can you at least tell your kid I'm not a total jerk?"

She frowned. "What happened with Erin?"

"She told me that I'd made you cry and heroes didn't do that."

"She was listening in when I was talking to my sisters and Dana. I know she was upset, but I didn't think she'd say anything to you."

"She did."

"I'll talk to her."

"Thanks."

"I shouldn't bother," she told him.

But she would because of Erin. Because it was the right thing to do.

He stood and circled around the table. She rose and moved away before he could reach her.

"Don't," she whispered.

"I wasn't going to do anything."

"You were going to touch me. I can't do that again, Mitch. I can't… It's not a game to me. I don't know what it is, but it's not nothing."

"It's not nothing to me, either."

"Then we should avoid it and each other until we can figure out what it is."

SKYE ESCAPED to the office where life made slightly more sense. It was easier to focus on the work to be done than worry about what was going on with Mitch.

She did believe he was sorry for dealing with Garth and that his offer to help her half brother had been born from pain and a need to lash out. But that didn't erase the sense of betrayal she felt or ease the feeling of loss.

She'd barely turned on her computer when T.J. called.

"Hey, beautiful."

"Hey, yourself."

"I heard about Jed. How are you holding up?"

"I'm doing okay. I hope you don't believe the stories. You should know it's not anything Jed would do or condone."

"I know. Jed's his own man, but he's also smart. He wouldn't risk his company with something like illegal arms. Are you having any trouble with the press?"

"Not yet. We've had a few calls to the house, but they get the machine and give up after a couple of tries."

"If you need anything, if I can help, let me know."

She smiled. "I will. Thank you for that."

"I'd like to see you again. You up for dinner?"

T.J. was a nice man. Funny, charming, uncomplicated. She should be all quivery at the thought of spending the evening with him. She was...sort of.

T.J.'s biggest flaw was that he wasn't Mitch. For all Mitch's betrayals and complications, he still made her blood run hot and her insides melt just by looking at him. If he touched her, all bets were off.

"Skye? It wasn't supposed to be that hard a question," T.J. said.

"Sorry. It isn't. Dinner would be great."

"I'll be by the house at six-thirty," he said.

"Why don't we meet at the restaurant," Skye told him. "It would be easier. Erin's only eight. I'm not sure she's ready for me to date."

There was also the issue of Izzy, but Skye wasn't going to mention that. She wasn't sure what her sister had going on with T.J. She just knew that Izzy was stubborn and would do almost anything to prove her point that she was the more desirable sister.

"The restaurant at seven, then," T.J. said. "I'll make reservations."

"An excellent quality in a man."

He chuckled. "I'll see you then. I'm looking forward to it."

"Me, too," she said, and they hung up.

She ignored the flicker of guilt that whispered that T.J. would never get her attention the way Mitch did. T.J. was the better bet. At least on the surface.

Although she could hear Izzy's voice in her head telling her she wasn't fooling anyone. That she was only pretending to be interested in T.J. because of Jed and the same could be said for T.J. That the only Titan sister he really wanted was Izzy.

"She's just playing a game," Skye whispered to herself. Izzy had always been the wild one and men gravitated to her. Yes, Jed had pushed Skye on T.J. but she refused to believe his charm was all a game. No one was that good. Izzy was just being a bratty younger sister.

"Do you have a second?"

Skye looked up and saw Trisha, her CFO, standing in the open doorway. "Sure. What have you got?"

"Nothing good," Trisha admitted as she walked in carrying a folder. "We've started the investigation. So far we've discovered there *are* two sets of books. They're running on the same program with all the same entries. The only differences are the bonuses paid to senior staff and the checks made out to you. The computer guys are telling me they think they've found the access point. It's remote, which means someone hacked in rather than uploading it from here."

Skye sank into her chair. "We're that vulnerable?"

"We're not supposed to be," Trisha said as she took the seat opposite. "I've been in touch with the security company responsible for protecting our system. At first they claimed it was impossible for anyone to hack in. But now that I've shown them it is, they'll be working to find out how. And who."

Skye already knew who.

"We'll figure it out," Trisha told her. "I believe that. But we have a bigger issue. This is the second problem with the foundation. People are starting to talk and ask questions."

Skye didn't want to hear that. "Donors or staff?"

"Both. People who work for nonprofits have a very specific drive to make a difference. They don't want to work their butts off only to discover the money being raised is going to buy someone a Mercedes. Donors don't want to be fooled, either."

"You think that's happening here? That the books showing the payouts are correct?"

Trisha gave her a small smile. "They can't be. I found a check to myself. I never authorized that. I'm the one who signs the checks and I know I didn't sign it and it sure never showed up in my bank account."

"That's a relief. But don't you sign all the checks?"

"Yes, but I review only a percentage of them. Otherwise that would be a full-time job. Payroll is computerized, as are payments to the local food banks and shelters we fund."

"So we don't know if the other questionable checks got through or not."

"I'm pulling all bank statements and reconciling them specifically with those checks. Unfortunately the rule of thumb is if a business is keeping two sets of books, that company also has multiple bank accounts. The money could come from anywhere."

This was a nightmare, Skye thought grimly. She hated that it was happening and didn't know how to make it stop.

"You're going to lose good people over this," Trisha told her. "I'm hearing rumors that people are looking."

"Are you?" Skye asked bluntly.

"Not yet."

She couldn't tell the world what was going on. Not only wouldn't it help their cause but she had a feeling that blabbing about Garth would only make him happy. Still, she could tell Trisha.

She leaned forward. "You know a little about my family. You've met my father."

"A couple of times. He's an interesting man."

"That's one way of putting it. About thirty-five years ago, he had an affair with a young woman named Kathy and she ended up pregnant. Jed wasn't interested in marrying her, which is where this all started."

Skye explained what she knew about Garth and his mother. While she didn't go into detail, she explained that Garth had been targeting the family from every angle.

"Someone sued my sister and her spa," Skye said. "This woman used to work for Garth. From what we can tell, he paid her to file a false suit. When Lexi confronted her, she dropped the suit and moved away. Garth will do anything to get us. He poisoned my guests at a cocktail party a few days ago."

Trisha looked shocked. "I heard about that. They said on the news that it was a frat prank."

"Garth admitted he'd done it," Skye said, "but when I told the police, they didn't believe me. Why would they? A man in Garth's position, with his money and clout, poisoning guests at a party? It doesn't make sense."

"Unless you know he wants the family taken down." Trisha sighed. "So he's coming after the foundation?"

"Apparently. He was behind the tip to the D.A. about money laundering. While we were cleared of all charges, think of the money wasted. We could have put our resources into feeding kids. Instead we were hiring lawyers and defending our reputation."

"I know why this needs to stay private," Trisha said, "but you have to brace yourself, Skye. People aren't going to understand and they're going to start leaving. For the senior staff, their reputation is their most important asset. If they think the foundation is going down, they won't want to sink with the ship."

IZZY WALKED through the high-rise condo. The tall ceilings and big windows gave the place an airy feeling. The decor was mostly black and gray with a few bright colors as accents.

She liked the ebony stained hardwood floor and the big fireplace in the corner. She wouldn't necessarily want to live here, but the place seemed right for T.J.

"Comments? Criticisms?" he asked as he went behind the bar and began fixing cocktails.

"You slept with your decorator," she said.

He opened a bottle of vodka. "That's it? You don't want to mention the view or that it seems so masculine. Just that I slept with my decorator?"

"Am I wrong?"

He laughed. "No. You're not wrong."

She slid onto one of the bar stools and rested her elbows on the granite surface.

"You're a player," she said.

"Is that bad?"

"Not in theory. I'm just not sure of your game. With me."

He pushed a martini toward her. "Do we need to have a game?"

Izzy thought about Skye. "We don't have to—that was *your* choice. How far are you taking this?"

His blue eyes brightened with humor. "I'm open to suggestions."

Izzy didn't have any. She wasn't completely interested in T.J., but she also seemed unwilling to walk away. He confused her and that didn't happen all that often. But how much of this was genuine interest on her part and how much of it was to prove a point to Skye? Although right now she wasn't sure what that point was.

"If you went to school with my sister Lexi," Izzy said. "You must also know Dana Birch."

"Oh, yeah. She was intriguing. Hot in a totally different way than Lexi, but I don't know anyone who was brave enough to ask her out. She made it clear no one was getting close."

Interesting, Izzy thought, knowing how Dana loved to date quiet, unassuming men she could boss around. The only problem was she easily got bored with them.

"Do you know why?" Izzy asked.

T.J. raised his eyebrows. "You're kidding, right? I'm a guy. I don't do motive."

"Or talk about your feelings?"

He shuddered. "No, thanks."

She laughed. "Fair enough."

"When do you go back to work?"

"In a few days. Then I'll be gone for almost two months."

"That's a long time."

"It goes fast," she said. "They keep me busy. Last time I was working on installing a new rig. This time I'll be repairing an older one."

"You're really a welder?"

"Didn't you see *Flashdance?* Welders can be sexy."

"No one is questioning your sex appeal. But welding?"

"It's fun. Being underwater gives it an extra punch."

"Which is important to you?"

"Of course. It's all about the thrill. Next time I'm off, I'm going cave diving."

"Seriously?"

"Want to come?"

"I'll do one or the other. Not both."

"Chicken."

"I don't have a death wish."

"Neither do I."

T.J. didn't look convinced. "Cave diving is a dangerous sport."

"That's what makes it exciting."

"So you're in it for the thrill?"

"I'm in everything for the thrill."

Their eyes locked.

"Why are you so fearless?" he asked.

A question she wasn't going to answer honestly. "Because it looks good on me."

He came around the bar and turned the stool so she was facing him. He put down his drink, set hers on the bar, then cupped her face and kissed her.

His mouth was warming and tempting. The kiss teased and promised. It was the kind of kiss that said sex was very much on the table.

She drew back. "Aren't you still seeing Skye?"

"Don't you know?"

"We've agreed not to discuss you. The conversation was getting awkward."

"We're having dinner."

Izzy didn't know how she felt about that. She and T.J. didn't have a relationship. They weren't dating. They were hanging out. She never asked the other men she saw if they had other women, mostly because she didn't care. She wouldn't care now except she knew Skye wouldn't get the game. She would look at T.J. as a potential husband, just the way Jed wanted her to.

"What are you thinking?" T.J. asked.

"That I can't figure you out. You can't have us both."

He leaned in and kissed her again. "That's okay with me."

Then his mouth was on hers again. The kiss was insistent, taking and giving with equal passion. Izzy wrapped her arms around his neck and parted her lips.

He deepened the kiss. He used his hands to roam

her body, then he discovered the side zip on her strapless sundress.

She felt the tug. Acting on instinct, she stood so when he pulled down the zipper, the dress fell, leaving her wearing nothing but a thong and high heels.

T.J. didn't miss a beat. He grabbed her hand and led her into his bedroom. While she pulled down the covers, he quickly removed his clothing. Then they were naked.

He pulled her to him and they fell onto the bed. His hands were everywhere, touching, teasing, pushing. He made love with an intensity that left her breathless. He drove her to the edge and pushed in right as she began to climax.

When they were done, he stared down into her eyes and smiled.

"I knew you'd be good," he told her.

"Yeah?"

But instead of contentment, she felt awkward and dirty. As if she'd done something wrong. Figuring out why didn't take an advanced degree in psychology. This had a whole lot to do with her competition with Skye. In theory, she'd just won the round. So why did she feel so much like throwing up?

CHAPTER THIRTEEN

SKYE EASED her horse west, heading for the larger herd of Cassidy cattle. Fidela had said Mitch was checking on them this afternoon. She hadn't been able to stop thinking about his visit that morning and thought if she saw him and talked to him and maybe he pissed her off, she could clear her head. She had enough going on that she didn't need to be mentally preoccupied with him, too.

She saw him on the north side of the herd. One of the dogs caught her scent, spun and barked. Mitch reined in his horse before turning toward her. She watched him ride closer.

He moved easily in the saddle, despite the loss of his leg and his time away from the ranch. Maybe that was something the body didn't forget. Maybe the movement was so familiar it was ingrained in the muscles. Like making love.

He looked good—like something out of a movie. Tall and straight. Powerful.

Sexy.

She didn't want to think about his body or touching him or how he made her feel things no one else had, but the images were there, along with the memories. The feel of his hands on her body haunted her.

He rode up to her, his cowboy hat shading his eyes.

"You're getting around," she said, motioning to the horse.

"He's trained special so he doesn't expect anything from my left foot. I can mount on the other side, as well. Which makes it easier."

"They can do that?"

He grinned. "A horse isn't born expecting a rider at all, Skye."

"I hadn't thought of it that way. Arturo find him for you?"

"Yeah."

"He's a good man. You're lucky to have him."

"I know."

She felt a little awkward and not sure what to say. She wanted to know more about how Mitch was doing with his leg. He was off crutches, which was good. But was he allowing himself to continue to heal? Was he pushing too much? Then she reminded herself it wasn't her business. That they weren't together. In fact, a case could be made that Mitch was the enemy.

"What's going on, Skye?" he asked. "You came looking for me for a reason."

There were a thousand things she could say, but she settled on the truth. "I thought we could fight."

"What?"

"I'm having a bad day. No. Make that a bad quarter. The foundation is still shaky. We've confirmed the second set of books were loaded remotely, which means Garth has been able to break through our computer security. I have staff members who are thinking of quitting. I told my CFO what's happening and, while she's sympathetic, I don't know how long she's going to stay. As she pointed out, in this business, reputation is everything. People think I'm dishonest. I can't stand that."

"No one who knows you thinks that."

"What about the grandmother in Indiana who sent in five dollars? What does she think? Or the kid in Reno who goes to bed hungry because instead of sending the food bank a check we had to pay lawyers and computer experts? What will they think of me?"

He moved his horse closer and touched her arm. "They don't know who you are," he said gently.

"Not specifically. But they'll hear that someone in the foundation took a bunch of money. They'll believe I did that to them."

"You can only fight the battle you're in. The others have to wait."

He was being reasonable. Talk about annoying. "I hate Garth. I swear, if I get the chance, I'm going to crush him like a bug."

"I'll help."

She looked at him. "I want to believe you."

"Give it time. You will."

She smiled. "Such confidence."

"You know me, Skye. Am I wrong?"

She shook her head. Given time and motivation, Mitch could do anything he wanted—especially where she was concerned.

"Besides," he said. "I owe you. You were there for me when my parents died. That was a hard summer. You made it bearable."

She wasn't sure she wanted to think about that summer when Mitch had suffered and she'd tried to help and they'd fallen in love.

"Anyone else would have done the same," she said.

"But it wasn't anyone. It was you."

"I wanted to help," she said. "Which isn't exactly a selfless reason, so don't make too much of it. I felt so trapped and spineless back then. Once I got home from finishing school, Jed started talking about me getting married. I felt like it was the 1800s and I was the plantation owner's daughter."

Mitch seemed to tense up, as if he didn't want to talk about that time. She'd left him because of Jed, so she couldn't really blame him for that. But before she could change the subject, he said, "That's how you acted. You could have stood up to him."

"Easy for you to say," she snapped. "You didn't know what I was dealing with."

"Of course I did. Come on, Skye. Jed's only as powerful as you let him be. You could have told him no."

"He's my father."

"Right, but he's not God. You need to grow a pair where he's concerned."

She'd thought she'd wanted to fight with him, but not about this.

"You're still doing everything he wants," Mitch continued. "You're dating T.J. because he told you to."

"You don't know that."

"Are you saying you haven't gone out with the guy and that you won't be going out with him again?"

There was judgment in his voice—and anger.

"If I'm going out with T.J. it's because he's picked up the phone and asked me out. On a date. He doesn't expect me to just have sex with him in a barn."

Anger flashed in his eyes. "I didn't expect it. I just took what was offered. You can lie to yourself all you want, but the rest of us know the truth. You're still jumping through daddy's hoops. When are you going to grow up?"

It was as if he'd slapped her. "You don't know what you're talking about," she said, glaring at him.

"I know it's time to get over your mother's death. That has nothing to do with you. You're not going to die if Jed gets pissed at you."

She didn't know how he knew her deepest fear but the fact that he would be so callous about it made every part of her feel under siege. She would give anything to have the shotgun back in her hands and this time she would happily use it.

"Let's talk about people in glass houses. You're not going to die because you lost a leg," she told him. "But you're sure bent on punishing everyone for what happened. Maybe you should adjust your own attitude before taking on mine."

"You really want to compare our situations?" he taunted. "Your biggest problem is which pair of three-hundred-dollar shoes to wear to work."

She told herself that a lot of this was frustration because of what had happened nine years ago and maybe because she had admitted she was dating T.J. Although that last one might just be wishful thinking on her part. But the reason didn't matter. She was done being his punching bag.

"You may not think my foundation means anything," she said, "but there are a lot of hungry children who would disagree with you. I might have made some bad choices because of things in my past, but at least I never betrayed my friends because I was angry at them. Erin's right. You're not a hero. You're just a jerk who used to wear a uniform."

She turned her horse and rode away.

By the time she got back to the house she wasn't exactly calm, but she was nearly able to convince herself she would be…eventually. Damn Mitch Cassidy. Why did it always have to be like this? Why did they fight so much? Why did she have to care what he thought about her?

If she didn't know better she would swear he was pissed that she was dating T.J. But it wasn't as if he wanted to go out with her himself. At least he wasn't acting like it. Not that she understood her own feelings for him. Maybe it was the past. There hadn't been enough resolution and, because of that, old feelings were coming to life again.

Just not the good ones.

She stalked into the kitchen and wished Erin were home. Being around her daughter always made her feel better. But Erin had spent the afternoon at a friend's house and Skye wasn't scheduled to pick her up for another hour.

She got a glass of iced tea, then walked toward the stairs. On the way, she ran into Izzy.

They looked at each other. They weren't exactly fighting, but they hadn't made up yet, either. Skye told herself she should be mature and say something nice. After all Izzy was heading back to the oil rig in a couple of days.

"Are you still dating T.J.?" Izzy asked flatly.

"What? Yes. We're having dinner tonight."

"You can't." Izzy twisted her hands in front of her waist. "You don't really like him. He's not your type."

Skye's temper rose. "I haven't dated since I was eighteen. I don't exactly have a type. As for not liking him, I barely know him. Which is the point of dating. To get to know him better."

"But you're seeing Mitch."

"Not on purpose. Mitch and I were over a long time ago." And they were never getting back together. That was obvious.

"You had sex with him."

Not that she was willing to admit to, Skye thought. "What is your point, Izzy? Where are you going with this?"

"You can't go out with T.J. Please."

"Why not? Because you're dating him?"

"We're not dating. Not exactly. But…"

"But what? Are you in love with him?"

Izzy crossed her arms over her chest. "I don't know if I even like him."

Skye rolled her eyes. "But until you decide, I should just step aside. Is that it? Or is the real point that you don't want him but you don't want me to have him, either?"

"It's not like that. I don't trust him," Izzy said, her voice tight. "Just go with this, Skye. I'm trying to help."

"I genuinely don't understand," Skye admitted. "Are you afraid of what will happen if I fall for the guy Jed wants me to marry?"

"Of course not. I don't care about this stupid house. Take Glory's Gate. Take the money. I never wanted any of it. Like you, I wanted a father—which

I'm starting to understand isn't going to happen. Is it remotely possibly I'm trying to help?"

"A few weeks ago I would have said yes, but you've been acting strange about T.J. from the beginning. Being a guy magnet has never been enough for you. Well, they can't all like you best. T.J. is interested in me and I'm willing to see where that goes."

"We slept together," Izzy yelled.

Of course, thought Skye bitterly. She wasn't even surprised. Izzy would do anything to make a point.

A part of her noticed she wasn't seriously hurt by the information. At least not on the T.J. front. Izzy's behavior, however, stung.

"Thanks for the share," Skye said, pushing past her sister.

Izzy grabbed her arm and stopped her. "It's not like that. I did it to see if he'd sleep with me and then still go out with you."

"You had sex with a guy I'm dating for my own good. That's really sweet. Thanks. But just to be clear, I don't need any more favors from you."

"I hate it when you get sarcastic," Izzy muttered. "Would you at least acknowledge the point here? T.J. isn't one of the good guys."

"Neither are you," Skye told her.

Izzy's eyes filled with tears. "Don't worry. I'm leaving for the rig soon."

"Not soon enough."

MITCH WIPED DOWN Bullet. The work allowed him time to think which was both good and bad.

What the hell was wrong with him? Why had he lashed out at Skye like that? Why did he keep wanting to punish her?

Part of the answer was easy enough to understand, but part of it meant going to a place he wasn't ready for.

Fact—nine years ago she'd walked out on him for no reason except her father had told her to. Jed was big with the ultimatums and Skye had been scared. He knew why, knew what had happened from her perspective, but still he couldn't seem to let it go.

Did he want her to hate him, because that's where this was headed. She would only come back so many times before she was gone permanently. Is that what he wanted? To chase Skye so far away he never had to think about her again?

To what end? Because it hurt to look at her and know what he'd lost? Because she deserved it? Because he was such a bastard that he took pleasure in torturing her?

He'd had to face who and what he'd become once already. Dealing with the loss of his leg and getting better, physically and mentally. Did he have to do that again, with Skye?

It was over between them. It had been over for years. Yes, she'd acted badly and he'd been hurt. So hurt he'd been unable to commit to anyone else. But was that her problem or his? At some point didn't he have to, as he'd so crudely put it to Skye, grow a pair and move on?

He replayed his conversation with Skye and winced as he heard his harsh words in his head. That is not the man he was. Where did he get off acting like that?

He looked at Bullet. "I'm a complete asshole."

The horse butted him as if pointing out it was about time he realized that. Mitch staggered a few feet and started to lose his balance. Bullet moved quickly, stepping closer and shoving his head into Mitch's side, catching him and supporting him.

He wrapped an arm around the horse's neck and hung on.

When he'd found his center of gravity again and straightened, Bullet butted him again, but more gently. As if showing he understood that Mitch wasn't the most coordinated human around. He patted the horse.

"A sense of humor is important," he said. "Thanks for getting that."

Bullet snorted.

Mitch reached for a brush. He'd defined the problem, which was step one. Now he needed a solution, which required a goal. What did he want from Skye? What did he want *for* her? Once he knew that, the rest would be easy to figure out.

THE RESTAURANT WAS crowded, but as soon as Skye mentioned T.J.'s name, she was shown back to a table.

She'd dressed carefully in a black cocktail dress she'd bought a year ago but had never worn. Although the style was very flattering, it was cut low enough to make her uncomfortable. In the safety of the dressing room she'd told herself it was time to be adventurous. But once she had the dress home, she'd lost her courage. Until tonight.

She'd curled her wavy hair, worn her favorite dangling diamond earrings and heels that hurt her feet before she left the bedroom. Maybe it wasn't going to be enough, but she wanted to do her best to show T.J. what he would never ever get.

He was already at the table, looking handsome and smooth in his custom suit. He rose when he saw her and seemed impressed with what he saw.

"You look great," he told her. "Beautiful and killer sexy."

"Thank you."

She took the seat across from his and dropped her wrap. His eyes widened.

The low-cut dress was also tight. Her curves seemed seconds away from spilling out. Skye figured she might as well flaunt the assets she had.

"I'm not going to be able to think straight through dinner," he muttered.

"Really?" she asked, smiling, then reached across the table and touched his hand.

"Seriously, Skye, you're gorgeous enough to be deadly." He glanced around the room as if trying to figure out what was going on. "Tell me again why we're here and not at my place?"

"Because you didn't ask me to your place."

His mouth dropped slightly. He might have been playing before, but he looked plenty serious now. "Do you want to leave?" he asked.

She leaned toward him. "Will you take me home?" she whispered. "Make love with me?"

He swore under his breath. "In a heartbeat. I thought you'd want to go slow."

"You thought wrong. Let's go."

He stood so fast, the chair went flying.

She rose and followed him out of the restaurant. She was pleased to see her car was still parked in front, as she'd asked the valet. Across the street she saw a flatbed truck pulling away with T.J.'s car on it. T.J. didn't seem to notice.

T.J. passed over his claim check, then put his arm around her. "I'm so ready for this," he murmured in her ear.

She pushed him away. "I'll just bet you are, you bastard. Did you really think you could sleep with my sister and then get me into bed? That's disgusting. I don't know what this is all about, but it stops now. You are nothing but a jerk and a loser. Were you going to keep Izzy on the side while you tried to talk me into marrying you? What did Jed promise you?" She threw up her hands. "You know what? I don't care. You lost Izzy and you lost me.

And by the time I'm done talking about you, you won't be able to buy a dog, let alone get a date, in this town."

He glared at her. "You think you're something but you're not. Without Jed, you're nothing."

"I'm still a Titan and I am somebody, with or without Jed."

He flushed. "The next husband Daddy tries to buy for you won't look as good as me."

She looked him up and down. "I'm not sure I could do worse. You're the kind of man who's never happy with what he has. I'll bet you cheat at cards, too. By the way, Izzy says you're the size of a peanut and lasted about thirty seconds. How disappointing."

Knowing she was going to regret her public tirade in the morning, but too happy with it now to care, Skye tossed the valet a twenty. He handed her her keys. She got in her car and drove away. As she turned at the corner, she pushed the button for her hands-free phone system, then spoke Lexi's name.

Her sister picked up on the second ring. "Hi. What's up?"

"I need to trash T. J. Boone all over town. Can you help with that?"

Lexi laughed. "You know I have a phone network that rivals the Pentagon. What do you want me to say?"

"I'm thinking we should start by mentioning an unfortunate lack of size in the male equipment department."

SKYE STOOD in front of Ray's grave and touched the impressive carved headstone. The quote, from Aristotle, had been one point of many she'd disagreed with. But Ray's children had never accepted her, had never been happy about their father's marriage to a much younger woman. No matter how she explained she wasn't in it for the money, they didn't believe her.

After his death, they'd discovered he'd left her only a few million which, from their perspective, had been practically nothing. Instead he'd divided his estate among all his children, including Erin. His children had never known that she had been the one to insist Ray write his will that way.

He'd wanted to leave her "taken care of," which in his mind meant thirty or forty million dollars. But she didn't need that. She still had a little money from her mother and she wasn't a big spender.

Erin's money had been left in trust for her. Skye had no idea what his other children had done with their shares. There was no contact, not even with their half sister.

She tried not to mind. Erin didn't know much about them and couldn't miss a relationship she'd never had. While Skye accepted they would always hate her, she was sad they would reject her child.

Ray had told her to give it time. She hadn't realized how little they would have together.

"I know you loved me," she whispered. Not that he could hear her, but it felt good to pretend he could.

That she would get an answer and then he would laugh. That big laugh of his that always made her feel better no matter what was going on.

"Mitch got in the way, didn't he? You knew he was in my heart, even when I didn't. Even when I tried to forget him."

Mitch had lived between them, a shadow they couldn't escape.

"I didn't love you enough," she said, tears filling her eyes. "And now you're gone. You would be so ashamed of me. T.J. turned out to be a real mess. Izzy tried to warn me about him and I wouldn't listen. It's my pride. I guess I've always had too much pride. Oh, Ray."

She clutched the headstone, wishing she could go back and change things. If only she'd gotten over Mitch sooner. Or at all.

But that wasn't her only regret. What she'd finally come to see was that she'd lost herself the day she'd chosen Ray over Mitch. She'd lost the essence of who and what she was and that might also be part of the reason she hadn't been able to love him as much as he deserved.

Ray had been good to her. He'd always encouraged her to reach for something. He was the one who had suggested she start the foundation. He'd helped her with all the logistics and had offered to give her more seed money. He'd been a lot older, but his heart and spirit had been young and he'd treasured her and Erin.

Now he was gone and she didn't know what was going to happen next. Except maybe it was time for her to take charge of her own life. To do what was right for herself and her daughter and not let every man around her tell her what to do.

CHAPTER FOURTEEN

SKYE WOKE to the sound of her cell phone. As she grabbed it, she looked at the clock. It wasn't even five yet. No good calls came at this time.

"Hello?"

"It's Dana. Sorry to wake you, but I wanted to give you a heads-up. They're coming to arrest Jed. You've got less than an hour. And no, he shouldn't run for it. He should call one of his five-hundred-dollar-an-hour attorneys. I wanted you to know because there will be press. Keep Erin away from them."

Skye sat up. She couldn't understand what her friend was saying. "Who's arresting Jed?"

"The Feds. They'll have local police assisting. It's for the smuggling. Shipping military weapons overseas isn't something that makes the government happy. They've pulled together some preliminary charges until they can make the big ones stick."

"This is all Garth," Skye breathed. "He made this happen. He did it all."

"I agree, but until we can prove that, Daddy's going to jail. You can't tell anyone I called you."

"I know. I don't want you getting in trouble. Thanks, Dana."

"You're welcome."

Skye scrambled out of bed. She grabbed a robe, then went down the hall and into Jed's room.

Her father was already up, showered and dressed. He sat at a desk in the corner, working on his laptop.

"Daddy, the police are coming."

He didn't bother looking at her. "I know."

How could he know and why wasn't he more upset? "They're going to arrest you."

"I'll be out of jail before noon. My attorneys are already working on it." He glanced at her. "Don't worry, Skye. I know what I'm doing."

She hoped that was true. "This won't help stock prices."

"Garth is playing hardball."

"You know it's him behind all this?"

"Of course."

"Then do something. Stop him."

Jed turned off his laptop and stood. "This is business. You wouldn't understand."

"I understand that he's doing his best to ruin us all."

"You'll be fine."

"Don't patronize me."

He shrugged into a suit jacket. "I'm about to be

arrested for an assortment of crimes, including treason, Skye. Do you think you could save your female tantrum for later?"

She left his room without saying anything and walked down the hall to Izzy's bedroom.

"You have to get up," she said as she walked in and turned on the light. "The police are coming and Jed's going to be arrested."

She and Izzy hadn't spoken since the afternoon Izzy had told her about sleeping with T.J. Skye hadn't yet shared how she'd walked out on him and had Lexi help her start rumors so that he would find it very difficult to ever get a date in Dallas again. But now was not the time.

Izzy sat up and blinked. "What? Arrested?"

"The smuggled arms. And who knows what else."

"Is he going to be charged with treason?"

"I hope not."

"They could execute him."

Skye walked into the large closet and pulled out a pair of black slacks along with the most conservative sweater she could find. In Izzy's collection there weren't a lot of choices that didn't scream *hot and sexy*.

"Why are you picking out my clothes?"

"Because the press will be here and if they get pictures of us, I want us to look respectable."

"Do you really think what we're wearing matters? Jed is going to jail."

"Appearance can make or break a situation," Skye

snapped. "We're Titans, Izzy. We have family pride and there is no way we are going to look anything but dignified."

"It's five-thirty in the morning. What has your panties in a bunch?"

"Just get dressed."

Skye hurried down the hall. She had to pull herself together quickly, as well.

She skipped a shower. After dressing, she brushed her hair back and secured it in a French twist. Minimal makeup took care of the circles under her eyes. She wore her mother's pearl earrings and low pumps. She was about to leave her room when Erin entered.

"Mommy? What's wrong?"

"Oh, baby." Skye hugged her. "Did all the noise wake you?"

"I don't know." Erin snuggled close. "I just woke up. Something's wrong, isn't it?"

Skye sat on the bed and set her daughter next to her. "Yes, it is, but we're okay. There's a bad man saying bad things about the family. We have to fix that and we will, but right now, it's complicated."

"Did you talk to the police? They'll help you."

"The police are…confused. They're going to take your grandpa away and ask him some questions. He'll be fine. But there are probably going to be some press people here, too. They'll be loud and rude."

"They shouldn't be rude."

If only thinking that would keep it from happening, Skye thought. "I know. I'm not leaving this house," she said. "But the police will be here soon. Can you wait in your room until they're all gone?"

Erin bit her lower lip. "I think I'm scared, Mommy."

"I'll wait with her."

Skye looked up and saw Izzy standing in the doorway. "You don't want to be downstairs?"

"No, thanks. You represent the family. I'll keep Erin company. We can play a game. When this is over, I'll take her out to breakfast." She turned to Erin. "Calico Café for French toast?"

Erin managed a slight smile. "Okay."

Skye hugged her. "I love you, Bunny Face. We're fine. You know that, right?"

Erin nodded. "Tell Grandpa I love him."

"I will."

Izzy led Erin away. Skye went downstairs. There were already a half-dozen cars and vans parked in the driveway. News crews gathered. Jed Titan getting arrested was a big story.

Skye waited until several police cars and unmarked sedans pulled up to call for her father. Jed walked down the stairs looking as well dressed and calm as if he were going to a cotillion.

Federal agents climbed the stairs and knocked.

"Let 'em in," Jed said.

Skye went to the door.

The second she opened it, lights flashed from

everywhere. Reporters crowded behind the officers, yelling and taking dozens of pictures.

"We're here for Jed Titan," the man in front said as he flashed a badge.

"I'm right here."

Jed had put on his jacket and stood ready. Skye opened the door wider. The man entered, read him his rights, then walked him out to the waiting cars.

The reporters crowded around, taking pictures and calling out questions. Jed ignored them. He walked with his head high, not trying to hide his face. Skye couldn't decide if it was pride or arrogance.

She went out onto the big porch to watch her father being driven away, which turned out to be a mistake.

When the police cars were gone, she found herself surrounded by reporters and several feet from the front door.

"Did you know your father was a criminal?"

"What else has Jed sold to our enemies?"

"Do you think your father is a traitor?"

"How much money have you stolen from your foundation?"

"Were you laundering money for him or for the mob?"

The questions flew all around her. She felt trapped and vulnerable and knew there would be pictures of her looking like a frightened deer.

"This is private property," she yelled. "You need to leave."

A couple of the reporters laughed. "Are you going to make me?"

A single shot cut through the early-morning air. Everyone turned and saw Mitch climbing out of his truck. He pushed back his cowboy hat and held his rifle loosely in his hand.

"You heard the lady. This is private property."

This was still Texas, where the tradition of using deadly force to protect property lived on. The reporters ran for their vehicles.

Mitch waited until the last one had left. He looked at Skye. "Dana warned me what was going on. She thought you might need some help."

She felt herself starting to shake. "It was a mob."

"Once Jed was taken away, there wasn't much of a show. They were looking to start a new one."

"Thank you."

"You're welcome." He hesitated. "Skye, about before."

She held up a hand. "I can't do this right now."

"I don't want to fight with you anymore. That's what I'm trying to say. The past is gone. I'm sorry for what I did, what I said. I was mad as hell. Seeing you again pushed all my buttons. I'm done trying to punish you."

Did he think that made it okay? "Who gives you the right to say it's over or not? Who gives you the right to punish me? Why do you decide?"

He walked to the bottom of the stairs and offered the rifle. "Want to shoot me?"

"This isn't funny. I can't do this anymore, Mitch. I'm exhausted and confused and close to my breaking point. You have to pick. Either be a bastard or be a nice guy. Just decide and then stick with it."

"I'm not going to be a bastard. I swear."

"Why should I believe you?"

She turned and walked into the house.

Izzy stood at the foot of the stairs. "Erin fell back asleep."

"Good," Skye murmured, wishing she had that ability. It would be nice to sleep until this was over.

"I heard a little of what Mitch said."

"I don't want to talk about it."

"You should give him a chance."

Skye put her hands on her hips. "Who says I haven't? Who says he hasn't been a complete bully since he got home? You don't know what he's said to me. You do know that he was working for Garth. Doesn't that mean anything to you?"

"Did he pass on anything to Garth? He was pissed, Skye. He reacted. Not everyone gets to think things through. He's having a tough time now. You should give him a break."

"If you're so interested in Mitch, why don't you go after him. Oh, wait. Maybe you have already. You know, for my own good."

Izzy stared at her for a long time. "I'm leaving for the rig in about an hour. I'll be gone two months."

"Good."

MITCH LOOKED up from his computer and saw Erin standing in his office. He hadn't heard her come in and he didn't know how long she'd been there.

He turned in his chair and looked at her. "Did you want to talk to me?"

Her eyes were big and sad. Her mouth pulled down.

"They took my grandpa away."

"I know, but he'll be back."

"Izzy's gone, too. To the rig. She and Mommy are fighting and maybe they don't love each other anymore."

"They're sisters. Sisters fight. But they love each other. I promise." As he said the words, he wondered if his promises meant anything to her. Or had she still not forgiven him for making her mother cry.

He wanted to plead his case, to convince her, but that wasn't his call.

She sniffed, then launched herself at him. He caught her and pulled her close. She hugged him as if she would never let go.

"I'm sorry," he whispered. "I'm sorry I let you down and I'm sorry I made your mom cry. I won't make excuses. Just know that I won't do it again."

"Okay," she whispered, her voice muffled against his shoulder. "My tummy hurts and I want it to be better."

"I know." He rubbed her back, then smoothed her hair. "How can I help?"

"Will you go riding with me?"

"Sure." He would have walked on water for her, if she'd asked.

"Can we go fast?"

"As fast as you want."

What he didn't tell her was that no matter how fast or far they went, they couldn't make it better. Not by running away. He'd learned that lesson the hard way.

IT TOOK JED a little longer than he'd planned to get out of jail, but by three that afternoon, he'd had a hearing and been released. The bail had been set at fifty million dollars and he'd had to surrender his passport, but he was a free man. At least until the trial.

Skye waited with Lexi while Jed was processed for release. Once again the press gathered. She did her best to ignore them.

"This is a total nightmare," Lexi murmured, staying close. "How did we end up in this mess?"

"One guess," Skye muttered.

"Right. I swear, we're going to get him."

Skye wanted to agree, but so far they didn't even know what "get him" meant. Get him back? Get him to stop? How could they stop Garth when they weren't sure of his goal. Annihilation of the Titan family was fairly general.

"Izzy's missing all the fun," Lexi said.

"She's heading back to the rig."

"At least she'll be safe from Garth."

Skye nodded. She wanted to be safe, too. She wanted all this to stop.

Jed appeared, flanked by two attorneys. Several reporters gathered around him.

"What happened, Mr. Titan? Were you charged?"

He held up his hands and smiled for the cameras. Despite what he'd been through, he looked good. Well dressed, at ease, confident.

"I know these charges are serious and I respect our judicial system. Because of it, I'll get the chance to clear my name. Because this is Texas, where a man's name and his word mean something, I give you my word that I'll be cleared of these charges. There are those who want to tear down what I've built." He looked directly into a television camera. "That isn't going to happen."

Skye listened to him talk and wondered how many favors he'd had to call in to be released.

She and Lexi waited until Jed was done to follow him to the waiting limo. They had to squeeze through the press to get into the car.

Jed had already poured himself a drink. "Vultures," he said between gulps. "Damn vultures. I'll show them."

Lexi fastened her seat belt. "Dad, we need to talk about this. Garth is coming at us from every side. We need a plan to stop him."

"I have a plan."

Skye and her sister looked at each other.

"Care to share it?" Lexi asked.

"No. Stop worrying. This doesn't concern you. I'm handling Garth."

Not very well, Skye thought, confused by her father's unwillingness to work with them. Did he honestly think they were incompetent or was it something more? Something he didn't want them to know?

MITCH WENT to see Garth that afternoon. He was tired of sitting on the sidelines and watching crap happen to Skye and her family. He was going to have it out with Garth. Besides, Jed's son had it coming. He'd played them all and that had to stop.

He found Garth's office easily. He'd timed his visit for lunch when most of the staff was gone and managed to slip onto the executive floor unnoticed. As he walked down the hall, he grabbed a file from a cubical desk and pretended to read the contents when he passed a couple of guys. They nodded at him and kept on walking.

The desk in front of Garth's office was empty and the door was partially open. He could hear bits of conversation.

Everything about his upbringing knew that it was wrong to listen in. Everything from his SEAL training pointed out that learning about the enemy was the first step in a victory. He saw another, less ornate door next to Garth's. He opened it and stepped into an adjoining conference room. There was a door that attached to Garth's office. Mitch cracked it a couple of inches and prepared to learn what he could.

"This sucks," some guy was saying.

"Sounds like it." Garth's voice was more amused than sympathetic.

"Oh, sure. Easy for you to say. You're not the one everyone is talking about. The rumors are everywhere. I'm either impotent, broke or I have a rash. According to word on the street I'm also gay, I beat my last girlfriend or I stole her dog. They're killing me."

"You have to admire their inventiveness."

"No, I don't," the other man complained. "They've ruined me."

"You pitted one sister against the other," Garth said. "You couldn't expect them to be happy about it."

"You told me to make trouble. I was following orders."

"You got caught. That's not my problem."

"You're a real bastard," the other man said.

"I know, but that's also not the point. You've been paid, and paid well. You came up with a plan, which I appreciate, but it backfired and that's not my responsibility."

"What? You're dismissing me?"

Mitch eased open the door a little more so he could see into Garth's office. The space was large, with an impressive view. Garth was visible, but not the other man. Mitch was determined to figure out who he was. The voice was familiar but he couldn't place it.

"You're done with me then?" the man asked. "Just like that?"

"You've finished the job. What else is there?"

"My reputation."

"I'm sure everyone will forget. Rumors come and go."

"Like hell. I want this fixed."

"I didn't break anything."

"But I can't live like this. Women are laughing at me everywhere I go."

The man speaking moved into view. Mitch stared into the familiar face of T. J. Boone. He didn't know if he should laugh or go punch the guy. Then he realized what T.J.'s presence in Garth's office meant and the humor faded.

His confrontation with Garth could wait. He had other business to take care of first.

He drove to Skye's foundation and parked. This time he didn't sneak. Instead he announced himself, hoping she would see him. He was shown right into her office.

Sunlight filtered in behind her, putting her in shadow. She was tall and curvy and beautiful. The blouse was buttoned up to her neck, which made him want to unfasten it, then pull it off and...

Not why he was here, he reminded himself.

"Mitch. What's going on?"

"I have to tell you something."

She grabbed the edge of her desk. "It's not Erin, is it."

He moved to her side. "No. She's fine. This is

something else." She needed to know and she wouldn't be happy. How likely was she to shoot the messenger? In her mind, he probably deserved it. Worse, would she be hurt? He knew Jed wanted Skye to marry T.J. Where did she stand on the subject? He would much rather she was pissed at him than upset she'd lost a boyfriend.

"I went to see Garth," he told her. "I wanted to…do something."

"Fight him?"

"I could take him."

"I'm sure you could and, while that's really sweet, this isn't your war."

"It became mine when he involved me."

Her mouth twisted. "You involved yourself."

"I know. But not the point right now. I went to see him and—"

Well, damn. Saying this was harder than he thought. Would she even believe him?

"T. J. Boone was there. They're in it together."

She went pale. "He's working with Garth."

"He was. Now he's complaining about something. His reputation being ruined and people laughing at him. Your doing, I hope?"

She sat on the corner of the desk. "Yes, mine. At least it was my idea. Lexi made most of the phone calls. We're saying terrible things about him. He could sue us."

"Only if he's willing to go to court to prove they

aren't true. Did you really come up with the idea of a rash?"

"That was Lexi. I said to tell people he stole my dog. This is Texas. A man doesn't do that here." She squeezed her eyes tight, then opened then. "I can't believe he's working for Garth. To do what? Make trouble?"

"Probably. T.J. mentioned he hadn't been paid enough."

She groaned. "He did it for money? He screwed with us for money? Izzy is going to be so pissed."

"Why Izzy?"

"It's a long story, but the bottom line is she slept with him."

"Why would Izzy have sex with a guy you're dating?"

"Because she was trying to make a point. She said that T.J. wasn't really interested in me. That he was pretending because of Jed. She thought Jed had made him the offer." She stood and walked to the window, standing with her back to him.

"She was right about his motive, but wrong about who was footing the bill," Skye murmured, as if she were talking to herself and not him. "Not my father, who was fooled by T.J., too. My half brother. T.J. didn't want to go out with me at all. He wasn't interested."

Mitch didn't know what to do. This was guy hell—should he move close and offer comfort or keep away? Worse, why was Skye upset? Was she just pissed or had she given her heart to that two-bit, cheating, suit-wearing—

"I wasn't even sure I liked him," Skye continued. "He was very charming, but there was no chemistry. Izzy was right. Why would a guy like that be interested in someone like me?"

That got him moving. He walked up behind her and put his hands on her shoulders.

"Have you looked in the mirror lately?" he asked. "Why wouldn't he be interested? You're beautiful. You're smart, you're funny, you're a great mom and you have a body designed to get men to sell their souls. I know. I've made a couple of down payments."

She hunched her shoulders. "You're just being nice."

"When am I ever nice?"

"Now would be an example. I fought with my sister because of a guy I wasn't even sure I liked. I was difficult and judgmental and mean because of him. And all this time, he was working for Garth."

Her shoulders shook slightly.

He turned her and pulled her close. "You fell for a smooth line. It happens."

"Not to me. I'm so stupid."

She was rigid in his arms but he didn't let go. "How could you know?" he asked.

"I should have guessed. If I wasn't trying so hard to be some guy magnet, which I'm not, I wouldn't have been such an idiot." She stunned him by socking him in the arm and glaring at him. "This is all your fault."

He took a step back. "What? How?"

"You came back and confused me. One minute you're the guy I remember, the guy I was in love with, the next you're a total asshole. You hurt me and kicked my heart to the gutter."

He held up both hands in front of him. "What does that have to do with T.J.?"

"Nothing, but it's still your fault." She started to cry.

He grabbed her and shook her, then he bent down and kissed her.

Her lips were soft and yielding. Then she pushed away.

"This is my office. I'm not having sex here."

"We're just kissing. No one said anything about sex."

"So you don't want me anymore? Was Garth paying you, too?"

He swore. "Skye, I swear."

"What?" she demanded, looking defiant and beautiful.

"You make me crazy."

"How do you think I feel?"

"Like you need medication?"

"Not funny." But the corner of her mouth twitched. "I could take you."

"On what planet."

"Zorgon."

Then she was wrapping her arms around him and kissing him as if she would never stop. She leaned into him, pushing her tongue into his mouth. He responded with a surge of passion that left them both gasping. They each pulled back and looked at each other.

"Better?" he asked.

She nodded.

"Good. Now, what can I do to help?" he asked. He was willing to do anything to help, although his first vote was for sex.

"I don't know. Can I get back to you?"

"Sure. I should probably let you get to work."

"Okay."

He started to leave, then turned around. "I'm sorry about T.J."

"No, you're not."

"I'm trying to be polite."

"I'll give you points for effort. I'm surprised, and I feel stupid, but I'm not hurt. We weren't involved."

Are we?

But he didn't ask. Mostly because he realized he didn't want to hear her say no.

CHAPTER FIFTEEN

SKYE MET Lexi and Dana for lunch at Bronco Billy's. She waited until they'd ordered to share the news.

"T.J. was working for Garth."

Dana paused in the middle of pouring sweetener into her iced tea. Lexi sagged back in her chair.

"Are you kidding?" Dana asked, then waved. "Don't answer that. Stupid question. T.J. working for Garth. Of course."

"It makes sense," Lexi said. "He waltzes into your life and Izzy's and totally messes up things. He gets between you and causes trouble."

Skye sipped her diet soda. "He didn't cause trouble on his own. We let him. I have to give him credit—he was really good. He pitted us against each other and all he had to do was sit back and watch the show."

Lexi leaned toward her. "Are you okay?"

"If you're asking if I'm hurt, I'm not. If you want to know if I feel like an idiot, absolutely. I can't even remember how the fight with Izzy started. She was defending me and telling him off and he came on to her and…" It was a blur. "She was telling me there was something wrong, she just didn't know what. I wouldn't listen. Her gut was right but all I could hear was that some guy wanted her over me and I was tired of being the dateless sister."

"Izzy will understand," Dana told her. "She's good that way."

"I know." Izzy would torture her for a few minutes, then let it go. Skye would be left wallowing in guilt on her own.

"I was so quick to jump to conclusions," Skye murmured.

"You were looking for a distraction and T.J. provided a good one," Lexi said.

"What do you mean, a distraction?"

Dana and Lexi looked at each other. The glance was quick, but Skye recognized it. It meant they'd been talking about her, that they'd figured everything out.

"What?" she demanded.

"You haven't been yourself since Mitch came back," Dana said. "I totally get why. It's a big deal. T.J. got lucky with the timing. If he'd shown up a month earlier, you would have caught on to him much sooner."

Skye didn't bother pointing out she hadn't caught on to him at all. Izzy had.

Was it as simple as Dana said? Had T.J. been nothing but a distraction? Skye knew she didn't care about the guy—they'd only gone out a few times. It was more what he represented.

"Score another one for Garth," Lexi said. "He's managed to come between us."

"I've sent Izzy a text message asking her to call me when she gets a chance," Skye told them. "I hope she doesn't wait too long. I want her to know. I just hope she wasn't too involved with T.J. This could hurt her." Which wasn't anything Skye wanted.

"But you're okay?" Lexi asked.

"Yes. On the surface, he seemed like the perfect guy. I'm more upset I was fooled."

"How did you find out?" Dana asked.

Skye told them about Mitch going to confront Garth.

Lexi sighed. "He's always been like that. A guy who gets things done. You have to respect that."

"You still in love with him?"

Dana's blunt question nearly made Skye choke on her drink. "Excuse me?"

"Should I talk louder?"

"No." Skye glanced around to see who was sitting close. Fortunately, they were early and the place was fairly empty. "I'm not in love with Mitch."

"You sure? It sounds like there's something going on."

"Don't push," Lexi said.

"Why not? The only reason she was involved with T.J. at all was because of Mitch."

"Don't forget that Jed wanted her to marry him. That would have had some weight."

"You think Skye is going to do that twice?"

Skye slapped her hands down on the table. "Hello. I'm sitting right here."

They looked at her and shrugged. "Feel free to step in at anytime," Lexi told her.

"I have nothing to say on the subject of Mitch."

"Which is part of the problem," Dana told her.

Their lunches arrived. Lexi had ordered a salad, and both Skye and Dana dug into burgers. Skye was feeling the need for red meat and fries.

"Mitch and I are friends. That's all." Friends who fought and made up and had hot sex in strange places.

"You're not friends," Dana said. "I don't know what you are, but it's more than that."

"You're still in love with him," Lexi said as she stabbed a piece of grilled chicken. "I don't think you ever stopped loving him, even when you were married to Ray, but that's just me."

Skye stared at her. "I'm not in love with him."

"Oh, please," Dana said, then frowned at Lexi's salad. "Your healthy eating is starting to get on my nerves."

"I'm pregnant."

"I know that, but jeez, don't you think you're taking it too far? I agree with giving up drinking and all that, but I saw organic yogurt and tofu in your re-frigerator the other day. Tofu? I'm starting to wonder how much longer we can be friends."

Skye couldn't believe it. They made an announce-ment like that then bickered about tofu?

"I am not in love with Mitch," she announced loudly.

Lexi looked at her. "Okay. If you say so."

"I'm not. I was, years ago. But we're both different people. We have a history. It will always be complicated, but I'm not in love with him."

She couldn't be. People change. They'd changed. "If I met him today, I'm not sure I'd even like him."

"Oh, you'd like him," Dana told her. "He's very likable."

"He can be a jerk," Lexi pointed out. "But he's dealing with a lot. His heart is in the right place."

"And other stuff." Dana grinned. "Or so I've heard."

"Who did you hear that from?" Skye demanded. "Is Mitch sleeping with someone else?"

"Ooh." Lexi looked delighted. "So you *are* having sex with Mitch."

Skye felt herself flush. "I really hate you."

"No, you don't. You love me and we'll stop teasing you now."

"He's not sleeping with anyone else," Dana said. "He's all yours."

"You make me insane. Both of you."

Lexi and Dana grinned at each other. "We know," Lexi said. "It's a gift."

SKYE GOT HOME a few minutes before the bus arrived with Erin. Her daughter burst into the house and began talking about her day.

"I got an A on my book report," she said as she

put down her backpack. "My teacher says over the summer I need to read books that are about more than horses." Erin wrinkled her nose. "I don't know why."

"She wants you to broaden your horizons."

Skye cut up an apple and put it on a plate, then added some cheese and crackers. They sat across from each other at the table.

"What else happened today?" she asked her daughter.

"We have to bring in somebody to school our last week before summer vacation. Like show-and-tell only about work. Mandy's dad owns a McDonald's and he's going to talk about that."

"Who were you thinking of bringing?" Skye asked, hoping it wasn't Jed.

"Mitch," Erin said, watching her. "He could talk about being a SEAL and his leg and stuff."

Mitch would shine in the classroom, she thought. "I think that's a good idea."

"You're not mad at him?"

Skye sighed. "No. Not anymore."

Erin nodded, then bit into an apple slice. "He made you cry."

"Sometimes people who know each other for a long time have fights. But we get over them and are friends again."

"So I can ask Mitch?"

"Yes."

Erin chatted more about her day, how she'd eaten

lunch with her friends and that maybe, just maybe, she would read a book that wasn't about horses.

Skye listened and talked, but she couldn't stop thinking about her conversation with Lexi and Dana and their assumption that she was still in love with Mitch.

It wasn't true, she told herself. She might not be able to totally define her feelings but they weren't love. They were complicated and rooted in the past. In time she would sort them out. Not that it really mattered one way or the other.

But as she listened to her daughter, she couldn't help wondering what it would have been like if she'd stood up to Jed and refused to marry Ray. If she hadn't slept with him and gotten pregnant. Where would she and Mitch be now?

MITCH STOOD outside the closed door. He didn't want to be here, didn't want to talk to a group of people he didn't know anything about. Joss waited patiently beside him.

"Let me answer the question," the other man said. "Yes, you have to."

"Technically, I don't," Mitch muttered.

Joss shook his head. "You're consistent. I'll give you that. Talk to me about the energy exercises I've given you."

Something else Mitch didn't want to do. He'd mocked and resisted and finally he'd given in and done them. Every morning he rubbed his hands together like a cartoon villain to start the flow of energy. He moved his hands up and down his body, including where his leg had been, matching his breathing to the motions. He held pressure points and cleared his mind and dammit all to hell, it had helped. His phantom pain was nearly gone. If he skipped a couple of days, it started to return.

"Because organic beef and free-range chickens aren't enough," he grumbled. "You've got me chanting and hugging trees."

"No one is asking you to chant. Now are you going in or are you going to continue to waste my time?"

He really wanted to waste Joss's time but knew that wasn't the right choice. He straightened, raised his chin and pushed open the door.

Inside were a bunch of people sitting in chairs pulled into a circle. The men ranged in age from maybe eighteen to sixty-something. At first glance they seemed to have nothing in common. Then Mitch noticed a hook here, a wheelchair there. They were a support group for amputees.

Joss had been pushing the group for a while now. He'd offered Mitch the choice of times and places, but not the option of not attending. Mitch had picked an all-male session with mostly vets. At least they would have that to talk about.

"This is Mitch," Joss said, walking into the circle and greeting several of the guys. "He's new."

An old guy in a wheelchair laughed. "Let me guess. He doesn't want to be here." The man patted his two stumps. "I don't want to be here, either. But every week I show up."

"Burt here is the leader of the group," Joss told Mitch. "He'll take care of you."

Mitch wanted to bolt. Instead he took a seat, knowing this was where he had to be. Joss slipped from the room.

"I'll start," Burt said when the door had shut. "I'm Burt. I got stupid when I was twenty and lost both my legs when I played chicken with a train and lost. I still dream I can walk. Just the other night, I was walking on the beach with Raquel Welsh. Now most of you young pups don't even know who she is, but trust me, she was something. A lady worth walking for."

Burt grinned. "Right now I'm in a good place. If I could get you gimps to let go of your anger, I'd be in a better place. But that's why we're here. I'm going to drag you kicking and screaming back into the world." His smile broadened. "Some of you I have to drag because you can't walk, but that's a different story. Who wants to talk?"

A man in his thirties raised his arm. The utility prosthesis glinted in the light.

"I wish I could dream about some broad," he said. "I keep dreaming about Iraq. Every time I close my eyes, I'm back there." He was still staring at the group, but his gaze seemed to turn inward. "I can't turn it off. It haunts me. All of it. Then I wake up feeling the pain." He glanced at Mitch. "My arm got burned off. It all comes back to me. Every second."

Mitch swallowed. "I'm sorry, man," he said.

"Yeah? Me, too."

Mitch waited for Burt to say something, to help, but the old man was silent. Finally the one who looked like he was barely eighteen said, "You try sleeping with a dog?"

They all looked at him. Even Burt seemed startled.

"Cliff, there are some things we don't need to know," a guy said.

The kid flushed. "Not like that. I mean get a dog. I got one from a shelter. A mutt. He's happy as hell and sometimes that bugs me, you know? But he's always there. Always ready to listen or play. He takes me out of myself. I'm saying a dog can help. They curl up next to you at night." He shrugged.

One guy mentioned tai chi as a way to deal with the pain. Another talked about the energy work Mitch was already doing. Nobody said he should get drunk and forget about it. Nobody assumed it would fix itself.

Over the next hour, problems were presented and solutions offered. A few men just wanted to talk, which Mitch couldn't understand, but maybe time would change that. When the session was over, he found Joss outside.

"What'd you think?" Joss asked. "You coming back?"

"Do I have a choice?"

"We all have choices. They're not always good ones, but we have them."

Mitch thought about the group, how they were all different but each understood the loss of a very real part of themselves.

"I'll be back," he said.

"Good." Joss shoved a brochure in his hands.

"What's this?"

"A crisis training seminar. You learn how to talk to people in trouble. It's a six-month course. At the end you're not a therapist, but you're somebody who knows how to listen."

Mitch dropped the brochure as if it were a live grenade. "What are you talking about? I can't help anyone else."

Joss stared at him. "That's where you're wrong. You're exactly the right person for someone in crisis to lean on. It's not easy and there are plenty who can't be saved, but when you pull someone back from the brink, when you see him build up his life again, it's a good day. Don't you want a few good days?"

Mitch looked from Joss to the brochure, then bent over and picked it up. "I didn't talk today," he said. "I don't want to talk. What makes you think I want to listen?"

"I have a gut instinct about these things." Joss grinned. "It's part of my charm. Just ask my wife."

"I'll pass."

Joss patted the brochure. "Think about it. The next class starts in a couple of months. By then they won't be able to shut you up in group."

"That will never happen."

"I know, but it's fun to think about. You've got someone to watch your back, Mitch. There are plenty of guys who don't have anyone. That's not right and it's something we can change—one vet at a time."

Joss walked back to the physical therapy center. Mitch made his way to his truck. He climbed in and put the brochure on the seat next to him.

Could he help someone in crisis? Did he want to? His first instinct was to call Skye and talk to her about it. Not that he would. She had enough going on.

Joss was right—someone had his back. Who had Skye's? Who would protect her from Garth's next move? Except it wasn't a difficult question and he already knew the answer.

He would.

THAT NIGHT, after Erin was in bed, Skye went to see Jed in his study. Her father was laying low these days. No parties had been planned, which after the last one wasn't much of a surprise. But he also hadn't been coming to dinner or showing up at breakfast. He was either at the office or in his study at home.

She knocked on the partially open door. Jed barely looked up.

"What?" he asked.

"I need to talk to you."

"This isn't a good time."

"T.J. was working for Garth."

Jed straightened in his chair and motioned for her to come in. "Where'd you hear that nonsense?"

"I know it's true. He was just one part of Garth's assault plan. He came between me and Izzy, which was his goal. Divide and conquer."

"You think Garth has a plan?"

"I'm sure he does. He's working all of us. You, me, Lexi. Even Cruz has had some trouble. No one is safe." Except Izzy, who was on the rig. "I'm sure T.J. isn't the first spy he's had." She didn't mention that Garth had approached Mitch. There was no point in distracting Jed.

"We need to have a family meeting," she continued. "We need to come up with a plan of our own to stop him."

Jed dismissed her with a flick of his fingers. "This isn't your fight."

"He's made it mine. Somehow he got into the computer system at the foundation. He's uploaded a second set of books that are completely false. But until I can prove that, we're under scrutiny from the government. We're at risk of losing our nonprofit status."

"No one cares about that," Jed said flatly. "You want to compare your silly foundation with the charges I'm fighting? I never understood why you're wasting your time with all that."

"Feeding hungry children? You consider that a waste? Oh, wait. Let me guess. These kids aren't worth saving. Is that it?"

"You should put your resources into something that matters."

"This matters to me."

"Then you're a fool. But fine. Keep your foundation. I'll find someone else for you to marry. You need a husband and more kids. That will keep you busy."

His total dismissal of who and what she was shouldn't have been a surprise, yet it was.

"You don't own me," she said quietly. "You're not picking out my next husband."

"Of course I am. Don't forget who you're talking to, little girl. This is my house. Glory's Gate is what you want and to win it, you have to play by my rules. Lexi played and lost the business. The same thing can happen to you."

She didn't know this man, she thought sadly. He was her father and she didn't understand anything about him. She didn't think he was deliberately cruel, but he *was* a bully.

"Does it occur to you that most fathers don't have to play the fear card with their children? Why do you think you have to buy us?"

Jed stood. "Be careful, Skye. You don't want to push me."

"I will if I have to," she said, and left.

On her way upstairs, she thought about how powerful her father was. He could be as ruthless as Garth.
This might very well be a battle to the death and she
had no idea who would win.

CHAPTER SIXTEEN

MITCH KNEW he'd made a serious mistake by agreeing to come to Erin's school and talk to the kids. He didn't have anything to say and he didn't want to scare them with his prosthesis. But Erin had insisted and apparently he couldn't tell her no. So he found himself walking down the halls of Titanville Elementary, looking for the right classroom.

What he spotted instead was a group of adults talking quietly in a hallway. He joined them, figuring this had to be the right place. A pretty blond woman with a name badge that read *Hi, I'm Monica* came up to him.

"Hi. I'm one of the teacher's aids."

"You must be Monica."

The woman frowned. "Have we met?"

He pointed to the badge.

"Oh, right. I forgot I was wearing it. Yes, that's me. My son is in this class. You are here with?"

"Erin Titan."

Monica's blue eyes brightened. "Erin's hero. It's nice to finally meet you."

If he'd been sure of his balance, he would have shifted uncomfortably. "I'm not a hero."

"Former SEAL?"

"Yeah."

"Wounded in action?"

"Uh-huh."

"Saved countless lives and you don't want to talk about it."

He shrugged. "Maybe."

"You have fulfilled the hero description. I'm sorry, but you're stuck with the title now. Come on. I'll show you where to wait." She led him to where the other adults stood and made a few introductions. Then she put her hand on his arm. "If you need anything, just let me know."

Her smile was sincere, her eyes wide with invitation. He might have been out of the dating game for a while, but he recognized interest when it slapped him in the face.

He watched Monica walk away, his gaze slipping to her butt, then down her legs.

She was appealing, he thought, belatedly realizing she hadn't been wearing a wedding band. He should probably take her up on her not-so-subtle come-on. They could go out. Get to know each other. Have sex.

All of which should have sounded really good... and it didn't. He didn't want blue eyes, he wanted green. A fiery redhead, not a blonde and the only fatherless kid he wanted in his life was Erin.

He swore silently. It had been nine years. Why couldn't he get Skye out of his head? Why did she have to be the one who got to him?

The door to the classroom opened and Erin came out. She shrieked when she saw him.

"You're here! You came."

"Of course I came."

She waved him into the room where they stood in back while a woman talked about how she rescued horses. A few minutes later, she finished and the kids applauded. Then Erin led him to the front of the room.

"This is Mitch Cassidy," she said proudly. "He owns the ranch next door and he's a real hero. He was a SEAL and fought in the war and protected our country and saved lots of lives." She started to go to her seat, then stopped.

"Oh. He lost part of his leg and now he has a metal one and it's really cool."

Several of the kids leaned forward eagerly.

"Can we see it?" one boy asked.

The teacher, a tall middle-aged woman, hesitated. "I'm sure our guest doesn't want to—"

"I don't mind," Mitch said, surprising himself and possibly the teacher. He drew up his jeans pant leg.

Several of the boys oohed while one girl covered her eyes.

"What happened?" a boy asked.

"I got in the way of an explosion. You don't want to do that. The explosion always wins."

"Did it hurt?"

"Before. Not now."

"Does your fake leg come off?"

"How do you stand in the shower?"

"Can you run faster or slower?"

The teacher raised both her hands. "Okay. One question at a time." She smiled at Mitch. "Unless you'd prefer to give your prepared talk."

"Not really," Mitch said. He had a few notes on what it was like to be a SEAL, but everything he'd written down had sounded stupid. Answering questions seemed easier.

"My leg comes off," he said. "I don't sleep with it. I don't run as fast as I used to, but I'm getting better. I can ride and walk and do pretty much anything you can do."

"What's it like being a hero?" one girl asked.

Skye slipped into the back of the room. Mitch looked good standing up in front of the class. Maybe too good. Looking at him made it tough to think.

She watched the emotions chase across his face and knew he was debating the whole "hero" part of the question. He accepted that Erin called him that but wouldn't think it of himself.

"I was doing a job," he said. "Taking care of my responsibilities. That's what people do—the right thing. Sometimes that meant being in danger." He settled on the corner of the teacher's desk. "Danger is a funny thing. It shows up when you don't expect it, so you don't have time to think. You act on instinct."

Several of the kids frowned, as if confused.

He saw it, too. "You just act. You don't have time for a plan. So you have to know what you're going to do before the danger shows up. Can anyone here tell me when you practice for danger?"

There was silence. The students got wide-eyed and looked at one another. Mitch casually pointed to the fire alarm on the wall.

"Fire drills!" one boy yelled.

"Right. You know how to leave the classroom and where to go in the yard."

"Did you have to practice?" a girl asked.

"Yes. All the time."

"So you could save people?"

"That's why I was there."

He talked about riding on navy ships and airplanes, about jumping from thousands of feet in the sky. He had them enthralled for nearly half an hour.

"I hate to interrupt," their teacher said, "but we have other special people here to speak. Thank you so much for coming."

Mitch waved at the kids. He paused by Erin's desk and spoke to her, then started for the door. Skye knew the exact moment he spotted her.

"What are you doing here?" he asked as he followed her into the hallway.

"I wanted to hear you speak."

"Why?"

"I thought it would be interesting."

They walked outside the building and stood in the parking lot.

She found herself oddly nervous. Had he always been so tall? Or maybe it was something else. Maybe it was Lexi and Dana's ridiculous claims that she was in love with him.

"Erin really appreciates that you did this," she said, staring at his chest. She couldn't seem to look into his eyes. "She was so excited that you were coming to her class."

"I was happy to do it. She's a good kid."

Skye risked raising her gaze. "I thought you'd hate her forever."

"For not being mine?"

She nodded.

"I thought about it," he admitted. "Then I realized if she was mine, she would be different and I don't want her to change."

It was the best thing he could have said.

"I'm glad," she whispered, then cleared her throat. "You were really good with the kids. They loved hearing you talk."

"Edited stories. The truth would keep them up for months."

She was sure of that. "You talked about rescuing people. Who rescued you?"

"A guy named Pete."

"A fellow SEAL?"

"Yes. He's a few years younger than me. Married. They're having their first baby." He looked past her. "He dragged me to safety, then went to get help. He could have been killed. He was shot himself, but did that slow him down? No way. He's back in Afghanistan right now."

He sounded angry. With himself?

"Mitch, you're getting a couple of medals for what happened. It's not like you just sat there and had a good cry."

He shrugged. "I laid down some cover. Got a couple of snipers."

While he was possibly bleeding to death with his leg blown off. Sure. Just another day at the office.

One of the teacher's aids walked up and joined them.

"Hi, Skye," Monica said. "Mitch, that was amazing. Thanks again for coming to speak to the kids. You were a hit. There's, um, going to be a reception later. You might like to come." Monica barely spared her a glance. "You, too, Skye."

A halfhearted invitation at best, Skye thought, trying not to step between Mitch and Monica. She saw the other woman's interest and, while she wanted to claim him as her own, she wasn't in any position to do that.

Annoyed, frustrated and not sure why, she gritted her teeth, excused herself and walked to her car. Monica and Mitch were still talking. Neither seemed to notice as she drove away.

Stupid man, she thought, turning the corner. He could date anyone he wanted. She wasn't interested in him. She never had been. He and Monica could get married and buy a house and she wouldn't care for one minute. They were both stupid and they deserved each other.

MITCH RODE that evening, after dinner. Sunset was later now that they were heading into early summer. He started toward the cattle, then turned Bullet and rode by the chickens.

Free-range chickens were held in by a perimeter fence that kept them from disappearing toward Oklahoma and protected them from predators. Coops traveled with them and as the sun set, the chickens bedded down for the night. He'd talked to Arturo and had discovered that Erin was right. The damn chickens were fed a coconut-based feed. All they needed was a little Reggae music and they could be on vacation.

But he'd grown used to seeing them on the land and he had to admit they left behind an effective fertilizer. Going organic had meant contracting with local farmers for certified feed. It was good business all around.

He stared at the land that stretched to the horizon. Now that he was back he wondered how he'd stayed away for those many years. Why hadn't he missed the Texas sky—bigger here than anywhere in the world? Why hadn't he wanted to ride by the herd, work the cattle dogs, eat Fidela's enchiladas and play chess with Arturo? He'd stayed away so long, he'd forgotten what home was like. Now that he was back he could see—

A dark shape moved across the open field, staying low and heading directly for the fence around the chickens. Mitch urged Bullet forward. He'd just checked the fencing a few days before. Was there a hole in it already?

He saw the opening seconds before the coyote dove for it. Without thinking, he reached for his shotgun, aimed and fired. The sound echoed in the night.

Inside their coops, the chickens began to shriek. The coyote, frightened but unharmed, raced in the opposite direction.

"Next time I won't fire a warning shot," Mitch yelled after it. The coyote didn't slow.

He slid off Bullet and walked toward the hole in the fence. The entire structure was moved every few days as the chickens ate the grubs and scratched at the grass. The corners and points of connection were vulnerable to separating, allowing coyotes and other predators a way in.

This opening was just the right size for a small coyote. Mitch fished out a few connectors and clamped them into place. It wasn't a permanent fix, but it would do for tonight. He and Arturo could put one of the guys on it tomorrow.

Then he turned back to Bullet, only to come to a

stop. There was no way he could get back in the saddle without a mounting block. The lights from the house twinkled in the distance. It was going to be a very long walk.

He grabbed Bullet's reins and led him a few feet. The horse stopped and looked at him. If Mitch didn't know better, he could swear the horse was telling him he was an idiot.

"Don't look at me like I'm stupid," he said. "I'm the higher mammal here."

Bullet shook his head. Mitch could swear he also rolled his eyes. Then he carefully lowered himself to the ground, crouching like a camel.

Mitch stared at him. "You're kidding," he muttered. "Why didn't anyone tell me you could do that?"

He settled on the saddle, hung on and Bullet struggled to his feet. When he was standing, Mitch patted his shoulder.

"I owe you, big guy. Oats for you, tonight."

Bullet turned his head and glanced at him, then headed for the ranch.

The house was in silhouette, a pretty place with welcoming lights. He could see Fidela moving in the kitchen. Arturo would be in his office or watching TV. It was a simple life, but it was his. For the first time in years, Mitch knew that he was home.

SKYE FINGERED the letter on her desk. "I wish you'd reconsider," she told Marianne. "We've done such good work together. You're an important part of what we do here."

Marianne coordinated all the local fund-raisers for the foundation and provided support for those interested in learning how to raise money to feed children.

She was barely thirty, with a new husband and a burning desire to make a difference.

"I appreciate the opportunities I've had here," Marianne said, not meeting Skye's gaze. "You've been really nice to work for and I really like all the people. I just feel it's time for me to make a change."

The last words were barely a mumble. If Skye hadn't been listening intently, she wouldn't have heard them. But she got the message and knew what it meant.

"Marianne, I swear to you, no senior staff has ever been paid a bonus and I have not taken a penny from this foundation. I don't even get a salary. That information is someone's idea of a bad practical joke. Trisha and our computer guys are working on solving the problem. We'll find what's wrong and fix it. Can't you give me a few more weeks? Haven't I earned your trust that much?"

She hated to beg, but in the past week, she'd already lost three good people.

"I have another offer," Marianne told her. "I start Monday. It's a smaller place and I won't make as much, but it's exciting and…"

"And you won't have to worry about your reputation," Skye said, trying not to sound bitter. "I understand."

In Marianne's position, she would probably do the same thing. Why not? Until Skye could prove her innocence, no one had any reason to believe her.

"I wish you the best," Skye told her. "If things don't work out at your new job, you're always welcome back here."

Marianne looked doubtful, as if she couldn't imagine wanting to return. Skye hoped that when the truth finally came out, she could salvage her reputation, but she wasn't sure. Garth had done some serious damage here.

Marianne left. Skye turned her chair so she could see out the window and wished she knew how to make things better. Where exactly had everything gone so wrong? At what moment had Garth decided to start his plan? Could he be stopped?

Her door burst open and a tall, geeky-looking guy stumbled into the room. His glasses hung halfway down his nose; his hair stuck up in fifteen directions and his clothes had a serious slept-in look.

"I found it," he announced with great pride. "I found it. I've been staying up all night and I wasn't sure I could, but I did." He paused, expectantly.

Skye stood. "Who are you?"

"Leonard." He pushed up his glasses. "I work in IT. I found where the breach is in the firewall. It's pretty slick." He said a bunch of stuff that didn't sound like any language she'd ever heard.

Skye raised her hands in the shape of a T. "Okay, Leonard. Talk more slowly and to those of us who barely know where the on button is on our computer."

"Oh. Right. Sorry." He smiled. "I got a little excited. The guy got through the firewall by piggy-backing on another program that we let in all the time. It's very complicated. A lot of work went into this. Once the Trojan horse got in, it went to work, opening up an easier access, then covered its tracks. So basically whoever is doing this can see everything we do online. Putting in a second set of books was a snap." He grinned at her.

It took her a second to absorb the information. "Can you stop it?"

"Sure, but I can do one better. I can send a program back that will start to capture information there. That way we can figure out who did this."

"Will it be legal proof?"

Leonard shifted uncomfortably. "Um, no. Tapping into someone's computer without a warrant isn't legal. But it would give you a place to start."

"I already have an idea of who's paying the guy," she said. "I just don't know who's cashing the checks and doing the actual work. How illegal is it?"

"I don't know."

Skye didn't, either. She didn't want Leonard or

herself going to jail, but she was tired of Garth being one step ahead of her.

"If we found out who was doing this, we could stop him, right?" she asked.

"Yes," Leonard told her.

"Give me a second." She grabbed the phone and dialed from memory.

"Why are you calling me at work?" Dana said by way of greeting. "Is this an emergency? Did you mean to call nine-one-one?"

"Is tapping into someone's computer really illegal or only a little bad? I mean are we talking about a slap on the wrist or time as Bubba's love slave?"

"You'd be in a women's facility, so you wouldn't know Bubba and I can't believe you asked me that," Dana said. "Don't ask me about illegal stuff. I do not want to arrest my friend."

"I have a computer genius standing in my office. He found out how Garth got into my system and can send a program back that will help us identify who he used to hack in and where he is."

There was a long pause. "Skye, don't ask me this. I'm serious. I love you, but I'm not breaking the law for you. And I'm not helping you do it, either. So just stop. We'll get Garth another way."

"I had a feeling you were going to say that. Okay. I'll talk to you later."

Dana hung up and Skye did the same.

"Leonard, I can't ask you to do this. It's illegal and I have no idea how much trouble we'd be in. You don't want to be a part of that."

He looked disappointed. "Yes, ma'am," he said. "If you change your mind, let me know."

"I will."

He left.

Skye sat at her desk and wished they didn't have to be the good guys. Life would be much easier to handle if they had the same lack of concern for the law Garth showed.

Her phone rang. "Dana, tell me you've had a change of heart," she said as she picked up the receiver.

"Skye Titan?" a man asked.

She could barely hear him. There was a horrible loud rushing sound in the background. "Yes."

"This is Daryl Green. I work with Izzy on the rig. There's been an explosion. Izzy's hurt. She's in a helicopter right now, heading for Dallas."

Skye stopped breathing. "Hurt? What happened?"

"We don't know what happened yet. There was a flash and then it all went to hell. She's alive. I know that much." He gave her the name of the hospital and then hung up.

Skye felt sick and scared and frantic. Izzy hurt? An explosion? That had to be bad. What if it was serious? What if she died?

Her fingers shook as she reached for her purse and keys. She had to get to the hospital so she was there when Izzy arrived. She had to tell Lexi and their father. She had to ask Fidela to pick up Erin at the bus stop.

Izzy, she thought as she hurried to the door. Izzy who had believed she was safe from Garth. That she had nothing to lose.

CHAPTER SEVENTEEN

LEXI WAS ALREADY at the hospital when Skye arrived. They hugged in the hallway.

"What do you know?" Skye asked.

"Nothing. She's in surgery. I can't get anyone to talk to me." Lexi looked pale and upset. "I can't believe this is happening. I can't believe she's hurt."

Skye held her close. She wanted to cry, but there weren't any tears. Just guilt. Somehow this was her fault. If she hadn't fought with Izzy over something totally ridiculous, none of this would have happened.

The familiar hospital smells reminded her of Ray's last days, and standing there was too much like the endless waiting she'd endured.

"She can't die," Skye breathed. Not Izzy. Not like this.

Rapid footsteps made her look up. Dana hurried toward them.

"How is she?" she demanded. "What are they doing?"

Both Lexi and Skye looked at her. "We don't know," Lexi said. "The doctors aren't—"

"Fine. I'll get information. You two sit down. What about Jed. Has anyone told him?"

"I left a message on his cell and with his assistant," Skye said, feeling stunned by everything. She couldn't think. Too much had happened too fast. She couldn't catch her breath. "I'll keep calling."

Dana led them to chairs. "Sit," she instructed. "I'll be right back."

Skye and Lexi sank down, then Skye sprang up and started to pace. "We have to do something. It's Izzy."

"I know." Lexi's eyes filled with tears. "What if she…"

"No!" Skye said. "She'll be fine. She's our sister and she'll be fine." If she wasn't, Skye would take out Garth. She didn't know when or how, but she would leave him broken and bleeding on the side of the road. Nobody messed with her sister.

Dana returned a few minutes later. "She's still in surgery. They should be finished within the hour. Her vitals are strong and she doesn't appear to have any internal injuries. There are a few burns from the explosion. We'll know more when they're done."

Lexi stared at her. "How did you get them to talk to you?"

Dana pointed to herself. "The uniform helps."

Skye hadn't even noticed Dana was dressed for work.

"Whatever it takes," Lexi murmured.

"Is Cruz coming?" Dana asked.

Lexi nodded.

"Good. We're going to check to see if he's here," Dana said. "Lexi, sit here and rest. We'll be right back."

Skye glanced back at her sister as they made their way down the hallway. "Do you think she's all right, with the baby and all? This is a shock and that can't be good."

"Lexi is strong. Once Cruz gets here, he'll fuss and that will help. How are you holding up?"

"I'm not. This is my fault."

Dana rolled her eyes. "Don't be an idiot. Garth paid some asshole to blow up an oil rig. Nothing about that is your fault."

"We fought."

"And if you hadn't fought Garth wouldn't have made this happen?"

Skye rubbed her temples. "Oh, sure. Use logic. That's fair. Okay. Technically, this isn't my fault, but I feel guilty. How's that?"

"Better." Dana glanced around, as if making sure they were alone. "Do you have the name and number of the computer guy? The one who could get into Garth's system?"

"Sure. Leonard. I have his number at work. Why?"

"As soon as Cruz gets here to take care of Lexi, I want you to give me the number." Dana's eyes blazed with fury. "No one hurts one of my friends and gets away with it. Garth crossed the line with this and I'll do whatever it takes to make sure he doesn't hurt you guys again."

Skye felt weary. "Dana, no. You're a deputy. You can't break the law."

"Why not?"

"Because you have more to lose."

"Izzy is like a sister to me. I could have lost her today. It doesn't get worse than that. Give me the number. If anyone asks, tell them I thought he was hot and wanted to ask him out."

Skye hugged her friend. Dana held on tight.

"We'll get through this," Skye murmured. "I swear we will."

"I know. And when Izzy's all better, we'll make Garth sorry he was ever born."

"I can't wait."

"I swear to you, Skye, I will personally arrest Garth Duncan and throw his ass in jail."

"I believe you."

IT WAS NEARLY TWO in the morning when Skye left the hospital. She drove to the Cassidy Ranch to collect Erin. Earlier, she'd spoken briefly with her daughter, who was concerned about her aunt but also having lots of fun with Fidela, Arturo and Mitch.

She parked in front of the house. The porch light was on, as was a lamp in the front room. The door opened before she'd made it to the porch.

Mitch stood there, looking strong and capable.

She'd been unable to cry at the hospital but the second she saw him, she felt the tears on her cheeks. She flew across the grass and launched herself at him.

He caught her and held on as if he would never let go.

"He could have killed her," she said with a sob. "She might be dead now."

Mitch kissed her forehead. When she straightened, he pushed the hair from her face and wiped her cheeks.

"But he didn't," he said. "She's okay, right?"

Skye gulped then nodded, feeling better in his arms. Knowing Mitch was with her meant she didn't have to be strong all on her own. She could lean on him a little. "It could be a lot worse. She has a lot of bruises, a few burns. Nothing's broken. But…" She stared at him. "She might be blind."

Mitch swore. "Are they sure?"

"Not yet. They say she's going to have to do some healing. In a few days we should know more. But the doctors made it clear it was a serious possibility."

Mitch put his arm around her and led her inside. She collapsed on the sofa and covered her face. "This is Izzy. She's so full of life. She loves adventure. She can't be blind. How can she go cave diving if she's blind? How can she swim with sharks and all that other stupid stuff she does?"

"You don't know she's blind yet," Mitch said, settling next to her and putting his arm around her shoulders.

"I know, but what if she is? What if she's never okay?"

He didn't answer. The truth was if she was blind, Izzy would deal. She would figure it out, make a life for herself and move on. That's what people did. Sure, a few got stuck in self-pity but eventually even that got boring. Not anything Skye needed to hear right now.

She leaned against him. "I have to be strong. I have to get it together. Izzy needs me. What have I got to cry about?"

"A lot and you don't have to be strong tonight. I'll handle things."

"Erin will want to know Izzy's okay."

"It's nearly three in the *morning*, Skye. She's a kid. Let her sleep. You can pick her up in the *morning*. Or better yet, stay here."

She sniffed. "Is she okay?"

"She was worried, but we kept her distracted. Fidela read to her until she fell asleep."

"Think that would work for me?"

"We can try it if you want."

"Thanks, but I need to get home."

"No, you don't." He stood and pulled her to her feet. "Come on. You can sleep in the second guest room. That way you'll be here when Erin wakes up. You'll both feel better being in the same house."

She hesitated, then nodded. He led her upstairs. He wanted to take her to his room, not to make love with her, but to hold her. He wanted to put his arms around her and physically keep her safe. But there was Erin to think about. If Skye's daughter woke up before them, it would confuse her to find her mom in his bed. So he kept going to the end of the hall and pushed open the door.

She stepped inside, then turned back to him. "Thank you," she whispered. "For everything."

He kissed her forehead. "Try to sleep. If you need anything, I'm across the hall. The bathroom is through there." He pointed to the door to the right.

"Okay, thanks."

He pulled the door nearly closed, then went into his room. Once there, he crossed to the window and stared out at the night. Garth had to be stopped. This had gone too far. Without evidence, the police couldn't make a move so it was up to him.

THE MAIN OFFICES for Cruz Control were done in red and black. All the artwork reflected the car theme and racing stripes led the way down the hall.

Mitch sat in Cruz's office, where car parts battled for space with every car magazine known to man.

"The local police are reluctant to get involved," Mitch told Cruz. "The explosion was in international waters and the oil rig is owned by a British company."

"Are they still considering what happened at Skye's party a prank?"

Mitch nodded. He'd spent a frustrating morning speaking with a detective who had been sympathetic but unhelpful. "Without definitive proof that Garth is determined to bring down the family, the events are all unrelated and seemingly random. Rumors aren't against the law."

"It's more than rumors," Cruz said, sounding angry. "What about doping Jed's horses and the lawsuit against Lexi?"

"Wasn't that dropped?"

"Yes, but that isn't the point."

"It is to them. Dana will do all she can, but we're pretty much on our own."

"You have a plan?" Cruz asked.

"Yes."

"Then consider me your partner in crime," Cruz said, his voice determined.

"Agreed."

SKYE SAT in the chair by the bed and stroked her sister's hand. Izzy lay on the hospital bed, her face nearly as white as the bandages around her eyes. There were angry red marks on her bare arms and bandages on her hands. One leg was propped up under the covers.

"That's starting to get on my nerves," Izzy said, pulling her hand free of Skye's. "You're patting me like a cat."

"And yet you don't purr," Skye told her. "Were you sleeping? It's hard to tell with the bandages."

"My personal fashion statement. No, I'm not

sleeping." She grabbed Skye's hand. "Just don't do the petting thing, okay?"

"You're so fussy. I'll have you know I'm wildly busy. You should be grateful I'm taking time out of my schedule to be here at all."

"Yeah, yeah. You were worried about me."

"Only a little." Skye did her best to keep her voice light. "How do you feel?"

"Like I got blown up and tossed in the Gulf. How do I look?"

"Battered and waifish. Do you need me to call a nurse?"

"Only if he's male and cute." She shifted and winced. "Otherwise, I'll pass." She gestured to the IV running into her other arm. "I have my own supply of drugs to dull everything. Life doesn't get much better than that."

Izzy had been sleeping steadily since her surgery two nights ago. When she woke up, she was coherent and as normal as could be expected under the circumstances. Every time she spoke and made a joke, Skye wanted to run into the hallway, telling the world her sister was going to be okay.

She managed to hold back, but just barely.

"You want to talk about what the doctor said?" Skye asked tentatively.

"No."

"We have to at some point."

"No, we don't."

"Izzy, you're going to need the surgery."

"Skye, I swear I can still kick you, so leave me alone."

"For now."

Izzy groaned. "I'm gritting my teeth. Do you see me gritting my teeth?" She drew back her lips. "Are you looking?"

"Very clenched."

"Good. Talk about something else."

They would have to talk about the surgery eventually, but the doctor had said there was time. Skye would listen to him, although what she really wanted was for Izzy to schedule it right away. To get it done with so she could be herself again.

"You were right about T.J.," she said instead.

Izzy sighed. "Being right is one of my favorite things."

"I know."

Izzy turned toward her. "Right in what way? Did he hurt you? I swear if he hurt you…"

Skye squeezed her hand and fought tears. "Nothing that dramatic. Oh, Izzy, I'm sorry we've been fighting. I've felt awful about that."

"I staged the explosion for just this reaction. I love it when a plan goes well."

"It worked perfectly. I was so angry at you and I can't even say why."

"I wasn't trying to hurt you or say you couldn't get the guy. There was just something about him."

"He was working for Garth."

"What?" Izzy nearly rose into a sitting position before falling back onto the bed. "No way."

"Oh, yeah. He was being paid and everything. I don't know if it was to actually try to get me engaged or to play us against each other."

"I'll bet he was just supposed to make trouble."

"And we played right into his hands," Skye said with a sigh.

"You more so than me," Izzy told her.

"As always, your support brings me such joy."

Izzy smiled, then the smile faded. "Working for Garth. That asshole."

"Tell me about it. Are you okay? Did you care about T.J.?"

"No. He was mildly interesting." She squeezed Skye's fingers. "I'm sorry I slept with him. I wasn't trying to hurt you."

"You were a little."

Izzy hesitated. "Maybe. You're very sanctimonious sometimes with your perfect life."

"My life isn't perfect."

"Of course it is. You're a great mother raising a great kid. You started a foundation to feed hungry children. How are the rest of us supposed to compete with that?"

Skye didn't know what to say. "It's not a competition."

"Sometimes it feels like it. Lexi is all smart and

business-y. You're like Mother Teresa with breasts and red hair and I'm the idiot who gets blown up."

"Don't say that," Skye told her, fighting tears. "You're my sister and I love you. I don't know what happened with T.J. I really don't. He pushed our buttons, that's for sure. You're all sexy and adventurous. Guys are into that."

"Maybe." She touched the bandages on her eyes with her free hand. "How did you find out about T.J.?"

"Mitch heard him talking to Garth. But I should probably tell you that after you told me you'd slept with T.J. and he was still planning to go out to dinner with me, I decided to teach him a lesson."

Izzy grinned. "Yeah?"

"Uh-huh." Skye told her about the dinner and the not-so-subtle invitation to bed. "He jumped at it, which is disgusting. He'd just been with you. So I told him off."

Izzy laughed. "On the sidewalk?"

"Right outside the restaurant. After I had his car towed."

"Go, Skye."

"Thank you. It felt good. Then I called Lexi and we've been spreading some very nasty rumors about him. Everything from him being bad in bed to embezzlement to having a dick the size of a peanut."

"So I was seriously flirting with danger by pissing you off," Izzy said.

"You were, but you've always been brave. Which

is why I know you'll want to schedule the surgery right away."

Izzy pulled her hand free. "That wasn't a very smooth transition."

"Come on. You know you're going to do this."

"I don't know. I have to think about it."

"What's to think about?"

"Total blindness."

"If you don't have the surgery, you'll be stuck where you are."

"Until the bandages come off, I don't know what that means. It's my decision, Skye. Back off."

"But you have to—"

Izzy pointed in the general direction of the door. "Aren't visiting hours over? Shouldn't you be leaving?"

"Izzy, don't. I'll stop talking about it."

"Just go. I'm tired. I don't want to talk anymore. Go on. You can come back later."

Skye wasn't sure what to do. After a few seconds, she rose and kissed her sister's cheek. "I'm sorry. I won't mention it again."

"Like I believe that."

"I'll be by later."

"It's not like I'm going anywhere."

Skye left. Everything had gone great with the visit, right up until the end. Why couldn't she leave well enough alone? Why did she have to push?

She paused in the hallway, not sure what to do. Should she wait and see her sister in a couple of hours or come back later? Before she could decide, she saw a man walking toward her.

Every part of her went still, as if knowing he was here made her world right again. She didn't have to decide on her own. She could ask his opinion because he would tell her what he thought and he thought things through. He was tough and difficult and smart and sexy and he made her laugh. He protected her and Erin. He was someone she could depend on. Just as important, she burned for him.

She walked toward him. When they were next to each other, he pulled her close.

"You okay?" Mitch asked.

"No. Izzy and I had a fight. I was pushing. Why do I do that? She's still in the hospital. I shouldn't be pushing."

He led her over to a couple of plastic chairs in an alcove. They sat down. He laced their fingers together.

"Why were you fighting?"

"She needs surgery. The doctors can't know for sure, but they expect her eyesight to be at about thirty percent when the bandages come off. It should stabilize there, but there's also a chance it could get worse."

"That has to scare the hell out of her," he said.

"It does. But it can all be fixed with surgery. They can repair the damage and restore her to full sight. She'll be better than new."

Mitch's dark eyes stared into her. "What's the downside?"

"If the surgery goes wrong, she'll be totally blind. The odds are tiny. The surgeon has never had it happen. But Izzy hasn't scheduled the operation. I was pushing her to get it done, to get everything fixed, then move on. She won't."

"It's only been a couple of days. Give her time. She's adjusting to a lot."

She wanted to snatch back her hand but was determined not to act like a five-year-old. "Are you taking her side?"

"Yes."

"Why?"

"Because there's no reason to rush the surgery. She has time. Let her come to terms with what's happened to her. It's a big shock."

Her gaze dropped to his leg. In his jeans and boots, she couldn't see the proof that he knew what he was talking about but it was there.

"Have I mentioned I hate it when you're reasonable?" she asked.

"No, but I'm not surprised."

That made her smile. She drew in a breath. "Fine. I'll let it go for now. You're right. There's no huge rush. It's just this isn't like her. She doesn't usually react so passively."

"She just got blown up, Skye. Give her a break."

"There's that logic thing again. She's my sister. I want her to be okay."

"She will be." He glanced at his watch. "Are

you going to stay here? Do you want me to meet
Erin's bus?"

Because her daughter would be home in a couple of
hours after her last day of school. Because someone
had to be there for her. But Erin wasn't his responsibility. Not that the information would stop Mitch.
He would do the right thing because that's the kind
of guy he was.

She thought about what had happened nine years
ago, when her father had scared her into leaving
Mitch. How she'd reacted without thinking and by
the time she could finally think it all through, it was
too late. She was pregnant with Erin.

She grabbed Mitch's other hand and held on tight.
"I loved Ray," she said, staring into his eyes.

He tried to pull back, but she didn't let go.

"I loved Ray," she repeated. "Not at first. But over
time. Sure he had issues—what on earth was he
doing wanting to marry someone so young? But he
was a good man and I appreciated that. I won't take
anything away from him by claiming not to have
loved him."

Mitch narrowed his gaze. "Is there a point to this?"

"Yes. I loved him, but I was never *in love* with
him. I never felt the fire, the passion. When he died,
I cried more out of guilt for not being able to give him
my heart than because he was gone. He wanted all
of me and I couldn't give him that."

She swallowed. "He's Erin's father, but I'm not

sure how long she'll remember him. His kids don't want anything to do with her, which is their loss, but a position they're unlikely to change."

He'd tensed. "Again, your point would be?"

"I never stopped loving you. Not for a minute. I pretended I did—I lived my life—but you were everything to me and you still are."

He jerked free and pushed to his feet. "Why are you saying this?"

She rose and faced him. "Because it's true. I want you to know that you have always been the one. I doubt I'm capable of loving anyone else. I don't expect anything, Mitch. I just needed you to know that I'm sorry I didn't have the courage to fight for you nine years ago. I'm sorry for what we both went through, and yet I wouldn't change it—learning to be a wife to Ray and having Erin have made me a better person. We're both so different now, but nothing in my heart has changed. I love you."

He'd come to terms with the past, and he was ready to be a good guy in her life—but love? Didn't she know those kind of words could kill? He didn't want to hear them. Not now. Not this way. Not yet.

He swore silently. She looked so damned sincere. As if she hadn't burned him down to his heart…the heart that doubted it could survive a second beating from her.

"I don't believe you," he said flatly. Because it was easier…safer.

She gave him a sad smile. "I'm not surprised. Why would you? Why would you trust me? If me loving you means anything, then let me earn back that trust. I'm happy to do the work. I'll earn your respect. I love you, Mitch. Nothing is going to change that. I've learned my lesson. I know what matters. I'm not going anywhere. Just think about it, please. Consider the possibility that after all this time, maybe we've found our way back to each other."

He didn't know what to say. It was everything he wanted to hear but it was also everything he was afraid of. Could he make himself that vulnerable to Skye, again? It was too much. So he turned and left without saying anything.

When he was back in his truck, he clutched the steering wheel hard enough to turn his knuckles white. It was that or put his fist through the window.

Why did she have to look so earnest? Why did he want to believe her?

His cell phone rang, but he ignored it. After starting the truck he drove back to the ranch. The phone rang every couple of minutes. Skye was nothing if not persistent but he needed time.

But when he pulled in front of the house, Fidela rush out to him.

"I've been calling," she said, sounding frantic. She twisted her hands together. "Oh, Mitch, I'm so sorry. It's bad. It's very bad."

CHAPTER EIGHTEEN

"PETE'S DEAD?" MITCH repeated stupidly. No way. Pete couldn't be dead. It wasn't right—he'd saved Mitch, he had a baby on the way.

"I'm sorry," Fidela told him, tears filling her eyes. "His brother called. I have the number."

Mitch couldn't feel anything—not pain or anger or regret. There was only a cold numbness that fogged his brain.

He took the number and stared at it as he tried to figure out the next step. Then he grabbed the phone and dialed.

"Hello?"

"This is Mitch Cassidy. I'm looking for Zane."

"That's me." The other man sounded tired. "Thanks for calling. You heard?"

"About Pete? I'm sorry. He was the best."

"I know." Zane's voice cracked. "Look, he talked about you all the time. We all know about you, how you saved his life."

Saved Pete? "He's the one who dragged *me* to cover."

"Yeah, but you held off the snipers. He loved you, man. I know you were hurt so I don't know if this would be asking too much, but we'd like you to come to the funeral. Lisa, his wife, wants to meet you."

Because they'd never met. Mitch felt he knew her, but that was all through Pete.

"When and where," Mitch said, the numbness wearing off. "Just tell me and I'll be there."

He wrote down the information and promised to call with the flight information. The funeral would be in three days. Full military. They wanted him to speak. He had no idea what to say.

"I'll call Skye," Fidela said when she hung up.

"No. Don't bother her."

"She should know."

"No."

He couldn't talk to her right now, couldn't talk to anyone. Rather than fight about it, he left and headed for the barn, where he saddled Bullet and took him out.

He waited until they'd passed the house before giving the horse his head and hanging on for the ride. It took Bullet a few seconds to realize he wasn't going to be held back, then he took off, his long stride covering ground. Mitch bent low over his horse's neck. Wind burned his eyes and pulled at his shirt. He wanted to go forever, but knew that no matter how fast they went, he couldn't outrun Pete's death.

Skye's car was parked behind the house when he

got back. Both he and the horse were breathing heavily, although Bullet had done all the hard work. He slid out of the saddle and walked his horse in, moving past Skye without speaking. She followed him into the barn.

"I heard," she said, coming up behind him. "I'm sorry, Mitch. I know Pete was your friend."

"Uh-huh."

"Fidela called me," she added, as if he hadn't guessed that.

"She should learn to mind her own business."

"She cares about you. I want to help."

He pulled off the saddle and the blanket, then began to walk the horse to cool him. His leg ached, but he didn't care. Nothing much mattered anymore.

"You're going to the funeral," she said. "Let me help with that. I'll make the arrangements. I can go with you, if you want. Or not. Let me help. There's not much else I can do, so let me do this."

He looked at her and instead saw Pete laughing. Pete had found nearly everything about life inherently funny. He enjoyed the early mornings, the nights of waiting, the rush of jumping out of a plane.

"His wife is pregnant," Mitch said.

"I know. That must make her feel both better and worse. She'll always have a part of her husband alive, but he won't know his child."

"Pete was so damn proud. He kept talking about how he came from a long line of good swimmers."

Skye frowned. "Don't you have to be a good swimmer to be a SEAL?"

"Sperm," he said. "He was talking about his sperm. Lisa got pregnant the first night they tried. We all thought the sonogram picture looked like an alien, but Pete claimed the baby was all him. Even had the family sports equipment." He glanced at her. "That means—"

"I know what it means." She gave him a faint smile. "He sounds like a good guy. Fidela told me when the funeral is. You can fly out that morning. Do you want to spend the night?"

"No. I'll come back."

"Fine. I'll make the arrangements."

She hesitated, as if she wanted to say more. Or maybe she just wanted him to say something. But he didn't have any words. Not yet. He couldn't think about what she'd told him earlier. Love? Not today. Not with Pete gone.

"Thank you," he said, standing next to Bullet and patting the horse's neck.

"You're welcome. If you need anything, just let me know."

He nodded.

She walked back toward her car. When she was nearly there, he called, "Wait."

She looked at him.

"Can you come with me?"

"Of course. I'll clear the day."

"I won't be good company. I'll probably act like a jerk."

"You do have practice."

One corner of his mouth twitched. "Nice. Potshots at the cripple."

"I do what I can." She opened her car door. "I'm sorry, Mitch. I wish there was something magic I could say to make it all better."

"Me, too."

THE RICH REALLY were different, Mitch thought as he moved down the steps of the private plane Skye had arranged for their flight to Phoenix. A black Town Car waited on the tarmac of the private airport. She joined him in the back of the car.

"You doing all right?" she asked.

"Nice car."

"I thought it would be easier to have someone else do the driving." She looked at him. "You don't want to tell me if you're okay?"

"I don't want to talk about my feelings." They were too close to the surface. The funeral was going to be hard enough to get through as it was.

"I understand," she said and touched his arm.

She'd dressed in a black suit and pulled her hair back. She looked dignified and serious. Did dealing with this make her remember Ray's death?

For the first time since he'd heard the news about Pete, he allowed himself to think about what she'd said to him. That while Ray would always matter, she'd never stopped loving him.

Was it true? Did he want it to be true? Could he trust her?

Not the time or place, he told himself, but he was glad she was with him.

She put her hand in his. "If you need to yell or fight," she said quietly, "just let me know. I'll argue or be annoying. I'm good at both."

He nodded. "Thanks."

They arrived at the church. Skye got out of the car, then waited for Mitch to join her. He took so long, she wondered if he'd changed his mind. Then he climbed out and stood on the sidewalk, looking as if someone had shot him.

There were well over a hundred people outside the church. Mitch stayed close as he introduced her to a few people he knew. They were all men, SEALs she would guess. Strong and confident, they moved easily through the crowd. But there was a restlessness about them—as though if they stopped *moving* they would have to deal with the loss of one of their own.

The service was difficult to get through, Skye thought two hours later, and she'd never known Pete. Several people had told *moving* stories about what he'd been like as a young man. Mitch talked about how Pete had saved him. He glossed over what must have been a terrifying and dangerous situation, instead focusing on how Pete was a funny, easygoing man who didn't believe he was a hero. Sort of like Mitch himself.

Once they went to the graveside, they stood through a military burial. At the end, an obviously pregnant widow came up and spoke to Mitch. Skye didn't hear what she was saying, but it was enough for Mitch to tightly hug her, then turn to Skye and say they had to leave.

He was quiet on the drive back to the airport. Once they'd cleared Phoenix airspace on their way back to Dallas, he leaned back in his seat and closed his eyes.

"It should have been me," he said quietly. "I should have been the one to die. Not Pete."

"You weren't even there," she told him. "How could you have taken his place?"

"I don't know, but this is wrong. He's a good guy."

"From what I learned about him today, he wouldn't want anyone to take his place. That wasn't his way. He died in a firefight, doing something he believed in. Am I wrong?"

Mitch didn't look at her. "It should have been me. He's got a kid he'll never see. A wife. A family."

Skye wanted to tell Mitch he could have all those things, too. It hurt so much to see him this way, to feel his pain, and not be able to do anything to help.

"You're the one who's here," she murmured. "Wouldn't Pete tell you not to waste the opportunity?"

"Maybe."

She wanted to push but didn't. Later they would talk, but for now she forced herself to stay quiet.

They'd driven together in his truck. When they reached Glory's Gate, she leaned over and turned off the engine.

"What are you doing?"

"Erin's spending the night with Lexi and Cruz. My dad is gone. Come inside."

He hesitated. "I won't be very good company."

"We're not going to talk."

She thought he might refuse. That he would wait until she got out of the truck, then drive away. But he didn't. He collected the keys and followed her inside.

She led the way upstairs, to her bedroom and closed the door behind him.

Once there, she stepped close and put her hands on his shoulders.

"I'm sorry," she whispered, then pressed her lips to his.

He reacted instantly, grabbing her around the waist, holding on as if he would never let go. His mouth claimed hers, demanding, taking, then suddenly gentling to barely a whisper of contact. He kissed her over and over again, tender kisses that offered every part of him.

Surrender wasn't necessary—she'd given herself to him the first time they'd made love nine years ago and there was a part of her she'd never reclaimed. It came to life now, burning for him, but also feeling, embracing, wanting more than just the passion that always flared between them. She wanted the connection.

He ran his hands up and down her back, then pushed off her suit jacket. It fell to the floor. He licked her lower lip. She parted for him and he swept inside.

Their tongues played a game of tag, teasing, dancing, before the need began to grow. She tilted her head. He deepened the kiss. She pushed off his jacket. It was the first time she'd ever seen him wear a suit and he'd looked good. But right now she wanted to touch bare skin, be close to him. Make love.

He stroked her face then moved his fingers into her hair. One by one, he pulled the pins free until her hair tumbled down her back. He buried his fingers in the soft curls.

She worked on his tie, first loosening it, then tugging it until she could let it drop to the floor. He unzipped her skirt and it puddled around her feet.

She stepped out of her pumps. He moved down her back to her butt, where he grabbed her and squeezed. She shifted toward him, bringing her belly in contact with his arousal.

He was already hard. She rubbed against him, wanting to feel his erection, wanting to know he wanted this, too. She was already wet and hungry.

He slid his hands under her blouse, up to her breasts. There he made quick work of the front closure on her bra. He pushed the cups aside and cupped her curves in his big hands.

He continued to kiss her. His warm fingers stroking her skin made it difficult to think. When he brushed her nipples with his thumbs, fire shot through her. She wanted to cry out, but contented herself with a soft moan, then closed her mouth around his tongue and sucked. He tensed. Then he backed her toward the bed.

When her thighs bumped the mattress, she lost her balance and abruptly sat. He unfastened the buttons and shrugged out of his shirt, then reached for his belt buckle, only to pause. His eyes locked with hers.

She didn't have to ask what was wrong—she knew. Just like she knew his hesitation had as much to do with him as with her.

They'd had sex twice before. It had been hot and fast and possibly safer for him because they'd never undressed. She'd never actually seen him naked since his return. She'd never had to deal with his amputation directly and he'd never had to deal with her reaction.

Without saying anything, while still holding his gaze, she pushed him back a step so she could stand. She pulled off her blouse and let her bra fall to the ground. Then she stepped out of her black panties. When she was completely naked, she took his hand and guided it to between her thighs.

"I want you," she whispered, moaning as he explored her swollen center.

He rubbed all over, sliding against that one spot of pleasure before thrusting a finger inside of her. She grabbed onto his shoulders to keep herself from falling. Her eyes fluttered closed.

He moved in and out, filling her, then leaving her empty and wanting. Her insides tightened around him, trying to get more. There was something about the way he touched her—it had never taken much to get her over the top.

"Skye," he whispered, as he withdrew his hand. "We have to talk."

She did her best not to whimper that talking wasn't what she needed right now.

She put her hands on his shoulders and smiled at him. "So talk."

"I'm having trouble concentrating. You're naked."

She smiled. "I know. I want you to be comfortable."

He glanced down at his erection. "Comfortable isn't the word I'd use." He returned his gaze to her face. "It's not horrible, but it's a shock."

"I'm pretty clear on what to expect." She'd been doing some reading online. She'd seen pictures. None of which had been Mitch, but she was reasonably confident she could manage without reacting.

"I want to be inside of you. I want to be on top." He hesitated. "I'm not sure how to make that work."

Why would he have a problem being...

Leverage, she thought, answering her own question. Everything would be different. He couldn't brace himself the same way.

"Then we'll just have to practice and practice until

we get it right," she said with a smile. "It's a sacrifice I'm willing to make because that's just the kind
of person I am."

He didn't return her smile. She read the worry in
his eyes and wished she knew how to make him feel
better. Probably the only way to reassure him was to
go through the experience.

She stepped aside and urged him to sit. Then she
knelt on the carpet and removed both his shoes and
socks. Underneath the left sock was the smooth
plastic of his artificial foot.

Unexpected sadness flooded her. Sadness for what
he'd been through and what he'd lost. He wasn't alone
in that. Hundreds of others had suffered the same way.

But thinking about that wasn't helping. She had
to focus on Mitch, on being with him, on letting him
know that she loved all of him.

She straightened, then reached for his belt, but
before she could touch it, he grabbed her around the
waist and pulled her close. He buried his face between
her breasts and groaned, then turned his head and
drew her right nipple into his mouth.

The sweet tugging caused her insides to clench. She
held on to him and lost herself in the sensation. Then
his fingers were between her legs, searching, finding,
rubbing, thrusting. He used his thumb to caress her
center while moving his fingers in and out of her.

She tightened her muscles as the need washed
over her. She was already close and getting closer by

the second. Her orgasm was just out of reach. A few more seconds and she would be there.

She cupped his head and ran her fingers through his hair as he moved from breast to breast. Almost, she thought desperately. Almost. Then she would—

She pulled herself away. It was agony as her body whimpered in protest.

"You're trying to distract me," she said, barely able to see straight.

He shrugged. "Maybe a little. You're also naked, Skye. What am I supposed to do? Ignore that?"

She unfastened his belt. "No. You're supposed to join me."

He pushed her hands away and stood. His suit slacks fell. She didn't look away from his eyes.

"Almost," she teased. "I'm talking naked, cowboy."

"You have to look."

For her or for him? Did it matter?

He sat back on the bed and tossed away his slacks. She sat next to him and looked down at the prosthesis, then he removed it and slid off the protective sock.

It was wrong, she thought sadly, staring at the place where his calf had once been. There was nothing there. Just a smooth curve of skin and a few fading scars.

"I thought it would be more dramatic," she said without thinking.

"Meaning?"

"At least some background music and a drumroll."

He stared at her. For a second she thought he was going to get pissed off. Instead he started to laugh. When she joined in, he put his arm around her waist and pulled her onto the mattress. Then he was on top of her and they were kissing and nothing else mattered.

He claimed her mouth with a desperation that left her breathless. His hands roamed her body, finding all the places that made her squirm. Well, all the places but one. No matter how she flexed her hips and silently willed him to *touch* her there, he ignored that place between her legs.

He moved lower, kissing her neck, then her breasts. He licked his way down her belly.

She knew where this was going, what he would do, and nearly screamed for him to hurry. Hunger burned inside of her. She'd already been close once—it wouldn't take much to push her over the edge.

Finally he moved between her thighs, parted her and then kissed her intimately. He used his lips and tongue to arouse her to the point of mindlessness, licking and sucking until she wanted to scream. At the same time he slipped a finger inside of her.

The combination was too much, she thought as her body tensed. She pushed toward him, wanting more, wanting all of it. There was a moment of certainty, a promise, then she was coming and shuddering, calling out his name, begging him never to stop.

He continued to touch her until she stilled, then he rolled away. Seconds later he was back, kneeling between her legs. She reached for him to guide him inside of her. As his thick hardness filled her, nerve endings began to dance.

It was perfect, she thought as she stared into his eyes. He fit her as if he'd been made for her—stretching her just enough, finding exactly the right, delicious spot when he thrust in all the way.

They quickly created their perfect rhythm. Their gazes locked. She felt herself getting closer again, but was determined to hold back until he was falling, too.

Familiar tension filled her. The need was there, pushing her onward. She found herself trying to think about other things, which made her want to laugh.

"What?" he asked, still moving in and out of her.

"I'm waiting for you."

He grinned. "I'm enjoying the moment. It's easy. I didn't know it would be easy."

What was he talking about?

Then she remembered. His leg. He'd been worried. She'd been concerned. But they were making love and it was exactly as it had always been. Perfect.

"Take your time," she told him, grabbing onto her self-control, determined to wait for him.

"You're really close?" he asked.

"Mitch, are you torturing me on purpose?"

"Uh-huh." His breath caught. "You ready?"

"I've moved on to desperate."

"That sounds bad. You can let go."

"Are you sure?"

He pushed in deeper and groaned. "I'm sure."

She felt the muscles in his back flex. She surrendered to her release and they lost themselves in each other.

SKYE WOKE UP alone in her bed the next morning, but she was okay with that. Being with Mitch the previous night had been like a renewal. They'd connected on a level she hadn't thought possible. While they hadn't talked about the future, she knew he was going to give her a chance. It had taken nine years and a lot of miles, but they were finally where they belonged.

She showered and dressed. It was Saturday and Erin would sleep in a little. Later she had a birthday party with one of her friends. Maybe Skye could sneak over and see Mitch again.

She hummed as she made her way downstairs. Everything was going to work out. She'd finally gotten her life together. All they had to do was get Izzy well and find a way to beat Garth. Then everything would be perfect.

"Not too much to ask," she said as she walked into the kitchen.

Her father was already there.

"Dad. You're home."

Jed sipped his coffee. "I still live here."

"You haven't been around much." Although it was the weekend and relatively early in the morning, he wore a suit, as if he had a business meeting.

"I've been busy," he said. "There's a lot going on. How's your sister?"

"Doing better. I know she'd like you to go see her."

"I hate hospitals. I'll see her when she gets home."

Skye glared at him. "She survived an explosion. You should make the time."

"Don't tell me what to do. I don't have time for distractions. A guy named Jack is going to call you later and ask you out. I want you to say yes."

She had reached for the coffeepot. Now she dropped her hand to her side and stared at him. "What?"

"You heard me. He's successful, which matters to me. I've heard people say he's handsome, which will matter to you."

"No," she said, too shocked to move.

"You'll go on a date, see how things go."

"Did you hear me? I said no."

Sunlight poured into the kitchen. Jed sipped his coffee again. "Do you think I care what you said?"

She stiffened. "You'd better. I'm not doing this again. I married Ray. He was a good man and I'm grateful for Erin, but I shouldn't have listened to you. I lost myself when I did that and it's taken me all this time to find my way back."

"That's a bunch of crap. Jesus, why do you have to be so emotional? This is business, Skye. You're going to do what I tell you because you like living here. You like the lifestyle. You gave away so much of your money to that idiotic foundation that you don't have much left. So you don't have a choice. This is a bad time for me and you're going to do what I tell you."

He didn't raise his voice, but it still seemed like he was yelling. She raised her chin.

"No," she said again. "I have plenty of money. As for the house—" She glanced around the room. "No, thanks. I'm not giving up my future so you can get the son-in-law of your dreams."

It wasn't the house, she thought sadly. It had never been the house. Staying here had been about being part of a family, of connecting. She'd wanted to give Erin that after Ray had died and maybe she'd wanted a little of that for herself.

"I'm not asking," he said as he put his mug on the counter. "Dammit, Skye, this isn't a negotiation. You're my daughter and you'll do what I tell you. You know all the shit I'm dealing with. Garth is everywhere. He's coming at me from all over. He wants me in jail. You know that, don't you." He stared at her. "Look at what he did to your sister."

She thought of Izzy lying in a hospital bed. "I'm very aware of that."

"Then help me out."

"Dad, I love you, but I won't let you push me into another marriage. It doesn't have to be that way.

We'll figure out how to defeat Garth. All of us. We can work together."

Her father looked at her for a long time. "That's not going to happen. You think I'd depend on the three of you? Lexi could barely handle her business. You're a constant disappointment and Izzy's no longer useful. Who wants a blind wife? You're going to do this. You don't have a choice."

He left.

She stood in the center of the kitchen. Despite the fact that it was warm and bright, she shivered slightly from the chill.

LATER THAT AFTERNOON, as Skye walked toward the staircase, she heard Jed call her name. She followed the sound to the library, where she paused in the doorway, suddenly unwilling to trust her father.

His words had haunted her all morning. He hadn't been the least bit subtle in his threat, and while she could tell herself she wouldn't give in, a part of her was nervous.

He motioned her forward.

She walked toward his desk. "What is it?"

He studied her for a long time, as if assessing her. "Do you think you're tough?" he asked at last. "Do you think you can influence me? You're a fool."

She took a step back. "Stop with the sweet talk, Dad," she said sarcastically. "Tell me what you really think."

"I will." He pointed to the files on his desk, then flipped open a couple and turned them so she could read the contents. "I didn't want to have to do this, but you're not giving me a choice."

She stared down at the papers. At first the writing didn't make sense. She read it a second time, then picked up a letter.

It was on printed stationery, from a doctor's office. The letter was addressed to Jed and detailed concerns about Skye's mental stability. About her ability to take care of Erin. The doctor recommended Jed get Skye a psychiatric evaluation as soon as possible.

The second folder contained something worse. Information from a panel of doctors, all claiming she was not only an unfit parent, but a danger to Erin and to herself. It recommended she be put away indefinitely.

"You have a lot of your mother in you," Jed said casually, as if they were discussing menus for dinner. "They think it goes back to when you were ten and found her body after she committed suicide. That would scar anyone. But you were weak, like her, and you never had a chance. It's too bad. Erin will miss you. But not to worry. I'll take good care of her."

She'd never known that terror had a taste. It was bitter and metallic, almost like blood. It filled her mouth until she thought she might choke on it. She looked at the man she'd loved all her life and saw a stranger.

"I'll do it," he told her. "Do you doubt me?"

"None of this is true."

"It's not about truth, Skye. Haven't you learned that? Who is going to fight me? A child is at stake. Don't you know what we do for our children?"

"Lexi and Izzy know it's all lies."

"If you get in my way, I'll hurt them, too." He smiled. "There's an easy solution. Break things off with Mitch and get together with Jack. I'm sure he's a nice guy. It will be easy. After all, you did it before."

She didn't ask how he knew about Mitch. Nor did she bother to point out that everything in the folders was faked. The documents looked real. No doubt he would have doctors prepared to tell any judge that she was crazy. He wouldn't be questioned—why would Jed Titan lie about his own daughter?

She thought of Erin reading upstairs. Love battled with fear.

"If you try to run, I'll find you and I'll use these," he said. "I'll lock you away forever and not give a damn. I'll destroy Mitch and take everything he has. And I'll have your daughter. Is there any part of you that doubts me?"

Nine years ago he'd threatened to withhold his love. When he'd worried that hadn't been enough, he'd threatened Mitch. Now he had a much more dangerous weapon. Erin.

She wanted to cry out that this was wrong on so many levels. She wanted to fight him with her fists, and drive him into the ground. She wanted to hurt him as he was hurting her.

If only she could. But she knew in her gut that Jed was willing to go places she couldn't imagine. That he had a streak of ruthlessness she could never match.

She would run, she told herself. But she needed time to make a plan. Time to make sure he couldn't lock her away from her daughter. Time had always been her friend, but now it was the enemy.

"Skye," he said impatiently. "You're starting to piss me off."

"I'll do it," she said.

Although the room was silent, she could swear she heard a door slamming shut. It was the door that trapped her in Jed Titan's particular level of hell.

"Good. You won't regret it," he told her.

She already did.

She left before she threw up on his desk. Once in the hallway, she did her best to catch her breath.

She'd lost. There'd been a game in play and she hadn't noticed in time to participate, let alone win. He would do anything—that was the difference. He would do anything, sacrifice anyone, including her. Or maybe especially her. Because she was easy.

Now he was going to force her into another relationship, but that wasn't what bothered her. What devastated her the most was that she was going to lose Mitch a second time. And she was going to have to make sure it happened in such a way that he believed it was over forever. She couldn't risk him getting caught in the cross fire.

Her happiness wasn't the only sacrifice. Mitch was going to lose, as well.

What if I was over before I even got started? I couldn't reach inside and...

For some reason we were only getting bits and pieces coming through as well.

CHAPTER NINETEEN

DANA BIRCH DID HER BEST not to grind her teeth. She'd already had to stop pacing because Leonard said it made him nervous. The computer genius kept looking at her over his shoulder, as if afraid she would suddenly karate chop him across the back of the neck. Sometimes being intimidating was a pain.

She glanced at her watch, then back at Leonard. The guy had been at it nearly twelve hours. She'd tried sleeping, but she was too wound up and nervous. This had to work. She had to figure out a way to get to Garth. Using his computer programmer against him was the only plan she had.

Three hours later, when she was so tired she was starting to get punchy, Leonard stood suddenly.

"I got it!" he yelled. "I'm in."

"Seriously?"

She raced to his side. They were in a hotel room just off the freeway. It was the kind of place that catered to travelers and offered not only a free breakfast but free Wi-Fi. No one had paid attention to them when they checked in and by the time Garth's computer guy knew what they were up to, they would be long gone.

She stared at the computer screen as Leonard sat back down. "I don't get it. It looks exactly the same. How can you tell you're in."

Leonard grinned up at her. "Because this is his stuff, not mine. Look." He led her through a menu then found his way into the guy's online personal information.

Dana made notes. She wanted an address for starters, then enough financial information to scare the crap out of him.

"See if you can find anything on Garth Duncan," Dana said.

"Like what?"

"A plan of evildoing would be nice," she muttered. "Whatever you can find."

After a couple of hours of playing with the guy's files, they'd uncovered enough to ID him, but nothing on Garth.

"That's just so typical," Dana said. "He's too damn good at covering his tracks. I swear, I will get him. I will park his ass in jail and I will stand there, laughing at him."

Leonard glanced at her. "You're a little scary."

"I know. It's one of my best qualities."

MITCH RODE OUT early the next morning. It had been a long time since he'd been so excited about starting a new day. He'd slept great and he felt good. Better than good. Everything made sense to him now.

When Skye had first told him she loved him, he hadn't wanted to believe her. He hadn't want to risk it, to go there. Not again. He'd given her everything he had and she'd walked away before.

They'd been kids, he reminded himself. Probably too young to be getting married. While he still believed she'd been wrong to side with her father, he accepted part of the blame. He hadn't bothered to find out why she'd changed her mind. He hadn't trusted her or their feelings for each other. He'd reacted and, by picking pride instead of love, he'd lost her.

A course had been set that had brought them to this moment. As a man who owned free-range chickens, he should probably say it was fate. That they were meant to be. As it was, he was happy to finally be back with her.

Skye was the woman he had always loved. Time and miles hadn't changed that. Part of his anger at coming back was knowing she would be close by. She was easier to ignore from ten thousand miles away.

He rode around the herd, sending the dogs to round up any strays. He checked for cows close to their time and looked for injuries. The sun rose higher, bringing heat to the day, but he didn't care. If anything, as the day wore on he felt stronger in his convictions. Everything about this was right.

He loved Skye. He'd always loved her. He wanted to marry her and have babies with her. Brothers and sisters for Erin, he thought, grinning as he imagined how she would love being a big sister. He wanted to grow old with Skye. He wanted to see how time would hone her beauty. He'd been damned lucky to find her the first time. What were the odds of it happening again?

He'd gone out before breakfast and hunger caused him to turn around and head back to the main house. He'd barely gone a mile when he saw someone on horseback. His heart recognized Skye before the rest of him did.

"You have it bad," he said aloud. "If Pete knew…"

He glanced up at the heavens. Maybe Pete did know. His friend would approve.

Pain joined the love, but there was room for both. Pete deserved to be mourned by those who had known him.

Mitch urged Bullet forward. The horse sped toward Skye and her mount. When they were within a few feet, he smiled at her.

"You're up early," he said.

"I have a busy day."

He started to ask her how she was feeling, only to realize there was something wrong. It was as if someone had burned the life off her face. She looked pale and tired.

"Didn't you sleep?" he asked.

"No, but that doesn't matter. We have to talk."

Was she angry that he hadn't said anything after they made love? Should he have told her then? Only he'd needed time to be sure.

"I agree," he said, then got off his horse.

She did the same. He reached out to touch her, but she took a step back.

"Don't," she whispered.

"Skye, what's wrong?"

Her mouth tightened. But she didn't speak. Pain seemed to radiate from her.

"Is it Erin or Izzy?"

"Neither."

"Then what?"

"It's us."

He'd hurt her. Sure. He'd been a typical guy— silent when she needed the words. She'd put herself out there and he hadn't responded.

"About yesterday," he said. "I shouldn't have waited. I wanted to be sure. I wanted it to be right." He moved closer and stared into her eyes. "It's always been you, Skye. That's what you need to hear, isn't it? I fought it for so long, but it was always there. Inside of me."

She winced and took a step back. "Don't say this. Don't say anything, Mitch."

"I love you, Skye. I want to marry you."

Tears filled her eyes. "No," she said harshly. "That's not going to happen. I won't marry you. Ever.

Do you hear me? Ever. I was wrong about everything. I don't love you. I can't. Last night showed me that. Look at you. You're a cripple. I need a whole man. I need someone who can take care of me. This was all a mistake."

He'd never been sure if he remembered the explosion or if he'd just been told about it enough to believe he did. Either way, the pain was real. At first there'd been nothing, then the exposed nerves had reacted. People described pain like fire, but flames would have a been a relief from what he'd felt.

It was like that now. Flames licking through him, only it was worse because there was nowhere to go. Nowhere he could escape. The agony ripped through him as she climbed back on her horse and rode away.

He couldn't breathe, couldn't do anything but stand there, watching her until she disappeared over a rise.

"Look at you. You're a cripple."

The words played over and over again. His good leg threatened to give way. What had happened? How could she have changed her mind? She'd sworn she loved him. She'd talked about the future. This was Skye. He'd trusted her.

In return, she'd shot him right in the heart then left him for dead.

SKYE SAT in Izzy's hospital room, trying to act normal. She was doing a reasonable job of fooling

Izzy, who has still fairly medicated and had bandages on her eyes, but Lexi kept looking at her.

"What?" Izzy demanded. "You're both distracted. I can tell. Do I have something in my teeth?"

"You're fine," Lexi said. "But Skye isn't. What happened?"

Skye did her best to smile. "Nothing. I'm good. Really. I'm great."

"Even I can tell you're lying," Izzy said. "What's wrong? You have to tell me. I'm injured. Possibly dying."

Lexi sat on Izzy's other side. She rolled her eyes. "You're not dying."

"I could be. Skye? Talk."

Skye didn't know what to say. For the rest of her life she would remember the shock and disbelief on Mitch's face as she'd said those horrible things to him. She'd offered her heart, convinced him to trust her, then had betrayed him.

"I think I'm going to throw up," she whispered.

"You're pregnant?" Lexi asked.

"What? No. I'm not pregnant. I'm a horrible person. I'm awful and mean and I hurt Mitch." She covered her face with her hands and wished she could cry, but there weren't any tears left. Between where she'd left him and the house, she'd cried until she had nothing left. Nothing but contempt for herself.

"What did you do?" Izzy asked, reaching for Skye's hand. "It can't be that bad."

"I told him I love him. I told him I'd never stopped loving him and when he finally believed me, I said that he wasn't a whole man and that I didn't want to be with him."

Bile rose in the back of her throat. She swallowed and pressed her free hand to her stomach.

"I devastated him. I ruined every chance we had for happiness."

"What did Jed do?" Lexi asked quietly.

Skye looked at her across the hospital bed. Of course her sister got it. "He threatened to have me declared a danger to myself and Erin and have me committed to a mental hospital."

"Goddamn son of a bitch," Izzy yelled. "What is wrong with that man?"

Lexi groaned. "I can't believe it. Why?"

"He wants me to go out with some guy. Marry him, I guess. He has letters from doctors. Tests. I don't know how he got it all, but I can't take the chance. Erin is my child."

"No one who knows you could ever think you're anything but annoyingly stable," Izzy said.

"The judge won't know me. Pru committed suicide and left me to find the body. Jed has it in writing." She pulled free of Izzy's hold and covered her face with her hands. "I'm going to leave. I'm going to figure out a way to get out of here and go where he can't find us."

"You can't run," Izzy told her. "You have to fight.

Of course, then you'd be taking advice from the blind girl and who does that?"

"You're not blind and you're not dead," Lexi said. "Stop making this about you."

"Who else is it supposed to be about?" Izzy turned to Skye. "You know I'm kidding, right? Just adding a little humor to the situation."

Skye nodded, then realized Izzy couldn't see that. "I know."

"Izzy's right," Lexi told her, looking intense. "You have to fight him. We'll help. You can't marry some other man because he tells you to. You're not his slave. You're his daughter."

Skye wondered if it was possible to explain the fear. "What if he takes her from me?"

"We won't let that happen," Izzy said. "We can fight this together."

He was Jed Titan. She wasn't sure anyone could fight him and win, although Garth was making a serious run at it.

"No. I'll agree for now," Skye told them. "It's the best thing. I'll work on a plan and then I'll disappear."

"Oh, sure," Izzy snapped. "Just give up. Suffer. You're really good at playing the martyr. God forbid you should stand up for yourself."

Skye glared at her. "That's very easy for you to say. You don't have a daughter."

"Yeah, and I don't want that big house. This is all about Glory's Gate."

"The house?" Skye was outraged. "You think I care about the damn house? Screw that. I need to protect Erin. I will not abandon her. No one is taking me away from my daughter. So until you can understand what I'm going through, keep your stupid opinions to yourself."

Izzy surprised her by smiling. "Better."

"What?"

Lexi shrugged. "You're mad now. That's a better place than defeat."

It was, Skye thought, feeling the rage engulf her. It gave her strength.

"You're right," she said, coming to her feet. "I'm not running. Who does Jed Titan think he is? He can't do this. I'm not crazy. There's nothing wrong with me. If he wants to show reports from five doctors, I'll get ten. Whatever it takes."

Lexi stood, walked around the bed and hugged her. "Good. We're with you. You know that, right?"

"Are you hugging?" Izzy asked, sounding pouty. "Is there hugging and sister bonding that I can't participate in? That's not fair. Blind girl here."

Skye squeezed her hand. "Thanks for pissing me off."

"It's a talent. You still running away?"

"No," Skye said. "I'm staying right here."

The feeling of empowerment continued to flow through her right up until she remembered what she'd done to Mitch. What she'd said.

"Oh, God." She sank back in her chair. "Mitch. I can't... He won't... I was so afraid and I ruined everything."

"You don't know that," Lexi told her. "Once you explain things, I'm sure he'll understand."

Skye wasn't sure. What she'd said, how she'd acted, had been unforgivable.

Jed had gotten his wish on one front. He'd made it impossible for her to be with Mitch.

SKYE FACED her senior staff at the foundation. Part of fighting back was not keeping so many secrets, she thought as she stood and tried to smile.

"As you all know, we've been having some trouble with rumors," she began. "First we were accused of money laundering. Once we were cleared of that, there were complaints that executives had been paid large bonuses and that I had taken out money for personal use. I want to talk about all this today."

She cleared her throat before continuing. "How many of you have received a bonus?"

There was a moment of surprise, then everyone looked at one another. No one raised a hand.

"It's all right," she said. "Just waggle a finger or two. Who has received a bonus?"

There was only silence.

"That's what I thought. I've hired an independent auditor to go over my entire financial portfolio. Once that is done, the company will certify that I haven't received any money, either. So what on earth is going on?"

Now came the hard part. What to tell and what to keep quiet.

"About thirty-five years ago, my father had an affair. Most of you have met Jed Titan at one function or another. If you haven't met him, I'm sure you've read about him. So it probably won't come as a big surprise to hear that he chose not to marry the young women he'd slept with, despite leaving her pregnant."

There were a few gasps. A couple of women whispered to each other.

"All these years later, Jed's illegitimate son has decided to get his revenge. That's what this is about. He's out to destroy all of us. You've seen what he can do. If it wasn't for Leonard's brilliant computer detective work, we wouldn't have found the source of the second set of books. We wouldn't have the beginning of proof to repair our reputation."

She glanced around the room. "I've told you this in confidence, to help you understand what's happening. There are probably going to be more difficulties. Ours isn't a business that weathers this sort of thing very well. In the nonprofit world, reputation is everything. Because of this, some of you will want to leave. Some of you may think about going to the press. I can't prevent either."

She smiled. "But I hope you'll stay. I hope you'll remember our mission statement, that we have a goal that no child in this country will spend a day hungry. That's what matters. That's what's important. My half brother will do everything he can to destroy what we've built. I'm not going to let that happen, but I can't do it alone."

She paused for breath. Trisha stood.

"You're not alone, Skye," her CFO said.

One by one the other staff members rose to their feet. They began to clap. Skye sighed in relief. One problem down, sixteen hundred left to solve.

CHAPTER TWENTY

IT WAS THE SECOND TIME in as many months that Mitch started the morning with a killer hangover. He didn't remember much about the previous night except he'd spent it with a bottle of Scotch and a burning need to forget.

A shower helped a little. He made his way downstairs where he shook off breakfast, grabbed coffee and started to leave.

"What's wrong?" Fidela asked. "What happened?"

"I don't want to talk about it."

She came up to him and cupped his face. "You mourn your friend. I know. Time will heal the wound. It always does."

Would time heal this wound?

"His wife is pregnant."

"Her baby will bring her much comfort."

"He'll never know his kid."

"He's in heaven. He'll know everything." She glared at him. "Don't you dare tell me you don't believe in God. You've been to war, Mitch. You've seen the pain and the miracles."

He kissed her on the cheek. "You're right."

"So believe in the possibilities."

He nodded because it was easier than arguing. Yesterday he would have believed. Yesterday he would have known that whatever happened, there was still good because he and Skye loved each other and they'd finally found their way back to where they belonged. This morning, the world was a shitty place and he was sorry he'd come back.

He stepped outside and winced as the bright sun seemed to pierce his skull. He limped to the barn and stumbled into his office.

Forgetting seemed impossible, he thought grimly. At least while he was here. He would have to go somewhere that didn't remind him of her. Assuming there was such a place in the world. If he'd had the faith Fidela had talked about, he would have offered God a bargain—his sorry self for Pete.

He sipped the coffee and thought about turning on his computer. Once he was online, he could pick a destination. Any one. Maybe Thailand. He could get lost in the jungle. He had money. Arturo would run the ranch. He didn't need Mitch.

"Hi!"

Erin bounced into his office.

"I don't have school today. It's the *summer*." She giggled, as if not knowing about her summer break was the funniest thing in the world. "Mommy said I could spend the day here and go riding."

Her voice was high and made his head throb as if it were stuck in the middle of a church bell.

"Can you keep it down?"

Erin looked confused. "Keep what down?"

He slumped onto his chair. "Nothing. I don't know where Arturo is."

"He's out riding the fence line. Fidela told me." She moved closer, then plopped on the floor next to his chair and looked at him. "Want to go riding."

"No."

"But it's nice out."

"I don't feel very good. My head hurts."

She pressed her lips together. "You can take something. Mommy takes something when she gets a headache. You buy it at the store. Or do you want me to get you a cold cloth? That helps." She sprang to her feet. "I'll go get a cold cloth. That will be nice."

He raised a hand to stop her. "Just go. I need quiet."

She ignored the instruction to leave. "I can be quiet."

"Not so far."

She sank back down on the floor and eyed him. "Are you sad about something?"

"What? No."

He would be sad one day. Right now he was beyond sad. Not beyond pain, though. The pain was right there, crouching in his gut, reminding him with every breath that he'd lost her.

Lost Erin, too, he thought, looking into her concerned face and wishing…what? That he could have been a part of her life? Sure. Why not? She was a great kid. He liked everything about her. Loved everything about her. He wanted to be a part of her world—helping her grow. Teaching her to drive and scaring off potential boyfriends. Who would do that now?

"Are you fighting with Mommy again?" Erin asked.

"Not in the way you mean."

"Huh?"

"No. I'm not fighting with your mother."

"She's not scared of you. I'm not, either. Sometimes people fight."

He rubbed his temple and wished he'd thought to swallow a half-dozen or so aspirin before leaving the house.

"Who told you that?" he asked.

"Izzy. She tells me lots of stuff. About my dad so I can try to remember him and what it's like to climb a mountain. She says that when adults fight I shouldn't get scared."

That got his attention. "Why would you be scared?" Was Ray not the paragon Skye had claimed? Had he frightened his wife and child?

Erin studied her shoe.

He put down his coffee and leaned toward her. "What is it? Who scares you?"

She looked up at him, her eyes wide. "Grandpa,"

she whispered. "Sometimes when he yells, I hide in the closet."

That bastard, he thought, reaching down to grab Erin and pulling her onto his lap.

"He's a big guy," he said as she snuggled close. "But he won't hurt you." If Jed tried, he would have to answer to him.

"Will he hurt Mommy?"

A reasonable question. Simple words, easily understood. Would Jed hurt Skye?

Mitch swore silently. Of course he would. Jed would do whatever it was he had to. If he thought there wasn't a choice. If he felt trapped. He would destroy anyone who got in his way. Even his own daughter.

He remembered making love with Skye. What they'd shared, how she'd touched him. How they'd truly been one. She'd seen him naked, had accepted him—all of him. He knew it in his gut and in his heart. She hadn't rejected him. She'd been afraid. Beyond afraid. Terrified. And there was only one thing that would frighten Skye into turning her back on him.

Erin.

"Mitch? Will Grandpa hurt my mommy?"

"No," he said firmly, putting her on her feet and standing, as well. "Not ever again."

"I don't understand."

He crouched in front of her and put his hands on her shoulders. "You're great, you know that? I think you're the most special girl I know." There was more he wanted to say. That he loved Skye and he loved her. That he would protect them both with everything he had.

But this wasn't the time. He wanted to get to Skye, to tell her that he'd figured it out and he was there for her. However Jed had threatened her, they would deal. Together. They would figure out a plan. She didn't ever have to be afraid again.

"I'm going to take you to the house where you can help Fidela make cookies," he said. "We'll go riding later, okay?"

"Okay."

They turned toward the door. She held out her hand, as if she wanted him to take it. He did. She was so small, he thought. Defenseless. But that didn't matter. She had her mother and she had him. They would protect her.

They returned to the house. He took Fidela aside to tell her she needed to keep Erin, but before he could say anything, she spoke.

"When Skye dropped Erin off, she was upset. Something's wrong. She said to keep her girl safe." Fidela grabbed his arm. "Mitch, what's happening?"

"I don't know but it has to do with Jed." He hugged her. "Don't worry. I'm going to find out and I'm going to fix it. I'll go get Skye and bring her back."

"Jed Titan is a powerful man."

Mitch smiled. "So am I. I didn't fight for what I

wanted last time. I let her walk away. I'm not going to do that again. I don't know what hold he has on her, but I'm breaking it today and for good." He glanced at Erin. "I said you'd let her help you make cookies."

"Of course," Fidela said. "Be careful."

Mitch started for the door. "If you're going to worry about someone, worry about Jed."

THE BAR WAS OLD, paneled and catered to rich men with influence. Jed ordered his usual Scotch from the bartender. He was meeting his lawyer for lunch. While he didn't usually enjoy sharing a meal with a lawyer, these days he didn't have much choice. They were a reality in his life.

As he took his drink and carried it toward an empty table, he saw another man sitting in the corner. Their eyes met. Jed changed direction and headed toward him.

Garth Duncan stood as he approached. He said something to the person he was with and met Jed in the middle of the bar.

"Afternoon," Garth said, looking confident. A faint smile pulled at his mouth, as if he had a secret.

There was power in knowledge, Jed thought, not intimidated by his bastard.

"You're not going to win this," he said, figuring there was no reason to waste time with niceties. "I've been playing this game longer than you've been alive and I always come out on top."

Garth gave in to the smile. "You talk tough for an old man facing treason charges. It's already over, Jed. You just haven't figured that out yet. But please, try to defeat me. I enjoy a good fight."

Jed saw the anger behind the smile, the rage and determination in his son's eyes. Was that because of him or did it have another source?

"You crossed the line when you hurt my daughter," Jed said. "Blowing up her oil rig was a big mistake."

Garth studied him. "I agree. Whoever did it was a fool, but it wasn't me."

Jed dismissed him with a shake of his head. "You think I'm an idiot?"

"A question for another time," Garth said. "I'll take credit for all I'd done. Your girls have given me a run for my money. You should be proud of them. But Izzy? She doesn't have anything I want, so I've left her alone. I didn't have anything to do with the explosion. You'll have to look elsewhere."

Which was true, but Jed wouldn't acknowledge it. "Why should I believe you?"

"I don't care if you do or not, Jed. That has nothing to do with the truth. It wasn't me."

Jed leaned close and lowered his voice. "I'm going to take you down, boy."

Garth looked more amused than afraid. "You're going to try. There's a difference. You're out of your league on this one. You don't even know what I want, so how are you going to stop me?"

"You want it all. Just like me."

Garth's amusement faded. "I'm nothing like you. You inherited a fortune and made it bigger. So what? I started with nothing and built an empire. You're used up and irrelevant."

"Then why are you trying so hard to beat me?"

The smile returned. "Because I can."

SKYE FORCED HERSELF to focus on the goal. Getting out. Erin was safely at the Cassidy Ranch, which meant she was away from Jed and right now that's all that mattered. Mitch would keep her safe. He might want to eviscerate Skye, but he would die to protect Erin. She was willing to bet her daughter's life on that.

Because no matter what, in the end Mitch was a good man. The best man she'd ever known.

"Later," she told herself as she collected her daughter's clothes and put them in a suitcase. Erin's toys and books were already packed and in the car. She figured she had the whole afternoon until her father returned, but she wasn't taking any chances.

Everything was finally clear to her. She was going to fight for what she wanted. She was going to fight her father and then she was going to fight for Mitch. But first she had to get out of Glory's Gate.

The irony didn't escape her. She'd spent her whole life trying to be worthy of these walls. Trying to feel as if this was really where she belonged. When the truth was, she wanted Jed's love. Something she'd never been able to find. Maybe it didn't exist. It hadn't for Pru.

She was his daughter and that should matter to him. It didn't, and the sooner she accepted that, the sooner she could move on. She'd already sold herself once for her father. She wasn't going to do it again.

When the suitcase was full, she closed it and carried it down to her car. Her things were already packed. She only had to go through her makeup and then she could—

"Going somewhere?" her father asked, coming in through the kitchen. "There seems to be a lot of luggage in your car."

She raised her chin. "I'm leaving. Erin and I are moving out."

Jed looked tired and his eyes were red. "I warned you what would happen if you tried that. I'm not going to warn you again. Skye, you will do what I tell you or I will—"

She cut him off. "Yeah, I know the drill. You'll have me locked up. Doctors will testify. Blah, blah, blah."

He glared at her. "Who the hell are you to talk to me that way?"

"I'm your daughter, Jed. The daughter you've used before, taken advantage of, put down. Oh, wait, you'll need more information. That describes all three of us."

"I don't know what you think you're doing, but

you *will* take your bags back inside and unpack or I'll make you regret every moment you're alive."

The fear was still there, but so was determination. She wasn't going to do this anymore. She wasn't going to be his employee or his bitch.

"No," she said firmly. "I won't unpack. I'm not staying. I wanted this to be different. I wanted us to be a family. But that's not possible with you. You want to take it all and give nothing in return. No one else matters."

"Oh, my poor little girl. Has your life been hard? Too many ponies to look after?" He stalked toward her. "I've taken care of you and you have wanted for nothing. All I want in return—"

"Is my soul."

"You've always been overly dramatic. You get that from your mother."

"A woman you drove to suicide."

"She was always unstable. And an idiot."

"She loved you so much that when she found out you wouldn't love her back, she killed herself."

"Not my problem."

"I agree. It's not. But it should have been. When I was little, I thought you were amazing. You could do anything. Now I realize you're nothing but a selfish jerk who doesn't care about anyone but himself. The only way you can keep me in line is to threaten me. What does that say about your parenting skills?"

"I swear I'll lock you up, Skye. You'll wish you were dead. Maybe you'll try to kill yourself, like your mother."

She ignored the words because they didn't matter. He couldn't hurt her unless she let him. And she wasn't going there.

"You can't lock me up. You have only yourself, because that's how you've always wanted it. That's your game. I have sisters who will scream from every street corner in Dallas. They know what you're trying to do and we'll work together to stop you. You have doctors? Fine. I'll get more."

"You don't have the money."

"I have plenty. Besides, it's going to be a little difficult to fight me from jail. That's where the government likes to keep traitors."

He swore. "You know I had nothing to do with that."

"You're right. I do. But does anyone else? If your family doesn't support you, what will the public think?"

He flushed. "*You're* threatening *me?*"

"How does it feel, Dad?"

She wouldn't go through with it, but it felt really good to say the words.

"I'm not running," she told him. "I'm moving in with Lexi until I can find a place of my own. I want you to know that so it's clear you haven't scared me away. I'll fight you and I'll win because I love my daughter and that's not anything you could possibly understand."

"You won't last a second without me."

"Then you have an exaggerated sense of your place in my life. I'll be fine. I have a foundation to run and a daughter to raise and a man to win back."

"You can't mean Mitch. Why would you want him?"

"Because he's my world. I'll do whatever is necessary to convince him that I had a moment of weakness and I acted out of fear. He'll forgive me." At least she hoped he would. In truth, she wasn't as confident as she sounded.

"Don't be so sure," Jed sneered.

"She can be sure."

The voice came from behind her. Skye caught her breath then turned and saw Mitch standing in the foyer.

"You're leaving?" he asked her.

"Just Glory's Gate. Not Dallas." She swallowed. What did it mean that he was here? "I'm moving in with Lexi."

"She didn't say anything."

"You saw her?"

"I've spent the afternoon with her." He held up a folder. "Interesting piece of information. Those so-called experts of your father's don't exist. Lexi came in this morning and copied down the names." He looked at Jed. "It's fancy printing and nothing else. Or as we like to say here, all hat and no cattle."

Her breath caught. "They're not real letters?"

Jed stared at her. "I'll still annihilate you."

"I can't believe he fooled me," she told Mitch ignoring her father as he stalked out of the room. "I'm an idiot."

"He threatened Erin. You weren't expecting that."

"Wait a minute. How do you know what's going on?"

He looked a little sheepish. "Your daughter stopped by this morning. Talking to her made me realize this had Jed written all over it. He was faking you out."

"And I fell for it. I'm so sorry."

"I know."

She moved toward him. "I didn't mean what I said. I was scared and I reacted and I hurt you. Mitch, I'm sorry. I feel horrible. I didn't mean it. You know that, right? I know that doesn't take away the words."

She wanted to sink into the ground. Humiliation clawed at her.

"I'm sorry."

He dropped the folder onto a chair and wrapped his arms around her. "I know."

"Really sorry. I was so stupid and I didn't think."

"I know."

"I love you. I'll do anything to convince you. Even beg."

One corner of his mouth lifted. "I can't see you begging. Well, maybe naked." He tucked her hair behind her ears. "Skye, I get it. Jed knows how to push your buttons."

"I won't let it happen again. I swear."

He stared into her eyes. "Next time come to me. We'll work it out together."

"I will."

"Good. So are you really moving in with Lexi? Won't that be crowded, with Cruz there and all?"

"It's actually Cruz's house and it's huge."

"I thought maybe you'd want to stay with me."

"Really? You still want me."

"Skye, I love you. Haven't you figured that out yet?"

Relief and happiness rushed through her. She leaned in and kissed him.

"Yes," she whispered. "I'd love to stay there and Erin will be thrilled."

"Good. You know that I would build you a house as big and fancy as Glory's Gate, if that would make you happy."

He would. Mitch was a man of his word.

She stepped back and turned in a slow circle, taking in the high ceiling, the antique furniture. She'd grown up here. The house represented so much to her. She'd lost Mitch once because of it.

"It's just a house," she told him. "I don't want another one like it."

He looked confused. "But you love this place."

"No. I love you. I don't want a house. I want a home, and that's where you are. The ranch."

"You know we have certified organic cattle and free-range chickens? We're practically tree huggers."

"I've heard, but I'm good with that." She kissed him again. "I love you, Mitch."

"I love you, too. Now get the rest of your stuff and we'll go get Erin. The three of us can ride into the sunset, just like in the movies."

She laughed. "That would be a perfect ending."

* * * * *

Don't miss Izzy's story,
STRAIGHT FROM THE HIP,
available in July!

IN THE MOVIES there was always a warning before something bad happened. Music swelled, the good guy promised everything would be fine now or the camera suddenly went into slow motion.

Life wasn't so tidy.

Izzy Titan sat in the window seat, as she had every day for the past month, staring out at the blurry world and feeling sorry for herself. While it wasn't a career choice everyone would make, it filled the day. She ignored her sisters' pleas that she join them for lunch or shopping or even come downstairs to dinner. Like a regular person. When it got too annoying, she pointed out she wasn't regular anymore—she was handicapped. If that didn't work, she slammed the door and locked it until they went away. She'd always given everything she had, so she was ready to become the self-pity queen, if necessary.

Finally her sisters stopped bugging her. Which should have been a really big clue.

There wasn't any warning. One minute she was sitting in her usual spot, the next someone grabbed her around the waist, pulled her to her feet, then tossed her over a very broad, very hard shoulder.

"What the hell do you think you're doing?" she yelled as blood rushed to her head, making her a little dizzy.

"My job. Go ahead and fight me if you want. You can't hurt me."

It was a challenge she couldn't ignore. But when she tried to kick her attacker, he wrapped one arm around her legs, holding her still. Wiggling didn't help, either. The man had muscles like rock and a month of immobilizing self-pity had left her girlishly weak.

"I swear," she began, as the guy turned and started walking. "Do you know who I am?"

"Izzy Titan. Hey, Skye."

Hey Skye?

Izzy raised her head and tried to make the room focus. Unfortunately, it was dark and blurry and she couldn't see any details.

"Skye?" she yelled. "Are you there?"

"Oh, Izzy." Her sister sounded concerned but not worried. Not afraid. "We didn't know what else to do."

"We?"

"I'm here," Lexi, her other sister, said. "This is for your own good."

"Having me *kidnapped?*"

"Nick comes very highly recommended. Your doctors wanted to put you on an antidepressant, which you'd never agree to. This is better."

"What?"

"You wouldn't leave your room or talk to us. It's been a month, Izzy."

"You're having me kidnapped because I wouldn't go *shopping* with you? Are you insane?"

They moved into the hallway. She could tell because the room got darker and her fingers brushed against the walls. Then they were going down, down, down into more darkness.

Each step jarred her entire body. If she'd had that lunch her sisters were so hysterical about she would be throwing it up, right about now.

"I'm not kidding," she yelled. "Stop this right now. All of you. Nick, I don't care what my sisters said, I don't agree to this. Put me down or I swear I'll throw your ass in jail for so long you'll actually learn to enjoy being Bubba's love slave."

"You signed a release," rock-guy said calmly, still moving through the house.

"What?"

"You signed a release. I've got it here in my pocket."

Izzy wanted to scream in frustration as she remembered Skye asking her to sign a few checks so her sister could pay Izzy's bills. "She tricked me. I'm *blind!* I didn't know what I was signing."

They went outside. She saw the blurry outline of trees and the welcome light and heat of the sun.

"You shouldn't sign what you can't read," Nick told her.

She could hear the humor in his voice and that really pissed her off. Seconds later, he opened a car door and dumped her onto a smooth leather seat. Before he could close the door, she pushed past him and bolted for freedom. She made it all of three steps before he grabbed her around the waist and pulled her against him.

It was like pressing against the side of a mountain... and not in a happy way. She kicked and tried to pull his arm free. Irritation turned to fury and betrayal. She turned toward the house—at least she could see something that big—and assumed her sisters were on the porch.

"How could you do this to me?" she demanded. "You're my *family.*"

"Izzy, we love you." There were tears in Skye's voice.

Good, Izzy thought furiously. She hoped Skye felt guilty for the rest of her life.

"We didn't know what else to do," Lexi called, sounding less than sure.

"I would never do this to you," Izzy screamed. "Don't think I'll ever forgive you. Ever!"

The last word was cut short as she was tossed back into the rear of a car or SUV. She couldn't tell which. The door slammed shut before she could run again. She lunged for the door handle, only there wasn't one. Nor could she open the windows.

Seconds later she discovered a thick, mesh screening behind the seat between her and the front of the vehicle. She was trapped.

FOR THE NEXT THREE HOURS, Nick Hollister drove ten miles above the speed limit. He wanted to go faster, but knew he couldn't outrun the inevitable. His pretty, dark-haired passenger was staring out the window with a determination that told him she was about ten seconds from losing it.

"You can cry if you want to," he told her. "It won't bother me." He'd seen a lot worse than tears.

Izzy didn't turn toward him. "I won't give you the satisfaction."

"You think I win if you cry?"

"Don't bullies always enjoy knowing they've hurt someone? You can't break me."

She raised her chin as she spoke, instinctively defying him. Good, he thought grimly. She was going to need every ounce of strength she had if she wanted to find her way back. Which was his job— to make sure she did.

"Break you?" he asked, ignoring that she'd called him a bully. He'd stormed into her life and taken her away from everything she knew. Hardly comfortable circumstances. He understood the fear of the unknown, although her unknown was a whole lot more controlled than his had been. "Dramatic much?"

"Hey, you're the one who tossed me into the back of a car."

"SUV."

"Whatever, this is kidnapping. I get to be however I want."

"Your sisters know where you are and what will happen when you get there."

"And I should find that comforting why?" She swallowed. "Don't even talk to me."

He heard the fear in her voice. He could see it in the way she kept herself stiff. In a second, he would smell it. Behind fear was terror and while he wanted her attention, he didn't need it that bad.

"My name in Nick Hollister," he said, using the same tone that calmed unbroken horses. "I run a school that teaches corporate survival training. That pays the bills. I also take in kids who have suffered a traumatic loss or have been victims of a violent crime. I teach them how I survive in my world. That helps them cope with their own."

Izzy stared out the window, obviously ignoring him. He wondered how much she could actually see.

"Your sisters asked me to take you on for a few weeks, to help you adjust to being blind."

"I'm not blind," she snapped. "I have thirty percent of my sight."

"You're acting like you're blind," he told her. "You've been hiding in your room for a month."

"It's not like I can do anything else."

"Your life is over? Because of one little challenge?"

"Shut up," she yelled. "You don't know what you're talking about. You can see fine."

"Look," he said. "They care about you. Your sisters," he added, in case she wasn't following.

This time she did glance at him, only to roll her eyes. The hazel irises were unmarred by her injury. "I'm more than capable of carrying on a conversation. I'm probably smarter than you," she said.

"I doubt that."

"Oh, please."

"How smart is sitting on your ass, feeling sorry for yourself?"

She straightened and glared at him. "I was in an explosion," she said, speaking slowly, as if to make sure he would understand. "I could have been killed."

"But you weren't."

"I was seriously injured and I lost most of my eyesight."

"Which you could get back tomorrow if you weren't such a girl about the surgery."

He glanced in the rearview mirror in time to see her narrow her gaze.

"A girl?" she asked softly.

"Yeah. You know. Chicken. Lacking in bravery."

"That's it!" she yelled. "Let me out, right here. Let

me out or I swear, I'll kill you myself. I'll rip you apart with my bare hands and feed you to the snakes."

"Snakes wouldn't eat human flesh."

"Shut up!"

"Skye didn't say anything about you being hysterical."

"Let me out!"

"No."

She grabbed the mesh screening and rattled it, but it had withstood a lot more than her.

"She did warn me you would be difficult," he said. "I charge extra for that."

Izzy sank back in the seat and resumed staring out the back window.

"If you won't have the surgery, then you have to survive with what you have," he told her. "That's where I come in. I teach you how I make it. You're staying with me until you can be on your own."

"What if I don't want to be on my own?"

"You think your sisters want you hanging around all the time? They have lives. You're what? Twenty-five? Twenty-six? You ready to give up so fast?"

"Go to hell."

"I've already been there."

He turned onto the familiar paved, private road and drove toward the two-story main house he'd bought on the run-down ranch nearly eight years before. Neighboring ranchers leased his pasture for their cattle, while he used the twenty acres of wilderness for his retreats. He kept a dozen horses in the big barn and had built several guesthouses where clients stayed. There were meeting facilities, a restaurant-grade kitchen that could serve up to fifty at a time and a big media room that rivaled a multiplex.

Not that Izzy would deal with much more than the barn. He planned to work her hard enough that she wouldn't have time to feel sorry for herself. The little he knew about her told him she would fight him every step of the way, but he didn't care about that.

He parked in front of the house and turned off the engine.

"We're here," he said in the silence.

REQUEST YOUR FREE BOOKS!

2 FREE NOVELS FROM THE ROMANCE/SUSPENSE COLLECTION PLUS 2 FREE GIFTS!

YES! Please send me 2 FREE novels from the Romance/Suspense Collection and my 2 FREE gifts (gifts are worth about $10). After receiving them, if I don't wish to receive any more books, I can return the shipping statement marked "cancel." If I don't cancel, I will receive 4 brand-new novels every month and be billed just $5.74 per book in the U.S. or $6.24 per book in Canada. That's a savings of at least 28% off the cover price. It's quite a bargain! Shipping and handling is just 50¢ per book.* I understand that accepting the 2 free books and gifts places me under no obligation to buy anything. I can always return a shipment and cancel at any time. Even if I never buy another book from the Reader Service, the two free books and gifts are mine to keep forever.

185 MDN EYNQ   385 MDN EYN2

Name	(PLEASE PRINT)	
Address		Apt. #
City	State/Prov.	Zip/Postal Code

Signature (if under 18, a parent or guardian must sign)

Mail to The Reader Service:

IN U.S.A.: P.O. Box 1867, Buffalo, NY 14240-1867
IN CANADA: P.O. Box 609, Fort Erie, Ontario L2A 5X3

Not valid to current subscribers of the Romance Collection,
the Suspense Collection or the Romance/Suspense Collection.

Want to try two free books from another line?
Call 1-800-873-8635 or visit www.morefreebooks.com.

* Terms and prices subject to change without notice. Prices do not include applicable taxes. Sales tax applicable in N.Y. Canadian residents will be charged applicable provincial taxes and GST. Offer not valid in Quebec. This offer is limited to one order per household. All orders subject to approval. Credit or debit balances in a customer's account(s) may be offset by any other outstanding balance owed by or to the customer. Please allow 4 to 6 weeks for delivery. Offer available while quantities last.

Your Privacy: Harlequin is committed to protecting your privacy. Our Privacy Policy is available online at www.eHarlequin.com or upon request from the Reader Service. From time to time we make our lists of customers available to reputable third parties who may have a product or service of interest to you. If you would prefer we not share your name and address, please check here. ☐

BOB09

SUSAN MALLERY

77347	UNDER HER SKIN	___ $7.99 U.S.	___ $8.99 CAN.
77420	FALLING FOR GRACIE	___ $6.99 U.S.	___ $6.99 CAN.
77305	SWEET TROUBLE	___ $6.99 U.S.	___ $6.99 CAN.
77314	SWEET SPOT	___ $6.99 U.S.	___ $6.99 CAN.
77297	SWEET TALK	___ $6.99 U.S.	___ $6.99 CAN.
77205	ACCIDENTALLY YOURS	___ $6.99 U.S.	___ $8.50 CAN.
77210	TEMPTING	___ $6.99 U.S.	___ $8.50 CAN.
77056	DELICIOUS	___ $6.99 U.S.	___ $8.50 CAN.

(limited quantities available)

TOTAL AMOUNT	$ _____
POSTAGE & HANDLING	$ _____
($1.00 FOR 1 BOOK, 50¢ for each additional)	
APPLICABLE TAXES*	$ _____
TOTAL PAYABLE	$ _____

(check or money order—please do not send cash)

To order, complete this form and send it, along with a check or money order for the total above, payable to HQN Books, to: **In the U.S.:** 3010 Walden Avenue, P.O. Box 9077, Buffalo, NY 14269-9077; **In Canada:** P.O. Box 636, Fort Erie, Ontario, L2A 5X3.

Name: _____

Address: _____ City: _____

State/Prov.: _____ Zip/Postal Code: _____

Account Number (if applicable): _____

075 CSAS

*New York residents remit applicable sales taxes.
*Canadian residents remit applicable GST and provincial taxes.

HQN™

We *are* romance™

www.HQNBooks.com

PHSM0609BL